Supe Slayer

by

J. M. Davis

Supe Slayer

Cover Art by *Abigail Owen*

The Wild Rose Press, Inc.
PO Box 708
Adams Basin, NY 14410-0708
Visit us at www.thewildrosepress.com

Publishing History
First Edition, 2021
Trade Paperback ISBN 978-1-5092-3365-6
Digital ISBN 978-1-5092-3366-3

Published in the United States of America

I caught a glimpse of a shadow swinging from the rafters, and instinctively, I raised Supe Slayer. It moved fluidly, like fog rolling across stilled water. A vampire.

I fired once, missing the vamp but blowing a massive hole through the aged roof. People screamed as splinters of wood rained down on them.

"You missed me, you missed me...now you gotta kiss me!" called a young voice. Angelica, the teenage vamp from Garon's district stood up on the rafters, her shock of blonde hair bright against the shadows of the barn.

I fired again, but she swooped from the rafter, her supernatural speed making it easy to dodge Supe Slayer's bullet. She clasped another wood beam and swung off, her body sailing smoothly through the air.

She landed in a crouch on the second level of the old barn. Her landing was so soft, it barely stirred a single dust mote in the air. She snarled, glaring down at me before disappearing toward the recesses of the barn.

"Angelica!" I shouted. Before I could make a move towards the ladder, I heard a woman's voice pleading, "Please, no" then a sickening crunch, like bone beneath a boot heel. Angelica's ghastly pale face emerged out of the dark shadows of the rafters, then, with the grace of a dancer, she took a running leap, silently dropping to the floor in front of me.

She watched me for a long moment, her eyes sparkling with a dangerous edge. It felt as if she could read my vitals by just looking at me. Counting each quick pulse pounding away at my neck and wrists. I tightened my grip on Supe Slayer and held my breath as I waited for her next move.

Dedication

To Gail.
Thank you for the inspiration.

Chapter 1

"Stop right there, asshole, or I'll shoot!" I aimed my Beretta directly between the eyes of a hulking man kneeling in the shadows. His head was slick-shaven, oddly reminding me of a boiled egg under the flickering security light. Thick shoulder muscles rippled beneath his tattered shirt as he pawed at something slender and distinctly feminine.

To the untrained eye, he looked like a regular guy, but I knew exactly what he was. Before I even approached him, I had loaded my gun accordingly. The iron bullets sitting inside the chamber were equipped with holy salt. You see, iron and anything blessed is a deadly combination to demons, which was exactly what this ugly motherfucker was.

The demon lifted his blood-smeared face and tossed an annoyed glance at me that clearly read, *fuck off,* before growling like a rabid dog.

I didn't waver though. I'd dealt with his kind before and smoked those assholes to ash without so much as a second thought. Or a single shred of remorse. I positioned myself into a firm stance, using both hands to keep the barrel trained on his forehead. If he made one wrong move, I'd pull the trigger, which would wipe him clean from existence. Well, not entirely clean. Being a demon, he'd leave a steamy smear of ichor behind, but that's nothing the Sweepers can't remove.

I gripped the gun tighter. "You know the rules, dipshit. You're only allowed to eat the souls of *sinners*. Not the innocent."

He sneered at me and went back to mauling the body below him. I flicked my gaze to the lifeless blonde, stifling a shiver as I imagined myself in her position. With that wheat-colored hair and lean legs, I could have easily been her. I gulped, taking a quick glance at the unmoving body. Lucky for me, I wasn't. Instead, I had the sights of my gun settled on the demon's skull, ready to make a wicked mess of ichor for the Sweepers.

Demons are malicious creatures who usually only feed off the fears and souls of sinning mortals, but sometimes, you get a greedy bastard who decides to make a meal out of an unsuspecting innocent.

And before you give me any grief about the whole debate that "*all humans' sin*" mumbo jumbo, let me tell you the definition of a sinner my team abides by: "a sinner is any being that chooses to act willingly against an Immoral Law." You know, premediated murder, pedophilia, and rape. The big no-no's of the world, human and unhuman alike.

"This is the last time I'm going to ask nicely," I said, curling my finger tighter around the trigger. "Put your hands where I can see them!"

The disgusting sound of wet entrails and slurping was interrupted by the sound of a door breaking open and the sharp clicking of high-heels on concrete. The demon's eyes easily tracked the sound, its nostrils flaring as it drew in the scent of the approaching figure. I held my breath, waiting and hoping the woman wouldn't notice us. I didn't feel like using the *Evap* on her, and frankly, I wasn't in the mood to mess with all the reports using the Memory Evaporator brings.

The woman emerged beneath the security lights, walking with clipped steps, each hand gripping fat trash bags. I divided my attention between her and the demon. His true form warbled beneath the human-male skin he wore as he considered his next move.

She tossed the bags into the dumpster with a loud *clunk* and turned to go back inside the building.

A low hiss, like a deflating tire, escaped the demon's teeth, and his eyes flooded completely black, indicating he still hungered for human flesh. Of course, he could have went for me, but when you're armed with a bad-ass gun that's been dubbed the *Supe Slayer,* I'm not exactly easy prey.

He shoved the dead girl aside and, with animal-like movements, crept on all fours toward the woman. He was going to make a meal out of her if I didn't stop him. So stop him, I did.

I squeezed the trigger, blowing his head completely off his shoulders, and sending his remains into an explosion of sticky goo. Hot ichor splattered across my face, burning my eyes. Stretchy strings of it hung from my hair. *Gross.* Then the stench of it hit me. My stomach stopped turning from it a long time ago. It's not as bad as one would think; roasted demon smells a lot like charred eggs.

I wiped the ichor from my eyes, slinging it from my fingers as I walked up to the steaming puddle of black demon pus. It sizzled on the pavement, looking very much like a streak of tar. I stood over it, watching it for a moment, feeling nothing but satisfaction. I remember thinking, '*Damn. I guess I've officially become numb to this job.'* Oh well, that's typical of all professions, I guess. You work at the Whacko Taco for too long, you'll eventually grow tired of burritos and nachos.

The PCI is no different. You stomp several dozen demon asses to the ground, and you become hardened and detached. Besides, it's not like the demon had a family at home. There weren't any little baby demons to feed, or a demon wife to support. Demons are spawned by evil and by Satan's black magic. They have no remorse, no souls, no manners, and absolutely no purpose other than tormenting humans. Slaying one is like squashing a cockroach.

I returned my gun to the holster at my thigh, the barrel still smoking and warm against my leg. Pulling the ichor from my hair, I took a quick assessment of the scene around me, relieved to find an empty lot. The woman must have high-tailed it inside when she heard the crack of gunfire. Music thumped inside the bar, but the back alley was thankfully desolate.

I went to the dead woman and sighed. *Now the part of the job I hate.* I unhooked the radio at my hip and spoke into the receiver.

"PCI Base, this is Detective James. I need a cleanup crew and an ID on a vic at two-oh-eight Gotty Boulevard."

A voice came through the radio airwaves. "Ten-four on that. Sweepers are on the way." Static crackled the night air, ending the transmission. I clipped the radio back onto my belt and waited with the mangled woman until the guys from forensics showed up.

It didn't take them long to identify her. Her name was Cindy Edwards. She was a regular customer of the

Loose Goose Bar, but she wasn't an alcoholic or anything. She just enjoyed karaoke and happy hour.

Vick Parsons, a fellow detective on my squad, stepped up beside me and asked, "What's the story this time?"

I shrugged. "Random act of violence?"

"Come on, Edy. Get creative every now and then. Your reports are always labeled *'random act of violence'*."

I cut my gaze at him. "I'm a detective, Vick, not a screen-writer."

He ignored me, his head cocked to the side as he studied the woman's battered face. "How about…tragically killed by a pack of wild dogs?"

I rolled my eyes.

"Bobcats?"

I huffed a breath of annoyance and walked away.

He laughed, calling out, "What?"

I kept walking, shaking my head as I went. *Fucking Vick.* That guy chapped my ass on a daily basis. He was harmless enough, but he shamelessly flirted with me and didn't know when to quit. I had already told him the only way he'd get me into his bed was to tie Hugh Jackman to it.

As I reached for the handle of my car door, my cellphone vibrated in my back pocket. I checked the ID screen and flipped it open.

"Hey there sugar lips," I said to my best, and only friend, Kay Abrams. The reason she's my only friend? I work crazy-ass hours, and tend to hang out with seedy Supernatural beings, aka *Supes*. I also have little time for a social life. To be honest, I'm surprised Kay held on as long as she did.

We've been friends since I was seventeen. I was forced to transfer to Pearlman High during my senior year of high school after I got kicked out my last school, Clanton High, for carrying a switchblade. It was an innocent mistake. I had used it to carve a notch in my dashboard after I blew Rory McGregor's mind in the backseat of my car.

After I added the eighth notch to my collection, I kicked Rory out of my car and slipped the switchblade into my book bag. Still riding the high of my early morning quickie, I strolled through the metal detectors without a single thought of the switchblade bouncing around inside my bag.

Long story short, the school went ballistic and expelled me an hour later. The only lesson I learned from that day was to stop documenting my sexcapades. Unless it's on film, of course.

Meeting Kay in the twelfth grade was a blessing. She was a great distraction from boys. If it wasn't for her, I'd probably have some gross STD by now. At Clanton, I chased tail more than a cat in heat, but at Pearlman, my focus wasn't so singular.

Kay had me participating in all the typical teenage antics: cutting class, sleepovers, and even Prom. With Kay tutoring me, I raised my GPA by ten points! Kay filled my time, where the boys at Clanton had, but it wasn't long before I had a short fling with the Resource Officer…but that's a story for another time.

I'm a rotten friend when it comes to socializing; I barely have time to hang out and rarely ever phone. But I loved Kay as if she were blood. The only secret I'd ever kept from her was my actual profession. She, along with everyone else in my family, thought I was a regular detective, solving regular mortal crimes.

I wasn't ashamed of my job, in fact, I *loved* it. I kept unassuming humans safe from the darkness of the world and ensured order amongst the Supes. But I took an oath five years ago to never divulge my true title, as a Paranormal Crime Investigator.

"Hey," Kay answered back. "What are you up to?"

"Finishing up a case." I sank into the car seat and stuck the key in the ignition.

"Feel like grabbing a beer?"

I pinched the bridge of my nose.

"You know how to handle it now, Edy."

I let out a heavy sigh. "I know. It just brings up a lot of old memories, that's all."

After I lost both parents in a car accident, I decided the best way to handle depression was to numb it with alcohol. Lots of it. For a while it worked. Whenever I got lonely, I'd down a whisky sour, or two, or three and before long that pesky emotion called sadness faded away. But then…the nightmares followed me in the daytime, so I'd splash some vodka in my coffee mug, and be on my way.

Captain was an observant old miser and quickly picked up on my daily buzz. He killed it in an instant with threats to fire me or toss me in rehab facility run by leprechauns who stay sober by gardening, scrap-booking, and stitching moccasins for the elderly.

"You know what? I shouldn't have asked," Kay said. "I'm sorry, Edy. I'm an awful friend."

"No, you're not," I responded, looking up through my dash window. "You're just a bad influence." Vick was strolling in my direction. I groaned and decided that anything, even being in a roomful of temptation was better than listening to the bullshit that spewed from Vick's mouth. "I'll meet you at Alex's."

"I'll be waiting."

I snapped the phone shut and stepped out of the car to face Vick. "What?"

"Got a call about a Sasquatch sighting just west of Bella Coola."

I closed my eyes for an irritated beat, and muttered under my breath, "Shit."

"Want me to come along?"

I gave him a hard look. "No, thanks." I got back into my car and slammed the door behind me.

Vick bent at the parted window. "You sure? That's a long, lonely drive, Edy."

I started the engine and revved the gas. "You'll just slow me down." I sped off toward the interstate, leaving Vick choking on exhaust in a flurry of thrown gravel.

Chapter 2

"Damn it, Carl. Why can't you behave yourself?" Leaves crunched beneath the soles of my boots as I paced the length of the clearing. I was miles deep in the Canadian forest, and aside from the filtering moonlight through the canopy of trees, my flashlight was the only illumination in the darkness. I swung the light up and shone it in the monster's face. He looked back at me meekly, like a scolded child.

"They were roasting marshmallows." He dug his big toe in the dirt. "I like marshmallows."

"Are you kidding me?" I stared at him. "Marshmallows?" I threw my hands in the air. "Why can't you be more like Nessie? We haven't seen, or even heard a peep out of her for close to a decade. *You* on the other hand...you keep popping up all over the place."

I began pacing again just so I could put some distance between me and the big guy. I wanted to slap some sense into that hairy head of his, but I was pretty sure it wouldn't do any good. "Did you know there's a reality show dedicated to finding you?"

"I'm sorry, Miss Edy," he said with a shaky voice.

I stopped, and raked my fingers through my hair, frustrated. It wasn't Carl's fault he kept being seen by humans. His beastly side overruled what little intelligence he had. Driven by hunger, his grumbling stomach is what got him into trouble. Sasquatches have a remarkable sense of smell. Carl could track a bologna sandwich from over a mile away, and making that trek was a cinch with those long, furry legs of his.

"If I mail you a package of marshmallows once a month, will you promise to stay out of sight?"

His big brown eyes twinkled with delight, and he nodded his head excitedly. "Oh yes, Miss Edy." His lips pulled into a wide, goofy grin over his sharp canines. Ordinarily, Sasquatches look fierce with those menacing teeth shining in the moonlight, but Carl was an oversized, teddy bear. His body was completely covered in wooly fur, except the palms of his hands, and the soles of his feet.

I figured once PBP relocated Carl, I'd get an address from them and send the big guy a monthly package of marshmallows. A sugary, special delivery for the Sasquatch who has a special place in my heart.

It's almost laughable how such a simple thing as marshmallows can keep this potentially dangerous creature in line.

"Now, you know we have to relocate you? *Again*."

He looked down that the ground. "I know."

"I've already called the PBP. Their representatives are on their way now." PBP was the Paranormal Being Protection Unit. It was their responsibility to research homesteads for the likes of Sasquatches, Abominable Snowmen, and other free-roaming Supes.

"Do you know where they will send me?"

"Probably farther north. There are some dense forests farther inland, several hundred miles from here."

"I want to go to New Orleans."

"New Orleans?" I asked incredulously.

"I like crawfish." He rubbed his stomach.

I considered it for a moment but quickly ruled it out. Having Big Foot in such a heavily populated area was a bad idea, besides the Lizard Man lived out that way. That would be twice the chances of one of the monsters getting glimpsed. I shook my head. "That's Glen's territory. I can't send you there."

Carl waved me away like an annoying horse fly. "Pah. That old eye licker ain't come out of the swamp since the eighties. He won't mind."

I shined the flashlight right in his eyes. "I said, *no*."

He squinted and shrank back.

"You'll go wherever PBP sends you, and this time, you'll stay out of trouble." I hated treating Carl this way, but I had to be firm with him. He had no concept of the possible consequences should his existence come into light.

Humans would capture him, study him, and exhibit him, all in the great name of science. He'd be miserable, and humans would question everything they've come to know about the tiny, self-absorbed world they live in.

The low hum of Segways came up behind me. I swung the flashlight in their direction, casting a faded light on the shiny machines. Three men maneuvered their way through the trees, branches snapping under the wheels as they glided across the forest floor.

These weren't typical Segways. Their wheels were all-terrain, and the motor could easily handle seventy miles-per-hour if needed. Paranormal precincts have the coolest toys and a seemingly endless supply of funds to build them with.

The Segways slowly circled me and Carl. They

could have been sizing us up, but I had a sneaky suspicion they were trying to make a dramatic entrance.

Finally, they pulled up next to me, each revving their engines as if I'd be impressed with the barely-there whirling sound that reminded me more of a computer rebooting than a souped-up scooter. I blew out a breath, growing increasingly impatient at the amount of time these jokers were wasting.

Kay was waiting for me, and to be honest, the PBP Unit annoyed the fuck out of me. Somehow they always recruited like-minded individuals. You know the type, the ones who force you to deep-throat their hippy views until you're ready to hack them back onto their sandaled feet. Their gluten-free bodies nourished their holier than thou souls.

One at a time, each motor was killed until we were all standing in an awkward silence. I switched the flashlight to my other hand. Carl hung his head.

The agents stayed stationed on their glorified scooters. I think they got off on looking down at me, like knights on gleaming, electric steeds. The agent in the middle removed his helmet and shook out a long mane of hair. I guess he thought he looked striking, but since I don't dig the "cheesy romance-novel hero" look, I just rolled my eyes at him, bored and down-right irritated with their theatrical arrival.

"Evening, Detective James," the long-haired agent greeted, unzipping the fanny back at his hip. He pulled out an electronic device that resembled a tablet. His eyes shifted to the monster beside me. "Carl. Nice to see you, buddy." He smiled at the hairy creature.

Carl waved.

"Hello, Agent…" I had no idea what the idiots

name was, though we had crossed paths a few times before.

"Franco," he offered with a frown. "You don't remember me?"

"Of course I remember *you*. It's your name that won't stick." I tapped my temple to illustrate the fact my mind won't grab ahold of such an insignificant detail as his name.

Agent Franco grunted, and powered up his device. The tiny screen glowed green in his palm. The other two agents removed their helmets. I recalled seeing one before. With his headful of black, tight curls, I thought his hair resembled a patch of unruly pubic fuzz. The other must have been new because I didn't recognize the portly fellow at all.

"Carl. Carl. Carl." Agent Franco *tsked* gently. "What are we going to do with you?"

The Sasquatch didn't reply. He merely stood there, staring down at his massive feet.

"In my old neck of the woods," Pubes drawled, "nuisance animals got euthanized."

Carl gasped, his huge eyes wide with terror.

I shot a deathly glare to the man who was dealt the unfortunate hand of having pubes for hair. He snickered, but it looked far from good-natured.

I reached for my trusty switchblade I kept hidden in my back pocket. Before any of them realized what was happening, I rushed Pubes and slid into the Segway with him, my body flush against his. I held the sharp point of my blade beneath his chin. "And dicks get circumcised. Would you like me to demonstrate, cupcake?"

"Whoa, hey!" Agent Franco shouted.

I ignored him, my focus solely on getting the bastard to piss himself. Pubes' eyes were on me, but he held his head absolutely straight, not daring to move. Not daring to test me.

Though I was lost in the moment, I was still keenly aware of the scene around me. Franco climbed off his Segway, while the other agent stayed put—probably too scared to get mixed up with a crazy broad like me. Pubes' nostrils flared as he breathed frantically, his upper lip beading with sweat.

"Detective James," Franco said at my elbow. "Put down the knife." I ventured a quick glimpse of him. He gulped, his hands shaking as he held his arms out in front of him as if he was trying to tame a wild beast.

"Not until he apologizes to Carl." The words slipped through my clenched teeth like poison. My body was electrified with anger. I'm still not sure what exactly set me off. The horror in Carl's innocent eyes? The way Pubes smiled that mocking smile? Or maybe it was culmination of the entire night's events, starting with the demon-mauled blonde at the bar. Either way it was the perfect cocktail for a shit storm named Edy James.

"All right," Franco said with the tone of a professional negotiator. He looked at Pubes, then with a nod, he said, "Nick. I think you better go ahead and apologize."

"I'm not apologizing to a mangy animal!" Nick practically spat the words in my face.

I twisted the blade into the fleshy part of his chin, nicking him just enough for a pearl of blood to bloom.

Carl's incredible sense of smell picked up the scent instantaneously. He loped over and touched my wrist gently, silently begging me to stop.

I glanced at him, his big eyes misty pools of amber.

"No, Carl," I said, not willing to let it go. "This dipshit owes you an apology, and I'm not leaving until he gives you one." I turned back to Nick. "Now, are we going to do this, or not? Cause if not, I'll be glad to shave off your pubes for you." I smiled big and flicked my gaze to his hair. "And I don't mean the ones attached to your head."

"What?" The agent's eyes blazed. I'm really not sure why he was so pissed. He knew he had pubes for hair.

I gave him a thoughtful look. "Actually, I think I'd be doing you a favor. I personally prefer to wax, but I'm fresh out the stuff right now. Looks like all I have is *this* to do the job." To demonstrate I ran the flat of my blade across his chin, lingering a second longer than necessary at his Adam's apple.

"Crazy bitch," Nick seethed.

"Nice of you to notice." I grinned. "Now, if you please, can we get this over with? My friend is waiting for me at the bar."

"The bar," he scoffed. "From what I've heard, that's the last place you ought to be."

In that moment, I saw white. White hot fury that blinded me, like the crack of lightning. I was just about to gut the guy when Carl shoved me out of the way. My shoulder took most of the impact, but I rolled over in time to see Nick's face drop, his eyes bugging out of his head with fright.

With a furious roar, Carl backhanded him right out of the Segway. Nick crashed into a tree with a thud and folded into an unmoving heap on the ground.

Franco rushed to Nick, his Birkenstocks slapping against the dirt as he ran. Dropping down beside him, he felt for a pulse. "Nick! Nick! Are you okay?"

Nick groaned. Luckily for him, Carl didn't use all of his strength. If he had, Nick would have been dead the moment Carl's huge hand connected.

Franco whipped his head to look at me. "What the hell, James?"

I shrugged. "I don't know, dude. I usually work alone." I realized in that moment that Carl was as close to a partner as I'd ever had. Since we deal with such dangerous creatures, PCI Detectives usually worked in pairs, but since I don't play well with others, Captain has kept me solo.

Franco faced Carl, his jaw set tight as he processed everything.

The big guy wrung his massive hands. "Carl sorry. I did not like the way he talked to Miss Edy. Miss Edy nice."

The new agent huffed from his Segway. I shot him a glare that made his shoulders slump and his eyes avert in unison.

"Look," I said to Franco. "I'm not going to let some asshole talk to Carl that way. And since it didn't look like you were going to do say anything—I did." I put my hands on my hips.

"There are civilized ways to handle such things, James. I was going to pull him aside once we got back to headquarters."

"Pull him aside? Oooh." I gave a fake shiver. "Sounds *so* severe." I rolled my eyes.

Nick stirred. Franco bent his head to check his vitals. "You okay, man?"

Nick pushed Franco aside. His eyes found mine, and with a curl of his lip, he snarled. His body warbled, flickering from human to demon in a fraction a second. I was the only one to see it. Without an explanation, I withdrew Supe Slayer from its holster, aimed, and pulled the trigger.

Chapter 3

Franco was covered in ichor.

"Again. What the hell, James?" Franco cried, wiping black goo from his eyes.

I returned Supe Slayer to its home and strolled over to him. "Wow," I said. "That demon was quite a performer. He deserved a fucking Oscar."

Franco peered up at me, his face streaked with the smelly aftermath of a blown-up demon.

I slipped on my leather gloves and sank down to my haunches. "How in the hell did you not notice him? How long has he been on the Force?" I dragged my finger through the puddle of ichor on the ground. It was thick, like congealed blood. I sniffed at my gloved index finger and quickly identified the demon as a Greater Demon.

Those demons normally rule a minor dimension, and typically stay unseen. They have minions that do all their dirty work. But *this* one…this one was different. He had an agenda, and it made my skin crawl knowing the infinite possibilities of just what that agenda might be.

"Nick." Franco cleared his throat. "I mean, *it* had been with the unit for about six months now. It gave no indication it was anything other than human."

I stood up, puzzled over why a Greater Demon would disguise himself as a human for so long. Why infiltrate a PCI relocation agency?

The new agent finally came off his Segway. His rotund belly hung over his belt buckle, the buttons of his uniform shirt barely hanging on for dear life. "Franco, what...what now?" He seemed genuinely frightened. Poor guy. This was probably the most action he'd ever seen on a shift.

"Go back to headquarters. Let them know what happened. I'll handle the Sasquatch."

"You sure?" On one hand, the man looked hesitant but on the other, relieved as hell to be able to tear out of here and not look back.

"Go. I'll be fine. I'll find a new location for Carl and be back to the precinct as soon as possible. Make sure they start combing the hotspots for demon minions to see if we can't shake some info out of them."

The new guy nodded, then jumped back on his Segway, and zoomed away, kicking up rocks and leaf litter as he went.

"Thanks for looking out for Carl," I said, offering Franco my hand.

After eyeing it for a second, he took it and climbed to his feet. "Sorry about that crack he made about...well, you know."

I lifted my hand to cut him off. "Don't." The demon knew mentioning my addiction would make my blood boil. Then I was struck with a thought. A *demon* knew I was an alcoholic. God, did *everyone* know?

After I relayed all pertinent information about Carl's case to Franco, I turned to leave him to do his job. The PBP may have a team of dicks running things on the field, but Agent Franco would find the perfect home for Carl and get him there safely.

I started to weave my way back through the woods, when I remembered my offer with the so-called Big Foot. I cupped my hands around my mouth, and shouted, "Don't forget our deal, Carl. Marshmallows in exchange for you staying out of trouble!"

He turned, lifting his hand, and giving me a thumbs up. I smiled and continued to pick my way back to my car.

When I finally slid behind the wheel, I was beat. I hadn't slept in twenty-six hours, and the drive back was going to be long and incredibly boring.

I swung through a gas station to load up on caffeine and sugar before I headed back to Cloverfield, which was twenty miles south of Seattle.

I cranked the radio up and settled into a steady clip of eighty mph down the highway. I thought about Kay along the way. After the call came in about Carl, I bolted without some much as a pause to phone her. I stood her up. Again. Boy, was she going to be pissed. I have to admit though, I was partially relieved. I honestly wasn't ready to face the temptation so soon after my sobriety.

I also thought of my mom, and how proud she was when I graduated the Academy. I could still hear her squealing from the audience as I crossed the stage and took the shiny badge into my hand. Dad's chest always swelled whenever he told his friends what I did for a living. Being a regular beat cop was fulfilling…for a little while.

However, five years into my career, I was blind-sided by a man in a crisp tan suit and cool sunglasses. I had just clocked out and was leaving the police station when I saw him leaning casually against the hood of my car, one ankle crossed over the other, completely at ease.

"Hey! Asshole. That's my car, you know," I said as I walked up. "You put a dent in her, and I'll be sure to put a dent in your ass in return."

The man's lips quirked in amusement, but he didn't move. He removed his sunglasses and tucked them into the front pocket of his expensive linen suit. His eyes, shockingly blue and quick, roamed over me from top to bottom. Before I could call him out on the very obvious and very unashamed assessment of me, he nodded, as if approving what he saw, and said, "Precisely as they described."

"Excuse me?"

"Your reputation far exceeds you, Kennedy James."

Yes, my name is Kennedy. My mother was obsessed with the famous family. She scoured every known interview, book, and television clip about them. She was fascinated by the allure of Camelot and said she named me Kennedy in hopes that I would become as successful as them.

When I was old enough to know who they were, I remember thinking my mother was insane. They may have been a family full of attractive, intelligent, and successful members, but the family was also cursed. At times I was even bitter.

Thinking, here, little Edy James was born, naively bearing the great Kennedy name. Instead of being a source of inspiration, the name would press down on me like a weight. I'd often force myself to shake off the pessimism, but to be honest, as time wore on, I think their unrelenting curse crept out and latched onto me as well.

"Your work has been…" He cast his gaze out across the parking lot as he groped for the right word. "*monitored* by my department, and officials seem to think you have the potential to be a valuable member of our team."

"What team?"

The corner of his lip inched up further. He stuck his fingers into his jacket's breast pocket and pulled out a business card. He held it out to me.

I eyed it for a moment, noting the steadiness of his hand as he held it out toward me, waiting patiently. Biting my lip, I reached out, and took it. My gaze skipped across the typed font.

Paranormal Crime Investigation. Commander Stiles Boddax.

I arched a cynical brow at him and snorted. "Vick really goes all out, doesn't he?" I turned my head to the left, and right. "Where is the idiot? Hiding behind the dumpsters?" I craned my neck searching for his auburn mop of hair, or his snarky little laugh.

The man just looked at me, his eyes warming a fraction. "First exposure to our sector is always the hardest to overcome." He straightened, retrieved his sunglasses from his pocket, and slipped them on with a sleekness that I almost envied. "You mean this isn't a prank?" I shifted uncomfortably.

"I'm afraid not. Far from it actually."

I ran my gaze across the business card again. *Paranormal Crime Investigation.*

I opened my mouth to speak, but Commander Boddax beat me to the punch, by saying, "Reality is sometimes more chaotic than fiction, Miss James."

"Paranormal? Like ghost hunting?" I asked, my stomach churning at the mere thought of it.

"Interview for the position and all your questions will be answered."

I used the corner of the business card to scratch at my cheek. Though my interest was piqued, I couldn't help but feel like I was the butt of a vicious joke. I wasn't about to risk looking like a fool, so I lifted my chin. "Sounds like a load of bullshit if you ask me. I'm happy where I am, thanks." I offered the card back to him.

He stood stock-still, his expression impassive. I wished I could have seen his eyes behind the sunglasses. To be able to find a hint of what was running through his head. The shiny lens only mirrored my own image, standing with slouched shoulders. Wispy pale hair, hanging like feathers down my back, and a scowl that emitted the clear reading of self-doubt, and contempt.

He ignored the card. "Call me when you decide to interview." He jammed one hand into a pocket and strolled away.

"When I decide?" I called. "Don't you mean, *if*?"

He didn't answer me. He just kept walking, his fancy Italian leather shoes reflecting the sunlight like tiny glowing orbs hovering above the asphalt. He moved like liquid mercury. Curiously sleek, like quicksilver in human form. I watched him until he cut a corner and disappeared entirely into a quiet alley. I looked back once more at the card, drawn to the simple black print. *Paranormal Crime Investigation.*

I called Commander Boddax a few days later out of curiosity, and the rest is history.

When I was officially hired by the Paranormal Crime Team, I wanted so badly to call my parents on the phone and share the wonderful news. But, they had died three months earlier in a head on collision. It wasn't until later that I learned that their death made me that much more desirable to the paranormal crime unit. Most of the team are either widows or loners.

Normal police work is dangerous, but replace regular convicts with ones who drink blood, shift into dangerous animals, or can cast a spell, and things get pretty hairy. Sometimes *literally.* It's better to not have a family to worry about you, or someone to have to explain your unfortunate demise to, should you get whacked by a Supe.

I don't remember undressing, showering, or crawling into bed that night, but I must have done all of those things. I awoke naked, buried to my chin in my comforter, with a headful of tangled hair.

I flicked my eyes to the clock on the nightstand. *Shit.* I was late. *Hours* late. At this point, it wasn't even worth rushing. Thirty minutes late, or three hours late, the Captain was going to be all over my ass either way. I went to the kitchen and started a pot of coffee.

I crammed a muffin that was well past its prime into my mouth and walked back to my room, fully aware the living room blinds were open. I didn't care. If anyone was peeking in my window, they just got an eyeful of a bare ass, and the unflattering sight of me scratching it as I strolled by.

I dressed in my usual garb. Skinny jeans, leather boots, shirt, and slim motorcycle jacket. Forgive me for not being a fashionista. Kay was far better in that department than I was. She kept up with the trends, and she loved anything flashy. I shit you not, her favorite color is sparkle.

The pot of coffee was finally done; I could smell it as I came out of my bedroom. I poured a cup, and after quickly downing the first mug, I prepared a second for the drive into work. Once there, I hustled through door, tossing around quick glances before I flung myself into my desk chair.

I didn't see the Captain, so I was hoping to appear as though I'd been there all along. I stripped out of my jacket, flipped open a few folders, and shuffled some papers around the desk. Then, I felt a pair of eyes burning into my skull, and I knew I had been caught.

I gritted my teeth and waited.

"James!"

I hung my head. *Fuck.*

"Can I see you in my office?" Captain shouted, not bothering to be discreet.

A low murmur spread throughout the room. I spun around in my rolling chair and shoved myself to my feet. *Here comes the tirade.* I felt every set of eyes in the room follow me as I made my way through the maze of desks toward Captain's office.

I stopped at the open door. He was leaning over his desk, both hands spread wide on the polished wood. He looked to be reading some sort of report.

I swallowed. "You wanted to see me, sir?"

He lifted his gaze. "Close the door," he ordered.

"Can I be outside of it when I do?" I gave a tense laugh.

He was not amused.

I shut the door behind me. I didn't move to take a seat, nor did he offer me one. That was okay, I'd rather be on my feet. It gave me a head start in case he reached across the desk to throttle me. That's what I expected him to do anyway: grow red in the face, sweaty under the pits, and maybe even shove a few papers off the desk, but all he did was lower his head and go back to reading.

Strange, I thought, peering at him as he studied the report with great concentration.

With the top of his head facing me, his bald spot was in full view. Several freckles and a liver spot were aligned just so, that it resembled a face staring back at me. I had to bite my lip just to keep from laughing.

"Spare me the excuse of why you waltzed your ass through my doors *four* hours late, James," he said to his papers. "I don't have the time nor the patience to be fed a mouthful of crap today. Just know, that I'm watching you. *"*

He raised his eyes and pinned me with a deadly glare.

"Dually noted, sir." I turned to leave, but before I could turn the knob, he spoke again.

"That's not the only reason I called you in here."

I faced him, curious. "Sir?"

He straightened, sighing deeply as he dragged a hand across his face. He looked older in that moment. The strands of silver hair far outnumbered the black now, and the lines in his face were as deep as a newly etched tombstone. "The inner-city district went over their quota."

"How much over?"

"Thirteen," he said flatly.

"That's Tina's district," I said, frowning. "She runs a pretty tight ship over there. There's no way she'd allow that many over-feeds."

Let me bring you up to speed. You see, the PCI gives vamp district leaders' human death allotments per year. These allotments are agreed upon by the vampire leaders based on their district population. Ideally, vamps aren't supposed to kill humans as they feed, but it's naïve to think accidents don't happen. Fifteen murders per month may sound like a lot to you but given that the United States logs more than six-hundred thousand missing persons each year, fifteen seems like a drop in the bucket. Plus, as sick as it is, with the amount of vamps feeding each day, fifteen "over-feeds" is merely collateral damage in the PCI's mission to keep vampires hidden from the mortal public.

Tina's district is relatively small in terms of vampire population. Many vamps choose to live on the outskirts of the city, rather than directly in the center of it. The reason? In the city, the prey is plentiful. Too plentiful. Many vamps can't handle the temptation of so many humans in one location, plus the chance of being outed as vampire is a bigger risk in the city, versus the less-populated areas of Washington.

Surprisingly, over-feeds rarely happen in the city. This is because of the copious amount of prey, overflowing the streets and crowding the bars. Ripe for the picking, or more appropriately, for the biting, the vampire's sole food-source is literally everywhere.

You may be asking yourself, what's an over-feed? Well, an over-feed happens when a vampire either purposely or accidently drinks too much blood from the victim, resulting in the human's death. Tina's monthly quota is fifteen, but typically PCI only reports one or two mortal deaths in her district each month. I scrubbed the back of my neck, pondering. "There has to be some sort of explanation. Maybe they had a rogue vamp stray through?"

Captain snorted. "And feasted on that many humans? If that's the case, then I want to see the poor bastard. He's probably got blood coming out every orifice right about now."

I wrinkled my nose.

"Find out what the hell is going on over there, and let your girl know that I don't take this reckless behavior lightly." He eyed me momentarily, surely catching the flinch that stung through me. "Remind her of the consequences of breaking Otherworld Laws. I'm sure the thought of being sun-fried won't appeal to the Mistress."

With a grunt, he plundered into his chair, the leather squeaking beneath his robust frame. When he lifted the receiver of his phone to his ear and began punching in a number, it became obvious I had been dismissed. I quietly let myself out and stalked back to my desk.

I sank into the desk chair, numb with the information I just received. *Twenty-eight people?* There *had* to be an explanation. Supes had been abiding the Otherworld Laws for decades. The laws were written and mandated by the Being Leaders. A collection of one respected representative from each species of Supe, as well as the mortal President at the time of its conception. A side note in case you're wondering.

The Laws were created in the early 1960s, and when they were finally honed and deemed acceptable by all, a young, dashingly handsome president penned his messy signature next to the paw print of Alpha

Werewolf, Thad Rodshadow. Take that info in, and let it marinate in your brain for a while. An odd Kennedy connection, that always made me feel as though I was destined for this job.

Anyway, with the Otherworld Laws agreed upon, each member signed the ordinances, swearing their people would obey them. The word of the Supe may not always mean much, but their mark upon something is eternally binding.

I needed to talk to Tina to get to the bottom of it. I stood and snatched my gun from my desk and shoved it into the holster. Slipping my arms into the sleeves of my jacket, I took brisk strides through the room, ignoring Vick's greeting as we passed in the hall.

Vick and I were both beat cops at my former precinct. I was recruited by the PCI two years before he was, and I remember the day he walked through the headquarters doors. I had just come back from a raid at a toy factory. (The place was overrun illegal nymphs who were trying to pass themselves off as Barbie dolls.)

"Well, I'll be damned," Vick said, sidling up beside my desk. "If it isn't Kennedy James?"

I kept writing my report.

"It's so nice to see a familiar face," he continued. "What do you make of this paranormal crime shit? Crazy right?"

"Yeah. Crazy. Now if you'll excuse me, I have a report to fill out."

"You're still mean as a viper I see."

"And just as deadly," I added, casting my eyes up at him.

He grinned. "Ooh. Now that's fucking hot." He slid his finger along my jawline. "One day, Edy. You will let your guard down, and when you do…I'm going to nail you. *Hard.*" He quirked his brow, giving me what he believed to be a sexy smirk.

I grabbed his finger and jumped out of my chair. Wrapping his arm into a submission hold, I slammed his face into the desk with a *thwack*! I felt Vick's bones crack in my grip, but I only gripped tighter, making sure he got my message loud and clear. Vick squirmed and let out a pained grunt.

"James!" Captain yelled from somewhere behind me. "Be nice to the new recruit, or I'll make him your partner."

That changed my tone real quick. I released my hold and righted Vick back into a normal position. Having him as my partner would be a disaster; one of us would not live to tell about it.

Vick rubbed his forehead, scowling. "Crazy bitch."

I drew my arm back, and Vick flinched away. My lips curled at that. Instead of decking him, like I wanted so badly to do, I reached into my back pocket and drew out my switchblade. The same switchblade that was confiscated all those years ago in high school. Vick's eyes shifted nervously to the blade in my hand. I smiled sweetly, and started toying with it, flicking it open and closed over and over. Captain, tired of my shenanigans, thundered, "James!" I pretended not to notice, snapping the switchblade into its full, and dangerous glory with a definite *snick* just before leaning close. I whispered with all the venom I could muster, "Touch me again, and I'll castrate you." Then, I shoved him one last time, before stalking away.

Chapter 4

With determined clips, I made my way to my car. I was still reeling over what Captain said. *Twenty-eight humans were dead?* Part of me was pissed. Tina and I had history, so I was a little peeved she'd pull that shit. Then, a clearer-headed version of me rationalized that something else was going on. Tina wouldn't jeopardize the good standing she'd earned at the precinct, and she just wasn't capable of blatant disregard of Otherworld Laws.

And no, my history with Tina wasn't a sordid one. We weren't lesbian lovers, although I'm sure she'd make one hell of a girlfriend. Tina had plunging curves everywhere and a sexy mole at the corner of her mouth. When I first met her, her lips were blood-stained. After meeting countless other vampires, with their pale mouths that seemed to blend in with the rest of their chalky white skin, seeing Tina's blood-red lips were a stark reminder of what she really was.

When I first joined the PCI, I was technically a rookie all over again, so I was assigned low-level crime scenes while I learned the ropes of the secret paranormal sector. One of my first missions was at a seedy dock along the coast. The crime involved a pick-pocketing mermaid. I was questioning a drunken sailor on the pier, who insisted a beautiful woman lured him into the water, where she molested him, then stole his watch and shoes. I remember looking down at his sodden socks, and wondering why in the hell would a mermaid steal shoes?

The mermaid who allegedly did all of those things was swimming in wide, lazy circles around the pillars of the pier. She looked utterly bored, and sometimes would "accidently" splash my expensive leather boots with mucky water. It didn't take me long to realize mermaids were nothing but trouble. They are not the angelic beings you think they are. They don't pluck underwater harps, salaciously sprawled across moored ships…no.

They're vile creatures, who'd rather poke fun at a man clinging to a sinking boat, than save him. They are the reason fisherman's bait gets lost, fishing lines get tangled, and tsunami's crash onto shore. They are pretty to look at, but they're downright nasty on the inside.

All evidence pointed to the mischievous mermaid, but of course, she feigned innocence and refused to get into the holding tank (the PCI's specially designed portable containers for unruly aquatic Supes). I had to jump into the water to attempt to restrain her, but of course, she fought back, biting me on the arm, and slapping me with her powerful tail. I wasn't much of a swimmer to begin with, but paired with wet clothes, and heavy boots, I soon became exhausted by the struggle.

The mermaid swore at me, using words that would curl even a weathered sailor's toes, and plunged under the water, pulling me along with her. My lungs burned, but if I screamed out in pain, I'd only ingest a mouthful of salty water. I drifted deeper, and deeper still, until soon I felt weightless.

Tina was…well, let's just say, she was 'enjoying her dinner' in a nearby hotel, famous for its ocean view. Vampires have incredible vision and hearing, so she saw and heard everything that was happening below. With lightning speed, she intervened just before the mermaid stuffed me under a concrete pipe. I was yanked from the dark waters and tossed onto the pier, sputtering and gasping for breath.

The mermaid escaped, disappearing beneath the rippling waves, but I was in no condition to go after her. I ached from head to toe, my limbs feeling like wet sand.

I muttered a quick thanks to the vampire, but I was pissed beyond reason that a stupid *mermaid* kicked my ass. I mean come on, she doesn't even have legs! I reasoned she was part shark and dragged myself to a stand, my saturated clothes sticking to my skin uncomfortably.

"You know you owe me now," Tina said, crossing her arms in front of her. "I don't do anything for free."

"Except test people's blood type," I shot, wringing out my jacket.

She smirked. "I think I like you."

I eyed her suspiciously. She was right after all. Vamp's rarely do good deeds just for the hell of it. It usually comes with a price, either in the form of a favor, a pardon, or an exchange of blood.

Her smile grew wider, revealing her fangs, which glistened dangerously beneath the moonlight. I thought she might pounce on me right then, but instead, she turned around so quick, her thick braid swung out like a round-house kick.

Tina walked away saying, "I'll collect payment

someday."

We've been *nearly* friends ever since. I say nearly because no self-respecting vampire would ever claim a human as a friend. Or a lover for that matter, so everything you've read is ludicrous. Vamps only see mortals as a food source. Of course, you may find a sicko vamp or two out there who'd have sex with a mortal, but hey, even the human world has a few twisted people who make goo-goo eyes at goats, so go figure.

Tina and I had an understanding. She'd keep her clan in line, and I'd leave her district alone. Until now, there hadn't been any major disturbances in her area, aside from complaints about Georgie, the vampire-stalker.

Georgie was a metal-head who wore nothing but black, save for the odd white contacts that made his eyes look like boiled eggs. Georgie suspected Tina was a vampire but never had any solid proof.

PCI had their eyes on Georgie for a while, briefly considering scrubbing his memory, but after surveillance proved him to be just a die-hard Goth, who dabbled in Satanism, they left him alone. He wasn't any danger to outing Tina as a vamp. He was just as clueless as the rest of the mortal society, and that's the way PCI planned to keep it.

What Georgie didn't know was the stuff he saw in movies was made-up. A vampire bite doesn't result in Turning. In order for a human to Turn, a series of complicated rituals had to take place. This includes blood-letting, denouncing all forms of faith, eating grave dirt, and a sacrificing. So Georgie would have been bitten all right, but he wouldn't have Turned.

Well, he wouldn't have Turned into a vampire anyway. He would have likely turned into a blood-less corpse.

As I pulled into Tina's apartment complex, I took note of the vampires chatting in the parking lot. Their keen eyes followed me as I crossed the pavement and climbed up two flights of stairs. I stopped at the last door on the floor and rapped it with my knuckles.

The door opened slightly, catching on the door chain. I found it funny a vampire used a lock in the first place. With their superhuman strength and senses, I figured vampires could easily fend off an intruder.

Tina peered at me through the gap, her eyes tightening at the corners as she gauged my rigid posture.

"We need to talk," I said, glaring at her.

Her mouth twisted, and she shut the door in my face. I heard the latch sliding, before the door opened again. She stepped aside, allowing me to push past her.

"You're here about the quota."

"What the hell, Tina? You're allotted fifteen per month. Isn't that enough? I thought we had an agreement?"

She shut the door and moved with the grace only a vampire could possess to her plush chaise lounge. She spread herself across it and regarded me like a regal queen upon a throne.

"Unfortunately, I do not have the answers you seek."

I arched an eyebrow.

"Efforts are being made to trace the killings."

I planted my fists on my hips. "This is PCI jurisdiction now, so I'll be handling the case from here on out. You can call off your goons and allow the professionals to handle it."

Her dark eyes scanned me, her face expressionless as she said in a monotone voice, "It isn't wise to delve into vampire affairs, Edy. This is *my* district and *my* clan. Little happens within the streets that I do not know about or learn about. Stay out of the way, and I'll report any pertinent findings to you as they come."

She snapped her fingers, and a blonde vampire emerged from the back bedroom. He wore only a black bathrobe, his skin pearly white amongst the splash of dark fabric. He dropped to his knees at her feet and began massaging her toes and instep. I ignored him and glowered at Tina, thoroughly ticked. *Did this bitch actually just tell ME what to do?*

I squared my shoulders. "Go ahead and continue your research, but I'll be doing a little digging of my own. I expect you to report anything suspicious to me directly."

I walked to the door. Save for the whisk of air whipping past me, I barely registered Tina's movement, until she was standing before me, blocking the door with her body.

She narrowed her eyes. "I offered you a warning, Edy. My conscious is telling me these killings were not by the hands of my clan. If that proves to be true, then any mortal who has the misfortune to face the one responsible, will be in great danger."

"Thanks for the concern," I replied as I reached for the doorknob. Tina allowed me to pull it open. Cool air drifted in, but of course, it didn't cast a chill on either vampire. I slid a venomous glare at Tina. "But I think I'll take my chances anyway."

I left, walking with furious steps back to my car.

Fucking Tina. Yeah, she saved my life once, but how dare she insinuate any incompetence on my behalf. Just because I was a human, didn't mean I couldn't solve the crime. Twenty-eight people were dead. Someone's fingerprints were all over this mass murder, and I was going to find out who.

The next night, a call came in from the sleepy town of St. Hoover. Several residents reported seeing a massive wolf-like animal running loose on their normally quiet streets. Since I didn't have any leads on the inner-city district killings, I took the case.

Before heading out, I went to the weapons room to select a few necessities, just in case. I scanned the shelves, knowing exactly what I wanted. Fairy Repelling Dust. *No.* EMF meter. *Nope.* Wing cuffs. *Not today.* My gaze ran across the rack of glistening Smite knives. For being so deadly, the specialized steel was oddly beautiful. It rippled with a visible aura, much like heat roiling off asphalt.

Blessed by Benedict monks, Smite was the only metal powerful enough to kill a vampire. Captain had recently taken a trip to Saint Ambrose Monastery, something he does every so often to keep the good-faith of the monks who provide such a vital weapon to the PCI.

I strolled to the shelf labeled WERES. I lifted two small canisters of *Were Mace* and snagged a box of silver bullets. *Hopefully I won't need any of this,* I thought to myself as I shoved everything into my coat pockets. As I was signing out the equipment, Captain came to the doorway. He leaned against it in an attempt to look casual, but I could tell by the tense set of his shoulders, something wasn't right.

"Something wrong?" I questioned.

"Topher is a bit out of his territory tonight," Captain said somberly. His eyes grave as he regarded me from across the space of the room.

"He's usually harmless," I replied, patting my pockets to make sure everything was where it should be. "I'll check it out. Have a chat with him."

"What did you learn from the Mistress?" he asked, unsubtlety changing the subject.

Captain always referred to Tina by her formal title. As reigning leader, she was called the district Mistress, and no other vampire dared to relinquish her of her status, unless they were ready to battle for it. Vampires have little democracy in their world. Leaders are often elders who have proven their right to rule by killing either a mortal of great importance or another vamp leader.

I'm not entirely sure how Tina came into power, but rumor has it, she finished what John Wilkes Booth started. Abraham Lincoln was gravely wounded in the theater that night, but theorists believe he would've survived if it hadn't had been for the massive blood loss. Blood loss that wasn't just from the gunshot wound, but from two puncture marks behind his ear. They were inflicted by an unknown source, but suspiciously resembled fang marks.

Generations later, the truth is still a blurred line. Most historians accept the facts that have been printed in black and white, but paranormal philosophers (yes, there is such a thing) insist there is a gray area that has Tina's teeth all over it. The closest thing to evidence I've ever seen is the way Tina locks her jaw whenever there is mention of the Civil War.

I wonder what she'd do if you handed her a five-dollar bill? Refuse it? Slap it away? Shrink from it? Maybe she'd hiss, and go all Nosferatu?

Captain cleared his throat, snapping me back to our conversation.

"She's aware the district went over," I answered hastily. "But she doesn't believe her clan is responsible."

"Then who is?"

I shrugged. "She's researching it. She'll be reporting all findings to me." My steady gaze faltered. "I have yet to find any of my own leads."

He unhitched himself from the doorframe and set a straight stare upon me. "Well find one."

I stared at his bald spot as he walked away, my fingers squeezing into fists. *Right. Because it's just that easy.*

****

The tires of my car were almost silent as they treaded the dirt-laden backroads of St. Hoover. Porch lights glowed eerily along the way, the only light in the deeply set, tree-surrounded cottages. The lack of civilization would prove to be in my favor. Since there weren't any streetlamps this far from town, it would be easy to convince the eyewitnesses that they didn't see, what they thought they saw.

I chatted with an old man and his wife first. They told me they were birdwatching on their sprawling wrap-around porch when a trampling of paws startled them. A huge "dawg," as the man called it, barreled through his turnip garden, and flung dirt across his freshly washed truck.

He gave chase at first, but when he noticed the

immense size of the animal, he backed away. He grumbled about his garden some more, before telling me he'd be waiting with his shotgun the next time that blasted *dawg* came around causing trouble.

The second witness was a widow, who thought the critter she saw was a coyote. She feared for her slew of house cats and insisted Animal Control do something about the vile creature.

The last witness didn't see the animal, but they heard the distinct howl of a wolf and mentioned that he caught a whiff of men's cologne as he was pulling in his fishing lines from the pond. An odd combination he'd never experienced out in the secluded area of St. Hoover.

I dispelled all of their wild stories by informing them a timber wolf got loose from an exotic animal breeder just outside the city limits. Professional trackers were hunting the animal and not to worry. All seemed pleased with my explanation, which was good. That meant I didn't have to use the *Evap* on anyone.

As I was driving to Topher's place, a blur of gray fur dashed across the road. *Shit!* I slammed on the brakes, skidding the car sideways, narrowly avoiding crashing into the line of bushes and small trees that ran along either side of the road.

Gripping the wheel, I searched the darkness beyond the windows. *Was that Topher?*

I opened the car door and stepped out into the night. Chirping crickets fell quiet, which sent a cold shiver of uneasiness through me. I squinted into the shadows.

"Topher?" I tested, my voice bouncing off the tree trunks.

I was greeted with only a steady silence, save for the hooting owl somewhere in the distance.

"Topher. Is that you?"

I ducked back into the car long enough to grab a flashlight from the glove department. I shined it into the wood line. I saw nothing except still leaves and untouched soil.

Assuming it was nothing more than a loose dog, I turned back around-unsuspecting of the crushing blow that came from behind-slamming me into the metal frame of the car. Pain exploded in my back and chest from the impact.

Two strong hands gripped my shoulders and flung me around. Dazed, I barely registered the drawn fist, but I clumsily blocked it, reacting just in time to swing my own fist up and across, connecting to the man's temple. He staggered but quickly shook it off, like it was nothing more than an annoying interruption, and kept coming for me.

In the tussle, I realized he was nude, his brawny chest full of curling sprouts of hair, his thick thighs like cuts of meat. He encircled me with his muscular arms, and I squirmed against him. The situation quickly shifted from dire, to awkward. *Eww. I'm fighting a naked guy.*

I gritted my teeth, totally skeeved out by that fact that his package was squished between us. I heaved my knee up in a swift motion. He grunted, and folded, but not before wildly swinging at me, knocking a closed fist into my side. My ribs suffered, and the air was snatched from my lungs. I fell against the opened car door, clinging to it just to remain upright.

He dove at my ankles, sweeping me off my feet.

My head clunked against the interior door compartment, and before I could gather my wits, the asshole pounced again. He straddled me, completely unaffected that his balls were resting against my gun belt. *Gross! I'm going to have disinfect my holster now!*

He glared down at me and raised his fist once more. My fingers felt around my pockets for the *Were Mace,* but before I could pull it out, another set of hands clamped down on the man's shoulders, jerking him off me.

I scrambled to push myself upright, leaning heavily upon the car as I watched Topher pummel my attacker into unconsciousness. It was a brutal beating and quite frankly, quick and clean on Topher's part.

When Topher pulled away from him, panting, it was then that I realized the unknown man was a Were. He lay unmoving, nothing but a heap on the ground. Blood trickled from his nose from where Topher had broken it.

Topher spat in the grass, then swiped the back of his hand across his mouth. "You all right?"

I brushed myself off, careful not to touch my gun belt. The memory of the Were's pubes made me crinkle my nose. "Yeah. Thanks."

"What are you doing out here?" Topher asked.

"Looking for you actually."

His brows lifted high. "Me?"

"Got some calls about a mutant dog-coyote thing, so I figured it was you," I answered, pressing two fingers to the smarting knot on the back of my head. I winced but was happy to find clean fingertips when I pulled back my hand.

"It was me," he admitted. "But I was only

hunting." He paused, his gaze ran over the Were, his lip curling in disgust. "Just, not for food," he snarled.

Chapter 5

I studied him. His snug thermal shirt was pushed past his elbows. His sandy hair was cropped short, which showed all the workings of his facial muscles as he adjusted his jaw and neck. Even the throbbing in his temples seemed more pronounced.

"What do you mean?" I asked.

He looked back at me again. "I think this is the asshole who mated with my sister. *Non-consensually.*"

A prick of anger flared within me. "You mean he *raped* her?"

"In mortal terms, yes. But there is no such term in the Were world. When you're in your animal-form, there is no basis of morality. Your hunger, needs, lusts, urges…they rule all your senses. You act in the moment and pay later for the consequences."

I rolled my shoulders, still checking myself for injuries. All bones appeared to be intact. "So then what's got your boxers in a wad?"

His brows met. "Weres don't *wear* boxers. The less clothes, the better."

I raised both palms. "I know. I know. The less, the better for easier transitioning." *Sheesh. Weres have no sense of humor.* "Anywho. So if Weres can act the part whenever they're in animal form, then why are you hunting him?"

His fists clenched. Even in the darkness, I could

see the whites of his knuckles bulging beneath his skin. "He was in our territory. If he hadn't trespassed, it never would have happened."

"So you don't know him?" I looked down at the Were on the ground curiously.

He shook his head.

"Isn't it rare for Weres to cross paths? I mean, don't you piss on everything to mark your territory?"

He scowled. "Something like that."

Chapter 6

I left St. Hoover with the knowledge that Weres mark territory with scent, not piss, and that the unknown man would have to answer to Topher's pack jurisdiction for not abiding by Pack Laws of announcing his presence and intent.

Topher said the Were would likely be forcibly implanted with a GPS tracker, so surrounding packs could keep tabs on him until they deem it safe to remove. I figured whatever other punishment they'd inflict was far harsher than what I could do at the PCI unit, so I allowed Topher to sling the knocked-out Were over his shoulder and haul him away, but not before I collected a sample of his hair.

What I didn't understand was why the stranger attacked me in the first place. He could have easily told me who he was or, better still, left me the hell alone completely.

*****

My body cursed me as I forced it to sit behind the desk for another two hours, tirelessly researching the Were's ID. The PCI lab was running the hair sample through the Supe DNA Database, so while I waited, I went through some case files by hand. Scanning each one for a description that resembled the six-foot mass of raging testosterone that attacked me.

The lab finally got a hit in Vancouver. Leopold, or

"Leo" Trevino, and by the looks of his rap sheet, he wasn't a nice guy. He'd been involved in multiple bar fights and also served time for assault and battery against a human. My eyes scanned the additional notes that were typed in the comment box. *Unpredictable. Disdain for humans. Dangerous.*

I rubbed my temples. *Lovely. Just what I need running around my jurisdiction.*

Spent from the night's events and still mentally exhausted from the trouble brewing the inner district, I decided to call it a day. I grabbed my jacket from the back of my chair and slipped it on. My muscles moaned in return. I needed the triple hot treatment. Hot shower, hot-oil massage, and a hot guy to give it. Since I hadn't had a single long-term relationship in my entire life, I'd have to settle for one out of three. *Hot shower.*

On the drive home, I punched the steering wheel when I drove past Alex's Pub. *Damn it!* I forgot to call Kay, and now she was probably so pissed at me she was giving me the silent treatment until I called her first. I slipped my cellphone out of my pocket and quickly dialed her number. She didn't answer, forcing me leave an awkward message.

"Hey, it's me. Sorry about the other day. Cop stuff. I know, it's always cop stuff, but really, I had to handle a special case. If you still—"

Her voicemail cut me off, then there was a dull dial tone ringing in my ear.

"Want to go…" I let my sentence trail off. I cursed and tossed my phone into the passenger seat. I was too tired to care anymore. I promised myself I'd call her soon, and with a heavy weariness that shadowed me across the lawn, into the house, and down the hall to my bedroom, the promise was enough. *For now*. It took all my attention just to step into the shower and wash myself.

I collapsed into bed, and almost as soon as my eyes fell shut, I was asleep.

****

I awoke to a sunny morning outside my curtains. Squinting, I held my hand up in front of my face, shielding my eyes from the beams of sunlight that poured in like lasers. I am not a morning person.

I swung my feet to the floor and massaged my achy shoulders and neck. I dragged myself out of bed, groaning, and shambled like a zombie to the window. And in case you're wondering, no, zombies aren't real. In fact, I'll settle this mess right now.

The crazy idea that the undead roam around searching for brains came from a cannibal in New Guinea that was accidently buried alive. The tribe thought he was dead, but he was actually unconscious from a venomous snake bite. He later came to and dug his way out his own grave. He must have looked like hell, covered in dirt, woozy on his feet, and exhausted.

He stumbled to the fireside, where a massive feast was being held. Just so happens, a couple of English men were there, doing research on the tribe and their rituals. Human innards, and brains were on the spit, barely even warm, when the cannibal crashed the festivities. He grabbed the brain from the fire and devoured it like a hungry animal. The researchers threw up in the bushes and spread the story of the dead rising from the ground and feeding on human brains.

Now, with that settled, I'd also like to dispel the rumor of any forth-coming zombie apocalypses. Listen to me. THERE ARE NO SUCH THING AS ZOMBIES. THERE WILL BE NO ZOMBIE APOCALYPSE.

If there were zombies, the PCI would probably enlist all military forces to wipe them out. There would be no questions asked and no details given. Their instructions would be "kill on sight," and believe me, when those orders are given from our department, that's all the military needs to hear before they come out with guns a-blazing.

Since zombies would likely lack intelligence, have zero reasoning abilities, or restraint, they would not be capable of adhering to Otherworld Laws, so in order to maintain harmony amongst the mortals and Supes, the zombie species would have to be eradicated. With zombie existence now clarified, I'll get back to my story.

After a cup of coffee and a cream cheese bagel, I returned to my bedroom to dress in my standard uniform. Random shirt, jeans tucked into boots, and a leather jacket. I checked my reflection in the mirror, almost satisfied with it, aside from the unruly hair. I pulled a brush through the length of it, wincing when I snagged it on a knot. Eventually, it smoothed, so I swept it up into a high ponytail and was almost ready to head to the station. I poured myself another cup of kick-starter, aka coffee, and headed out the door.

As I strolled through the halls of the precinct, I couldn't shake the feeling that everyone was looking at me expectedly, as if they knew something I didn't.

Then…I knew why. I halted at the double doors leading to the squad room so abruptly the coffee sloshed out my cup and onto my shoes. I glowered through the glass, my hackles rising with sinking realization. *So, that's why everyone was staring at me. They're waiting for my reaction.* I gripped the cup in my hands tighter and shoved the doors apart.

Captain was talking with a leanly muscular, dark-haired man at my desk. The stranger had his butt planted on top of my desk, his posture relaxed, and full of confidence. The Captain's arms gestured around him, as if giving him a seated tour of the office. I stomped my way toward them. Captain turned to acknowledge me, but I ignored him, glaring at the man instead. My eyes went from a dead stare into his eyes, to a pointed look at his ass.

He didn't seem to register what I was relying with my heated gaze, so I gladly informed him.

"Your *ass* is on my desk."

He regarded me with round eyes for a moment, but then his mouth drew into a smile. His gaze traveled down the length of me, before returning to meet my stare.

"So it is." He slid off the desktop and took up a casual stance beside the Captain. I divided my simmering glare between them.

"Once again, James, your first impression is stellar." Captain raked his eyes across me, his expression bored or irritated, I couldn't tell which. Maybe both. "With the inner-city case being…unusual, I've decided it would be best handled by a team, rather than a solo investigator."

I scoffed. "Unusual? Aren't all our cases, *unusual*?" I sat my coffee down and crossed my arms tightly over my chest.

He stood, unmoved by my comment.

"This is Seth Grooms," he said, unbuttoning the cuff of his sleeve, and methodically rolling it, inching it up and over his meaty elbow. "He'll be assisting you with the case." He began to work on the other sleeve, his tone authoritative, as if daring me to challenge him.

I didn't want to disappoint him, so I shot back, "I work better alone. Let Newbie here handle something more his own speed." I flicked my gaze to Seth.

The guy crammed both hands into his pants pockets, and his brows lifted in interest as he quietly listened. His collared shirt was crisply pressed, his badge winking up at me from the belt loop of his dark denim jeans.

Fucking collared shirts, I thought bitterly. *I hate collared shirts.* They reminded me of preppie, man-bag toting men and dusty old guys. My lip curled involuntarily. *At least he's not wearing khakis.* "Maybe the juvenile cyclops who are dining and dashing?" I offered, teasingly.

Seth's mouth twisted as he fought back a smile.

The Captain's gaze shifted to Seth fleetingly, before frosting over with scorn. "Good luck with this one," he said as he jerked his chin in my direction. "I apologize now for whatever comes out of her mouth." He bustled away, grumbling something about insubordination and opinionated females.

I dug my nails into the leather fabric of my jacket, anger coursing through me. "Damn it," I muttered, stomping my boot heel into the floor.

Seth appeared entertained. His eyes sparkled, and his lips curved into a small smile.

"What?" I barked.

"You hate me for no reason." He pulled up a chair

and sat down.

My gaze iced over. "That shirt gives me reason enough."

His smile drooped. "What's wrong with my shirt?"

I snatched my chair out and sank into it heavily. "The real question is, what's *right* with it?" I threw my legs onto the desktop, crossing my ankles.

He looked down at his chest, bothered. "Is it the color?"

I slid my gaze to him, trailing it across the dark green, vile shirt. "Going golfing today…*Grandpa?*" I grabbed a pencil from the desk and twirled it through my fingers.

"Oh. So, it's not *cool* enough for you. I get it." He flipped the collar up, ala Elvis Presley style. "Better?"

I snorted a laugh, then abruptly snapped my jaw shut. *Did I really just laugh?* I fixed my mouth into a scowl and vowed to myself that I'd never do such a stupid thing again.

He snickered into his fist but wisely didn't say another word.

Together, but separately, we poured over the inner city's crime reports. Silently, we alternated paperwork, each privately searching for missing clues while the other scanned over the tiny list of suspects. Frustrated, I shoved the papers into a folder and slammed it shut.

Nothing made sense. The best, and so far the *only*, possible explanation I could come up with was a rouge vampire was on the loose, somewhere in the inner-city district. Perhaps the vamp was too sly for the Mistress?

Cleverly evading her cronies as they viciously, and illegally, fed on thirteen humans over the districts allotted quota. Maybe the mystery vampire was already gone? Perhaps they simply passed through, ravaged the town, and had moved on?

I gnawed on a pencil as I thought, ready to snap it in two, when all the phone lines in the precinct rang, almost simultaneously. Blinking lights of alternate lines lit up on the phone pads, signaling more in-coming calls.

Seth's brows bunched, and he looked just as confused and wary as I felt. Something was wrong.

Everyone in the room paused, eyes switching around nervously before Detective Stromberg, a seasoned investigator with a perpetual frown, and a pinched face, reached out to the phone in front of him. He picked up the receiver, silencing the trilling ringing. One by one, the rest of us followed suit. Slowly lifting the receivers and hesitantly pressing them to our ears.

Seth watched anxiously as I said, "PCI." That was all I could muster.

"Yes, who is this?" a female voice demanded. I sensed a trace of English accent amongst the panic.

"Detective Edy James."

"Detective James, there's been a murder."

"Who? Where?" I pulled the inner-city districts crime folder back in front of me. I waited with pencil poised to jot down the information.

"Tek Ronboi," the voice said.

I dropped my pencil. "Tek Ronboi?" Tek Ronboi had been the leader of the quiet section of the western rural district. Once a native of Zimbabwe, Tek came to the US sometime in the fifteen-hundreds. He was a nice guy, as far as vamps go. He always had a blinding white smile, which of course bared his fangs, but somehow he made them look friendly.

"Yes ma'am," the caller continued. "And word amongst the town is he's not the only leader who's been eliminated."

The voice on the other end was right. Each call that night was reporting a murder. As if that wasn't strange enough, the real head-scratcher was all the victims were vampire leaders.

I jumped up and snatched my jacket from the chair. I tried to ignore Seth as he leapt to his feet and fell into step beside me. *Fucking Captain. I could smack him for pairing me with this idiot. He knows I hate the whole partner thing.*

"Where are we headed?" he asked.

"*I'm* responding to a call. *You* are staying here." I picked up speed, putting some space between me and the Newbie.

"Edy," he called. "Wait up."

Of course I didn't. I slipped into my jacket as I half-jogged through the hallway. Shouldering the front doors apart, I burst into the night. The air was crisp, and the moon was hidden by dark, rolling, gray clouds that resembled smoke, making it nearly pitch-black outside. The perfect night for vamps.

My boots tapped down the precinct's front steps, and from behind me, I could hear Seth's footfalls rushing to keep up. "Edy," he said. "You can't leave me behind. We're partners now."

I rolled my eyes and kept moving. My car was parked a few spaces away. As I covered the asphalt, I wondered how I could shake Seth. *Can I unlock the door, slip inside, and lock it before he gets there?* I glanced back at him. *Fuck.* He was too close. I stepped beneath the flood of security lights that spilled across the pavement and dug my keys out of my pocket.

I could douse him with Were mace, I thought, reaching inside the pocket that still held the aerosol can. *That would definitely do the job, but then, I'd probably lose mine for using it on him.* I decided it wasn't worth it, so I left the can where it was, unlocked the car door, and sank inside. I quickly jammed the key in the ignition, pursing my lips together as the passenger door pulled open. *Damn it!*

Seth tossed a black duffel bag that was stamped with the PCI logo to the floorboard and sat down.

I gripped the steering wheel and turned toward him. "Get out."

He glared at me. "Hell no," he said stubbornly. "Like it or not, Captain made us partners." He slammed the door shut and reached for the seatbelt. "You're stuck with me, Edy. I'm not going anywhere, so you better get used to it."

I scowled at him, squeezing my hands tighter around the steering wheel, imagining it was the Captain's beefy neck beneath my fingers.

"Just stay out of my way," I snapped as I put the car into gear and floored it, tossing him back against the seat.

Chapter 7

If I wasn't so pissed at the Captain for arranging this *forced* partnership, I would have snickered when I saw Seth clinging to the dashboard out the corner of my eye. I whipped in and out of the lanes, jerking him back and forth like a rag doll.

I didn't slow at the train tracks like I normally do. I gritted my teeth as the undercarriage of the car scraped and bounced over the metal tracks. Seth's head knocked against the window, and he cursed under his breath.

I didn't have to speed. The case wasn't considered an emergency. Suspects weren't being obtained, and the victim was dead. I mean, *really* dead this time. Truth is, irritation grated me like a rusty file across skin, and I *needed* to release it somehow. Speed usually soothed that need.

As I turned into the Madame Isabelle's parking lot, I slowed the vehicle down, casting my gaze all about, searching for something out of the ordinary. Security lights reflected off puddles of engine oil pooled on the whorehouse's asphalt. I turned my attention to the stretch of buildings to left of the bordello. Stores, just two with flashing neon OPEN signs in the windows, while the others sat quiet and dark. Of course, the only two opened after midnight were a hash store and a coffee joint that offered the ridiculous services of bikini-clad baristas.

"A bordello?" Seth questioned, clearly shocked. "The murder was here?"

"Why is that so hard to believe?"

"It's not really," he answered. "It's just not the sort of place I expected a district leader to be."

I arched an eyebrow. Seth was right. Most leaders had legions of admirers, vampire and mortal, surrounding them. Why was Tek in a bordello? Surely he didn't need the company. Besides, word around town was Tek recently Bonded with Claudette, the second-in-command to the Hillside District.

With her mocha skin and velvety voice to match, she was a stunner. Big, bright eyes that hold you captive in their gaze, like the way cobras mesmerize their prey just before they swoop in for the kill. Claudette was just as lethal as a cobra. The sword in the hand of Garon Walker, she was the chess piece that moved about the board, making deals, and sealing allegiances with her sharp-wit and even sharper teeth.

She was a hellcat in the streets, gaining her the nickname, She-Devil. Her Bond with Tek reeked of plots and power moves. I couldn't help but think Garon hoped to gain control of Tek's territory through the Bonding. There could be no other explanation.

The Hillside district once covered only the rolling hills and mountainous regions of Washington, but over the last few decades, it's expanded to the heavily populated cities. That was largely in part of Garon. He was a tough SOB who most folks, human or Supe tried to steer clear of at all costs. During his thirty-year reign, he either eliminated the lesser districts' leaders entirely or convinced them to dissipate their control and converge into a larger, mightier clan.

Surely that had to be why Claudette Bonded with Tek? It certainly wasn't for love. Don't believe the books you've read or the movies you've seen. Vampires do not fall in love, and Bonding is rare. Bonding is the vampire equivalent of mortal marriage, and since vampires are fickle creatures who are more promiscuous than a tomcat, Bondings are more inconvenient than they are valued. *Unless there's something to gain?*

I put the car in park and killed the engine. Since Seth didn't look like he was going to be persuaded to stay put, I fisted the keys, and said, "Let me do the talking."

He didn't say anything. He just grabbed his duffel bag and stepped out into the night. I jumped out behind him, determined not to let him get to the bordello doors first. My boots crunched along the pavement as I hurried, echoing across the nearly empty parking lot. Up ahead, I saw the Sweepers hard at work. They wore baggy jumpsuits that resembled hazmat suits.

They were busy removing equipment and bottles from the back of their response van. To mortal eyes, it was a plain van. Nothing fancy. Nothing interesting. But inside, it was a trove of cleaning equipment. Industrial carpet cleaners, pressure washers, and bottles of special disinfectants. Potent solvents that could dissolve any trace of Supe blood from every surface you could think of.

Sweepers weren't just a housekeeping unit. They were a highly classified and extremely important division of PCI. Their duty was to ensure the crime scene was swept clean of all evidence that a supernatural being had been there. They restored order, and normalcy back into the mortal world.

As I approached, one of the Sweepers acknowledged me with a nod but kept diligently working, unwinding an extension cord. Another was wrestling what looked to be a carpet-cleaner out the back of the van. I touched her on the shoulder and gave her a two fingered salute. She smiled behind her protective mask.

I helped her unload the heavy machine, grunting as we set it on the ground. Sweeping was often a thankless job, so I tried my best to show my appreciation whenever I could.

Seth was several paces ahead of me, so I hurried to catch up. As soon as I walked through the bordello doors, I saw the house's Madame herself, pacing the length of the mock living room. It was a cozy place, much like a Victorian home in the eighteen-hundreds. Of course, with the Madame being a vamp, this was probably the way she designed her home back when she was human and just chose to keep it that way.

Expensive candlesticks, and dainty teacups lined the fireplace mantel. Artwork with frames stripped of their glass hung on each wall. Unpolished silver trays were decorated with vases of fresh roses and lilacs. Nearly every item that could hold a reflection was either removed or allowed to tarnish until it was too murky to shine.

The old speculation that vampires don't have a reflection isn't exactly true. They have a reflection. It just ain't a pretty one. You see, when a vampire drinks blood for the very first time, the blood permanently stains their papery skin. The blood eventually fades, but the stain flares vividly each time the vamp is either angry or hungry.

When receded, the stain isn't visible to the human eye, unless it's seen in a reflection. See why vampires avoid mirrors at all cost? If mortals see their true form, all hell would break loose.

The Madame halted when she saw me, her eyes wide and red from crying.

I introduced myself with the professional curtness I've groomed myself into using each time I question a witness. I've found the nice cop technique does not suit me. Go figure. Sensing Seth coming up behind me, I deliberately ignored him and went into "bad cop" interrogation mode.

"Are you here to arrest me?" the woman asked, her English accent thicker in person than it was on the phone. She was wringing a lacey handkerchief in her hands, resembling more of a traumatized widow than a ruthless vampire. Her cheeks were glossy, wet with tears, and her hands shaky.

"Is that the start of a confession?" I asked, resting my hand on my holster.

"*Smooth* people skills," Seth whispered.

I whipped my head to flash him a glare. He flicked his gaze at me briefly before turning his attention to the woman. She wore a silver silk bathrobe that fell around her thighs. Her auburn hair was twisted into a messy bun, with sultry tendrils hanging loose around her temples and neck.

"I didn't kill Tek," the vamp said quietly as she worried at the handkerchief. "But I am familiar with the PCI and their prejudices. Evidence could clearly point elsewhere, but as long as there is a vampire around, suspicion will always be diverted to them." Her eyes focused on me, squinting at the corners as if accusing me directly.

I shifted my weight to show her a clear view of the Supe Slayer sitting snug against my hip. "You think PCI is prejudice of vampires? Lady, you got it all wrong. We are suspicious of *everyone*. Mortal. Immortal. We don't discriminate."

Her eyes darkened. "I know my people are merely tolerated by the lawmen."

"If humans didn't provide subsistence for *your* people—"

Seth held a hand up in front of my face, blocking me from the vampire. That move *really* rubbed me the wrong way. I gritted my teeth and sucked in a deep breath trying to harness my anger.

"Pardon me, Miss…?" Seth questioned politely.

"Isabelle."

"Right. Miss Isabelle, what my partner is trying to say is, PCI regards all species with a cautious eye. We have to. But we allow the evidence to lead the way, and justice always prevails."

She smiled and dabbed at her cheeks with her handkerchief. "Of course, Detective."

I rolled my eyes and turned away. "Of course, Detective," I mouthed in a quiet, mocking tone. If I wasn't there, and *if* she was wearing panties, I was willing to bet a hundred bucks she'd drop them for Seth in a minute.

"Now, can you tell us what happened here tonight?" Seth asked her.

I stalked through the room, pretending to be scouring the place for evidence. I wasn't. I just wanted space from Seth.

"I was...*entertaining* Tek when someone came to the door."

I glanced over my shoulder, gauging her body language. It was difficult to tell when a vamp was lying. They didn't do all the normal things a mortal did when being deceitful. No twitching, no eye-shifts, no sweating. She only clutched the top of her robe, as though she just realized she was indecent.

"At first, we ignored the knocking, but they persisted," she explained. "Tek yelled that the bordello was closed, but whoever it was kept knocking, so I dressed and came downstairs to send them away." She drew her robe tighter around her neck. "When I opened the door, they were gone." Her eyes narrowed a fraction. "But I smelled Supe blood."

"Supe blood?" Seth reiterated, pulling out a small notebook from his back pocket. "Did Tek have any enemies, Miss Isabelle?"

"Heavens, no." She dabbed at her nose with her handkerchief.

"Was he involved in anything illegal?"

"Aside from banging you while Bonded to Claudette Klemmings," I interjected, running my finger along the fireplace mantel.

Seth gave a nervous laugh. "That's hardly illegal, Edy."

"Did you know Tek was Bonded?" I asked the vamp.

Her eyes grew icy. "Yes."

"So then why were you..." I marked quotations in the air. "*Entertaining* him?"

"Tek and I are not strangers, nor are we a business matter."

I noted she was still referring to him in present tense. *Is it a mere slip, or is she in denial?* "You mean he wasn't paying you for your services?"

Seth gave me a pained look.

She took a measured breath. "Tek has never been a *customer.* Our rendezvous have spanned across many, many years. Far more than a simple mortal can comprehend." Her small hand fisted around the delicate lace of her handkerchief, and the stain of her first taste of blood flared red. The streak ran from the corner of mouth, down to the hollow of her throat. "*We* should have been Bonded."

My eyebrows shot up, and her green eyes flashed when she realized her mistake. She gave me far too much information. My brain quickly compartmented her words, and I reached for the vampire cuffs that were nestled against my hip. *She's jealous of Claudette. She's a prime suspect.*

"So why weren't you?" I strolled closer to her.

She cleared her throat quietly. "Aside from this bordello…" She cast her eyes to the floor. "I don't have much of a dowry to offer. Tek wanted to expand his district…peacefully."

Seth was writing furiously in his notepad.

"What do you mean, peacefully?" I left the vamp cuffs where they were.

Her eyes met mine. "Claudette approached him with the idea of combining districts. He only agreed to keep the peace. If he hadn't, Claudette would have taken his district by force." Her voice shook.

I knew what that meant. Claudette would have challenged Tek or possibly killed him in cold blood. Tek was basically bullied by Claudette into the

Bonding, but why him? There were dozens of other districts in the area.

I studied Isabelle, with her pale, smooth as cream complexion, and scarlet-streaked chin, wondering if she held the answer.

"Of all the districts," I asked her. "Why Tek's?"

She glanced down at her handkerchief. "She was intrigued by his ability with dark magic."

"Dark magic?" Seth said, surprised.

She nodded. "Tek's human ancestry consists of generations of witch doctors. I believe Claudette wished to harness that power for her own dealings."

Chapter 8

"What happened after you answered the door?" Seth questioned.

Isabelle touched her handkerchief to her chin, dabbing at it as if she could wipe away the blood-red stain. "Then, I went back upstairs. Right away, I sensed something was amiss. The room was far too quiet. Too still."

Her gaze grew distant. She licked her lips and paused for a beat. "I found Tek dead. His head completely severed." Her breath caught, and for a moment, I thought she might collapse to the floor.

My gaze touched Seth's. His eyes slowly shifted to the staircase, then up to the second floor.

Before he could make a move, I started for the stairs. I grabbed the shiny banister, propelling myself hurriedly up the steps, taking two at time. I paused at the landing, listening to Seth still below, calmly encouraging Isabelle to spill her guts.

I was surprised by how natural it was for him to get her to open up. How comforting and compassionate he was. What was more surprising, was she was actually telling him everything. Normally, vamps are vague to the point of being maddening.

I ducked my head into each room I passed, noting nothing out of sorts. They were each equipped with the normal bordello décor. Plush bed, fitted with slippery satin sheets, dim lighting, and a coat-rack full of feathery boas, riding crops, and other creepy sex toys.

The last room had to be Isabelle's. I stepped inside and was hit with a wall of stench that I could only describe as "porn set filth." It was a combination of musky incense, fruity lubricants, greasy foreplay, and cigarettes. I gagged and covered my nose. Tek was sprawled out naked on the bed.

The sheets beneath him were covered in dark, almost black blood. His head was resting on the pillow, in line with his lifeless body but detached from his neck. His eyes were closed, which was good because I actually respected Tek and didn't want to see him staring back at me with blank eyes.

I scanned the area. The window was open, causing the curtain to flutter like a ghost in the soft wind. There was no disturbance in the room. Nothing indicating there was even an ounce of struggle from him. It was like he had been lying there oblivious, waiting on Isabelle. His neck sliced before he even knew someone was in the room. But that was impossible. Tek was a vampire. His hearing was sharp, and his senses keener than any wild animal. *How could someone slip in without his knowing?*

I rounded the foot of the bed and stood beside the nightstand. I peered down at the lethal wound. It was clean, telling me the weapon used was especially sharp, and the one delivering it had to be strong enough to deliver the blow with one deathly swipe. The arteries, nerves, and skin were cauterized neatly, as if done by an extensive medical procedure. *That's weird*, I thought to myself. *The murderer took time to cauterize the wound.* Whoever killed Tek, wanted to make sure he wasn't coming back.

There are three ways to execute a vampire: exposure to natural sunlight, piercing the heart, and severing the head from the body. Vampires are a lot like lizards in the fact that they can regenerate, but only under special circumstances. Sunlight fries the vamp until the point of ashes, leaving no possible way they can recover.

However, their flesh and organs have evolved to regenerate if a crude weapon is used on them. Wooden stakes, common swords, and knives...they only maim the vampire, thoroughly pissing them off as their cells instantly being morphing, until the tissue, muscles, and skin begin knitting themselves back together. The wound must be cauterized to prohibit the cells from regenerating.

The PCI has sole access to a special steel called Smite, which instantly cauterizes vampire flesh to keep such a thing from happening.

I withdrew a fingerprint kit from my pocket and sprinkled the dust around the base of the windowpane and across the curtain. I was finishing up when Seth came in, Isabelle a few paces behind him. She kept her eyes adverted, and her fingers twisted in knots in front of her.

"Whoa," said Seth as he stepped up to the side of the bed. He pulled out his cellphone and snapped a picture of Tek's neck.

"Clean cut," he said in a hushed tone, probably for Isabelle's sake.

"She's a vamp, you idiot," I told him, disgusted. "Whispering is pointless. She can hear a canary fart in San Diego."

Isabelle jutted her chin out and let out a prissy humph. "I'll be downstairs."

I waited for her footsteps to disappear before I turned back to my work, swishing the duster around in loopy swirls. As the prints emerged, almost lifting from the powder, I smirked. *Bingo.*

I retrieved the PCI print scanner from my back pocket and powered it on. This wasn't an ordinary print scanner. Mortal scanners are for mortal fingerprints. The PCI print scanner could read not only fingerprints, but also pad tracks left by Weres and other shape-shifting creatures.

"You always carry your equipment on you?" Seth questioned.

I tossed a pointed glance to his duffel bag. "It's easier than carrying that stupid thing around."

"I take it you don't carry a purse either?"

I faced him. "What?"

"Nothing." He shrugged and shifted his eyes nervously. "I mean, you just don't look like the type to carry a purse, that's all."

"It's a good thing I don't, because by the looks of things, I'm going to be too busy carrying your weight." My heated glare narrowed dangerously. "Focus on the damn case, will you?"

He frowned, but smartly didn't say a word.

I set my attention back to the print scanner, grumbling curses. I swiped the device across the fingerprints, the infrared lighting illuminated them, like glow sticks. Digital ID numbers, names, and aliases blinked and scrolled in a frenzy of flashes across the screen.

Of course, Isabelle's print matched, but I

impatiently pressed *CONTINUE* on the screen, and the device quickly skipped through more of the Supes in the database, eventually rolling back through the names again. *Damn.* No other hits.

I shut it off and shoved it back into my back pocket.

"Get a match?" Seth asked, walking up to me.

"Just hers," I said.

"You don't honestly think she did it, do you?"

I brushed past him and shoved the curtain aside. "No," I answered honestly. I peered out the window and down at the manicured garden below. "Quite a climb. Definitely rules out a mortal."

He came up beside me and glanced down. "Could have brought a ladder?" he offered.

"Tek would have heard that for sure. Plus, look at the wound. It's perfection. No mortal could deliver a death blow to a vampire like that."

He pursed his lips and nodded in agreement. "Yeah. The scene reeks of Supe, but which one?"

"The vamp mentioned the smell of Shifter."

"Her name is Isabelle, and she also said she couldn't tell which one. After you ditched me, and left me downstairs with her, I questioned her about it some more. She couldn't tell me what she sensed, only that it was Shifter. Gathered no leads from it."

"I thought you wanted time alone with her," I said, purposely ignoring his gaze as I moved away from the window and went back to the bedside. "Besides, you were down there with her almost ten whole minutes." I peered back down at the wound.

He gaped at me. "You timed how long I spent with the witness?"

I scoffed. "Witness."

He stood on the other side of the bed. "What?"

I dipped my fingers into the front pocket of my jacket and removed a latex glove. I pulled it on, wriggling my fingers as I snapped it into place. "What nothing. You seemed more interested in batting your eyes at her, than questioning her." I began probing around Tek's neck.

"That's ridiculous."

Now bored of the conversation, I wiped my fingers across the lacey pillow sham, smearing congealed blood across it. "I thought I'd have to mop up your drool for you."

He laughed. "Are you...*jealous*?" He spread his hands out on the bed and leaned over Tek's body. I ignored the fact that our faces were inches apart and pretended to be engrossed in Tek's exposed spinal cord. "Damn Edy, we just met, and already you're jealous of other women? That cold shoulder you've been giving me is just a ruse, isn't it? I got to say, you had me going." He grinned like a loon and winked playfully.

I jerked upright. "Are you nuts?" He startled, straightening to his full height. I yanked off the latex glove and tossed it at him. It hit his chest and slinked down him like a jellyfish. "I'm not interested in you Newbie. I'm calling you out on it, so you can get your shit together."

He looked taken aback, but I plundered on, the words gushing out before I can even consider stopping them.

"Focus on the case and keep your *little* fella in tow while on the job!" I skirted around the bed and stomped through the hall. My boots clunked loudly, echoing off the walls as I scurried down the stairs. I didn't slow until I was outside, standing below Isabelle's window.

Fucking Seth…fuck him and fuck the Captain for putting us together. If you haven't noticed by now, I'm a bit of a hothead, and when you pair that trait with being crippling anti-social, you get a toxic blend of bitchiness. And did I mention, I *really, really* hate being forced to work with a partner?

I craned my neck up to the window, judging the culprit's way of entry. A supernatural being could easily scale the side of the house. I was about to dust for fingerprints when I noticed a print in the dirt. I knelt and touched my fingers to it. It was big and definitely canine. I searched the ground around me. There was no other visible track. *Doesn't give me much to go on, but it's a start.*

I took my cellphone out to snap a photo of the print, but it rang in my hand before I could. It was Captain, so I didn't hesitate to answer.

"Captain?" I said, feeling that familiar surge of adrenaline running through me whenever I sensed bad news.

"Eleven leaders were murdered tonight."

I gulped.

"One of them was the inner-city district Mistress."

I didn't need a mirror to tell the color had drained from my face. "Tina," I whispered.

Chapter 9

"Got any leads?" I asked, straightening.

"No," Captain said, sounding exhausted. "How's things going at your scene? Anything panning out?"

"Got a track…probably Shifter."

"It's not much, but it's something."

"Who's handling Tina's case?" I asked, tossing a quick gaze around me.

"Vick and Marty. Listen, James. I want everyone to report back to headquarters ASAP to start comparing notes. This reeks of an organized mass murder."

I cut my eyes to the print in the dirt. "Be there in twenty." I ended the call and snapped a quick photo of the track, using my hand as a size comparison. *No way is this a regular dog.*

Seth rounded the front lawn, finding me examining the side of the house. "Want me to dust?"

I ignored him, squinting up at the old wooden slats of the window shutters. From where I stood, nothing seemed out of place.

He sighed and disappeared for a minute. He returned with a borrowed ladder from the Sweepers. He rested it against the second story window then bent to dig through his duffel bag. After rummaging through it a moment, he produced his print kit and set to work dusting the side of the house as well as the window's outer ledge. I waited impatiently below, strolling the grounds, searching for another track, but came up empty.

Seth also came up empty. Whoever climbed through the window was careful not leave any prints behind.

"Come on," he said to me as he zipped up his duffel bag. "The scene has run cold."

I nodded and headed back to the car while he gave the go-ahead to the Sweepers to begin their work on Isabelle's room.

I sank into the car and cursed, wracking my brain on the pitiful clues we procured that night. *One fucking print and a cauterized death blow. What the hell can I gather from that?*

I started the car, slammed it into drive, and whipped out of the parking spot. *Unfortunately, it targets the Shifter community,* I thought to myself. *Which means Seth and I have long hours of questioning local Were clans ahead of us.*

I stomped on the brake, screeching the car to a swift stop. *Shit! Seth! I left him behind!* I flicked my gaze to the rearview mirror and caught a glimpse of him jogging toward me across the parking lot. I touched my forehead. *And this is why I work better alone.*

He opened the car door and sat down, panting. "I thought you were ditching me."

"I wasn't ditching you," I replied. "I just…forgot you."

"Even better." he tossed his bag in the back seat.

Before he could put his seat belt on, I punched the gas. He slammed back into the seat, muttering a curse. Maneuvering onto the highway, the car slipped into the flow of traffic, and I booked it at a steady ninety mph.

He scrambled to draw his seat belt across him, clicking it with visible relief. "Damn it, Edy. You're bound and determined to make me shit myself."

I smirked and continued to drive the only way I knew how. *Fast.*

"So what are your thoughts about the case?" he asked, nonchalantly reaching up to grip the handlebar on the car ceiling.

I pursed my lips, refusing to give into his mindless chatter.

"Want to hear mine?"

I gave him a sideways glance. Short bursts of light from the overhead interstate signs, lit up the cab of the car as we passed beneath them. That's how I noticed for the first time, his eyes were hazel, and he squints when he ponders. I found myself actually curious to hear what was running through his head, but instead I just lifted my shoulder in a bored shrug.

That didn't dissuade Seth from telling me though. He shifted in his seat and leaned toward me slightly, as if ready to tell me a juicy secret. "No prints on the side of the house point to a flyer or leaper of some kind. A ghost, winged Shifter, or even a Were with superb jumping abilities."

"Or they could have worn gloves?" I said in my best, *well duh* tone.

"Gloves are too slippery. It would have been hard to get traction."

I nodded because he was actually right about that. As he rambled on about nonsense, I zoned out, dwelling on the facts of the case. No fingerprints. Cauterized wound. Shifter track. Oh, and the fact that every vampire leader in the surrounding districts were all murdered on the same night.

We got back to headquarters, finding our colleagues reflecting on the large corkboard in the center of the room. They were trying to make sense of the murders, searching for some sort of connection between them. I made my way through the clustered bodies, regarding the assembled facts and scrawled, jotted notes as I drew closer.

"James," Captain bellowed, stepping out of his office. His eyes skipped across the room, landing on Seth. "Grooms. Let's hear your report."

All eyes switched between me and Seth. He opened his mouth to speak, but I hurried to say, "The only print we lifted was a Shifter print in the dirt." I glanced at the corkboard to the images of the decapitated vamps. Each neck wound appeared to be cauterized, just like Tek's. "Death blow…the same as the rest."

Murmuring broke loose.

"Someone is trying to gain mass control of the districts," Vick said above the din.

I flicked my gaze to him, pissed that he was saying, what I was thinking.

"So now we have to figure out who," said Yolanda Reynolds, a blonde detective in a pencil skirt. I never understood how she could work in a skirt. All the running, stooping, hiking, and ass-kicking seems easier in pants, but whatever.

"The only connection so far is the cauterizing of the skin and vessels," Captain said, strolling to the corkboard with a steaming cup of coffee in hand.

"And the time of death is almost simultaneous," Seth added.

We exchanged theories for the next two hours. My

crime scene was the only one to leave a track, so I volunteered to question Topher's pack about it. Seth didn't seem too eager to meet the pack leader. After deciding to break for the night, I asked him about it.

"Weres are so damn unpredictable," he said as we walked out of the office. I was glad to be away from the stale, air-conditioned atmosphere of the building, and out in the crisp night air. I wouldn't call myself an outdoorsy girl, but I enjoy my time in nature, where it's quiet, and less crowded with people.

"Plus," he continued. "I think they smell Princess Peachy Keen on me…"

I arched a brow. "Princess Peachy Keen?"

He didn't flinch, instead he glared at me defiantly as if I'd just insulted his grandmother. "Yes. She's a Persian."

I laughed behind my fist. "You got to be kidding me. You have a cat named Princess Peachy Keen?"

"She had that name when I adopted her, okay? So what? Did my cool rating just go down another notch?" He paused at an old hotrod. It was covered in primer and obviously a work-in-progress. It had sleek, shiny exhaust pipes and a mean looking front grill. My panties grew wet just looking at it.

He reached through the parted window and unlocked it.

Stunned, I pulled my gaze from the hotrod. "That's yours?"

He glanced at the car. "Yeah." His tone came out unsure, as if bracing himself for a snide remark about how beat-up the paint job was.

I gathered my composure, slacking my features, and shuttering my obvious ogling with an indifferent bat of my eyes. "Your cool rating hovers at the same spot, Newbie. I'll overlook Princess Peachy Keen...but only because of your choice in cars."

His lip curved into a smug but boyishly charming smile. "Thanks." He scrubbed at the back of his neck. "I think."

I strolled away, leaving him standing there, watching after me with a lopsided, stupidly sexy grin on his face.

Chapter 10

The next day I was on my way to the precinct when I got a call from Kay.

"Hey slacker," she said when I answered. "Where the hell have you been?"

"Working," I replied, happy she was finally over her tizzy, which meant no more silent treatment.

"Typical," she said, almost bored.

"Did you call for a reason or just to bitch at me?" I eased the car into a parking spot and killed the engine.

"Both," she answered.

I leaned back against the headrest. "What do you want from me, Kay?"

"Nothing. I just like giving you shit."

I lifted my head, gazing out the windshield at the station building. On the outside, it looked like a regular brick building, with its generic sign that read STATION and its concrete steps leading to the double glass doors.

To mortals, it was indeed a functional police station. The uniformed secretary behind the desk at the entrance handled any walk-ins. She'd screen the mortal crimes from the paranormal crimes and call the Liaison Squad to ensure they were filtered to the proper precincts.

"I'd be hurt if you didn't," I said, shoving my keys into my pocket.

"Didn't what? Give you shit?"

I chuckled. "Yeah. Somebody's got to."

I could sense her smile, even through the phone.

"I think you ought to go to happy hour with me tonight. To make up for dropping me like a hot potato the other day."

"I had to," I countered. "I had to work. It's not like I did it on purpose."

"Yeah, yeah. Just meet me at Alex's at six."

I screwed my eyes shut for a moment. *Fuck.*

"Edy?"

I opened my eyes. "Okay," I said through tight teeth. "I'll see you at six."

"Great," she said. "Can't wait to see your face."

"Now it's my turn to say, 'yeah yeah,' " I replied grumpily.

She giggled. "Love that bubbly attitude of yours. See you tonight, and don't you dare stand me up."

"I won't," I promised, opening the car door, and stepping out.

"Oh, and Edy?"

"Yeah?" I made my way across the asphalt, shielding my eyes from the bright sun.

"You're strong enough."

I knew exactly what she was talking about. "I'm glad *you* think so."

"You are. You're the strongest woman I know. But, if you honestly think you'll be tempted, then let's just forget about it. We can do something else."

I paused at the station's doors. "No. I can handle it. I'll be there."

"You sure?"

"I'm sure. You just better save me from any creeps that might be lurking around."

"*Fine*." She exhaled a long sigh. "I'll be your pretend lesbian lover…*again.*"

"You could do worse you know," I shot back, smiling.

"Hey, if I dug vajayjays, you'd be quite a catch. But since I don't…you're sort of killing my game, Edy. Just cause you're content with a lifetime of one-night stands, doesn't mean I am."

For some reason, Seth with his crooked grin, came to mind. It lingered, like an annoying fly buzzing around a picnic lunch. If there was any time to wonder if I was schizophrenic that moment would be it. Part of me wondered what type of lover he was, but the other half of me balked at just the mere image of our two naked bodies tangled in lovemaking.

My smile dropped into a scowl. I pushed through the doors and said, "I'll have you know, I haven't brought a guy home in weeks."

She gasped dramatically. "What! Edy's gone celibate?"

"Hell, no. I just hit a dry spell, that's all."

The secretary at the desk lifted a brow at me; her pen stopped scribbling long enough for her to shake her head in disgust. She was discussing something with Detective Chase, a redhead with farm-built muscles and a neatly trimmed goatee. He just transferred to the precinct from a PCI unit located in southern Texas. He tipped an invisible cowboy hat at me, and said with his throaty twang, "I'd be happy to water your crops, Miss Edy."

I flipped him the bird and kept walking.

"Look," I said shouldering through the doors to the office. The room was buzzing with activity as everyone was dissecting the vampire murders. "You just worry about your own sex life and let me worry about mine." I sank into my desk chair.

She laughed. "Okay, okay. I think I've given you enough hell for now. I'll see you tonight, Edy."

I blew a breath through my nose. "Later." A second later I heard the click of her hanging up, and I pulled my phone away from my ear, with a half-relieved, half-irritated sigh.

"So, why are you worried about your sex life?"

I whirled around in my chair to face Seth. He was standing over me, his hands jammed innocently in his pockets. He seemed to have taken care to pick "cool" clothes today. He wore dark denim jeans (that were not yet broken in), a plain thermal shirt, and black sneakers that he inevitably polished at the end of each day.

"I'm not." I glared up at him. "And don't eavesdrop on my conversations."

His lips curved into a grin. "I didn't mean to, but you're not exactly quiet, you know." He pulled up a chair, swinging it around backwards before sitting down. His legs were sprawled wide, and he rested his forearms on the back of the seat. "So why are you worried about your sex life?"

"I *said*...I wasn't." I spoke through clenched teeth, turning back around to my desk. I slid some papers in front of me, trying hard to focus on the words written upon them. For some reason, I couldn't.

My cheeks flared with warmth, but I couldn't tell if was from annoyance or from embarrassment. I am far from being a prude but talking to Seth face-to-face about sex was a little unnerving.

"A girl like you shouldn't have to worry about

that."

My spine straightened like a rod. Pausing to regain control over my temper, I glowered at him from over my shoulder. "What?"

His eyes widened marginally. "I just mean…" He lifted a shoulder. "You know." He gestured to me with a flick of his wrist. "When you look like *that*…" His brows scrunched tighter and tighter the more uncomfortable he grew, but I wasn't about to let him off the hook that easily.

"Like what?"

He ran a hand through his dark hair, mussing it from its perfectly combed style. "Oh, forget it."

"No." I twirled the chair around, so we were facing one another and crossed my arms over my chest.

He swallowed. "Well. I mean. Have you ever *looked* in a mirror?"

The corner of my mouth twitched, threatening a smile. I don't know what it was about Seth that brought out these rare moments. Honest to goodness smiles, and a lightness in my chest, that wasn't forced or fake in any way.

"James," hollered Captain.

I jumped at my name. Captain came thundering through the room, his face red with impatience and worry. He must have been getting pressed by the vampire community to solve the mysterious murder cases, and not to mention he was still pacifying mortal law enforcements since the allotted quota was surpassed by the inner-city district just days before the simultaneous crimes.

"You plan on sitting there, batting your eyes all day at Grooms, or are you going to get some damn work done?"

I gritted my teeth.

Captain looked around the room. "Get to work. All of you." His stormy eyes settled on me. "I want Topher questioned. Get it done or I'll be calling his ass to heel myself." He stomped back to his office, ignoring anyone who tried to speak to him on the way.

I muttered a curse and grabbed the phone, noticing Seth squirm in his seat. "Don't worry," I said drily. "Topher's not going to eat your cat. He's a Were, not a damn Retriever."

"They're both canines," he mumbled. I couldn't respond because the phone stopped ringing, and Topher's voice filtered through the receiver.

"Hello?" he said.

"Topher. It's Edy. I need to ask you a few questions. Is there any way we can meet?"

"What's this about?" His tone was strained, but he kept careful control over it. "Is it about the wandering Shifter?"

"I'm not sure. Maybe?" I took up a pencil and tapped it on the desktop.

"Has something happened?"

"I'll explain later. When can we meet?"

"I'm out of town right now."

My head buzzed. *Out of town? Did he kill Tek and then decide to skip town?* "Where are you?"

"I don't see how that matters, but if you have to know, I'm in Karlson, handling Pack business. I'll be back tomorrow. We can meet then, at my ranch."

Figures. Shifters always made you come to them. They were more comfortable and not to mention less venerable on their own turf. "You been gone long?" I couldn't help myself. The detective in me was searching for an alibi.

"Two days. Why?"

I brushed off his question, responding with a clipped, "I'll be at your place at eleven."

He allowed the line to go completely quiet for a few drawn out seconds before saying, "That's not entirely ideal, but fine. Tomorrow at eleven."

I stilled my tapping and replied. "Good. See you then." I hung up and turned to Seth. "You don't have to come with me you know."

He frowned. "What kind of partner would I be if I let you go onto Were territory alone?"

I cut my eyes at him. "I can handle Topher. I've been handling him for years."

Seth quirked a questioning brow.

"Oh, for god's sake," I said pushing myself away from the desk. "Not like that. *Jesus.*"

"I've always been curious what Shifters are like in bed," he wondered out loud. "Most people assume they're wild in the sack, but I've never been able to prove or dispel that rumor."

"Well, from someone with firsthand experience," Vick said gloatingly as he strolled leisurely toward us. "The rumors are all true. Last year, I met a little number who could shift into a lynx." He slid his eyes to me and winked. "It was fitting, cause that girl was a total wildcat." His eyes roamed across me. "Although..." He licked his lips. "For a mortal chick, Edy...you're a real fox."

I rolled my eyes and stood up. "Honestly," I huffed. "If it wasn't such a hassle, I would slap your ass with a sexual harassment suit."

Vick puckered his lips. "Hmm," he purred. "I'd love for you to slap my ass."

Seth raised a hand. "Okay, that's enough." His tone was cutting and dominant. My lower region responded to the authority in his voice. I pictured myself shoving the papers from the desk and taking him right there. Startled by the primal need Seth brought out in me, I clenched my fists.

Seth stared Vick down, puffing his chest out protectively. His usual mild-mannered nature reminded me of Clark Kent. As I raked my gaze down the length of him, I had to bite my lip to keep from panting. The lean muscles in his back bunched tightly beneath his shirt. His cheeks flared hotly, and eyes shone just as brightly as he backed Vick up a few steps.

"Calm down, man," Vick said with a snide smile. "Edy's enough woman for the both of us."

Seth crowded Vick's space. "Edy's a lady, and she'll be treated as such."

Vick snorted. "A lady? She's got the naughty parts of one, but that's about it."

Seth's shove came out of nowhere. I didn't even see him lift his arms, but he must have, because Vick was stumbling backward. He crashed into a desk, its metal legs scraping across the floor as he did. Vick's face read as shocked, and he was totally thrown off his normal uppity vibe.

"Next time you make a statement like that," Seth hissed. "You'll be paying for it with teeth."

Vick glowered at him, and the tension in the air peaked. For a several drawn out minutes, there was a battle of wills between the two men, but when Seth refused to back down, Vick lowered his gaze, like a weaker animal relenting to an alpha.

Disgusted by Vick, but turned on by Seth, I decided I needed space from both. "I'm going to the weapons room," I said. My gaze shifted between him, and Vick. "Alone." I stalked away, eager to let off some steam by blasting a few holes in some paper dummies. And I knew just whose face I was going to imagine on the target...

Chapter 11

After shredding about half a dozen targets, I cleaned my gear and went back to work. For the next few hours, I read over the other crime reports. All were eerily similar. No forced entry. No prints. No witnesses. The only lead so far was the Shifter track I found outside of Miss Isabelle's Bordello. If this was organized by the Pack, what was the motive? Why would a Shifter want to eliminate vampire leaders? They can't gain control over their clans, so how would they benefit by killing off the leaders?

It was just after six o'clock, and most of the office had cleared out. Only a handful of detectives remained, and they were dealing with minor crimes—like fairies looting and Chupacabras purposely stumping wildlife biologists by pooping in their tents.

My phone startled me, ringing loudly in the nearly deserted office. I scurried to quiet it.

"Hello," I answered with an irritated edge to my voice.

"Forget something?"

Shit. I sank my forehead into my palm. "No…"

"That's funny," Kay said. "I don't *see* you here with me." Sarcasm oozed from the phone line.

"I got caught up going over clues of a case I'm working on." I shut the folder in front of me. "I'm leaving right now." I stood from the chair and flicked my gaze around the room. Seth had left an hour earlier, and now all that remained were Chase, Reynolds, and a couple of new recruits.

I tossed a wave to everyone that was about as artificial as my enthusiasm for meeting Kay for happy hour. I walked briskly through the building and out to my car.

"I'll be there in ten," I said, sliding behind the steering wheel.

"Ten?" she snorted. "Only if you floor it."

I felt my lips slip into a smirk. "Make that five."

Seven minutes later, I pulled into Alex's Pub, slightly annoyed that my time was compromised because of some old dude in a sedan creeping his way down the road.

I climbed out of my car and paused to check my reflection in the window. I was still in my work clothes, but thankfully, it didn't resemble a uniform. Slim, gray-washed jeans paired with a loose-fitting blouse that tended to slip off my shoulder could actually be passed off as a legitimate outfit.

I ran my fingers through my hair a few times and thought, *this is as good as it's gonna get.* After adjusting my jacket, I headed for the pub door.

As soon as I walked in, I took a quick scan of the room, searching for Kay's curly auburn hair. The pub was pretty empty, save for a couple regulars I recognized and a table full of old men snacking on onion rings over their frosty bottles of beers.

The small foyer I waited in was broken up by three steps that expanded into the rest of the room. The pub was cozy with its country cabin-like feel, and welcoming staff, but the combination of alcohol and greasy food in the air made my stomach turn.

"Evening," called a middle-aged hostess from a booth. She was rolling silverware in napkins and appeared relieved for a break. She hoisted herself from the bench chair and tucked a loose strand of hair behind her ear.

She stopped at the landing, not bothering to climb the steps. I towered over her by at least a foot. "Bar or booth?" she asked with a cheerful smile.

I pointed to the bar and said. "Bar. I'm here to meet a friend." I spotted Kay sitting near the end of the bar. Her springy curls were bouncing with excitement as she chatted to an attractive blonde who smiled a little too broad and leaned in way too close. But I noticed she was laughing a bit too loud, so the shameless flirting was mutual.

Ugh. I hesitated, dreading being the third wheel, but before I could back away, Kay sensed me. She turned around and waved me forward. Her smile was sweet and genuine, making me feel guilty for wanted to bail on her again.

"Well, okay then," the hostess said, her smiling never faltering. "Tucker is the bartender tonight."

My eyes impulsively skipped to the man with shoulder length hair. *Damn it.* I had forgotten about Tucker. He hadn't noticed me yet, as he was busy mopping up a spill on the polished wood bar. His thick arms bulged under his thinly spread t-shirt. Somehow even in the Washington smog and rain, he always kept a great tan.

I knew Tucker well, unfortunately. I used to frequent the pub, often leaning upon his shoulders as I stumbled into the backseat of a taxi. One night, instead of hailing me a taxi, Tucker offered to drive me home himself. We had an explosive night of drunken sex, but when I came to my senses the next morning, I blew him off.

Well, actually, I told him to quote, "skedaddle" around a mouthful of cereal. A bowl in one hand. A spoon in the other. I had no idea how sensitive he was. He pouted like a punished kid.

I obviously hurt his *very* fragile feelings or his *very* flimsy manhood. He cursed at me for being selfish, cold, and yada yada yada as he snatched his clothes from the floor and bustled out my house. For a big guy, he handled his heart like a bitch.

"Holler at me if you need a menu," the woman said, drawing me back to her.

I dipped my head in a polite nod, and she walked away, leaving me to stand there alone, weighing my options. *I could leave now, but then I run the risk of Kay never speaking to me again.* I took a step forward. *I could tell her I'm not feeling good and need to go home?* Another step. *No. She'll know I'm lying.*

With Tucker there, this night just got a whole lot shittier. Not only did I have to control my urges to swig back a tray of shots, but I'd have to wade through the tense air Tucker would bring and pretend I was having fun for Kay's sake.

I drifted down the steps, and Kay grinned.

Or I can suck it up. I sighed inwardly and resigned myself to the enviable. My shoulders slouched as I made my way begrudgingly to the bar. I knew I was going to be bored out of my skull while Kay flirted with this guy all evening. Then, one of two things were going to happen. She'd grow tired of Blondie and cut the line, or she'll get desperate enough to go home with him. Either way, I was staring down the barrel of endless hours of small talk, refusing drinks from strangers, and boredom that would only fuel my crankiness.

Kay whispered something to Blondie, and I stifled a cringe as I felt the weight of their stares on me as I crossed the floor toward them.

"Hey," I said as I closed in on them.

"Yay. You're here!" Kay slid off the barstool, rushed forward, and wrapped me in a quick hug. I gave her my usual limp pat in return, catching a whiff of her hair as I did. She smelled of coconut shampoo, her scent of choice since high school.

Kay looked great as usual. Her sweater matched her pale blue eyes, and her throat was draped with multiple silver chains. A past birthday gift from me. When you're a PCI detective, you tend to give presents that secretly ward off Supes. Mundane gifts, such as silver jewelry, wrought iron décor, and clusters of garlic cloves, are all cleverly disguised Supe deterrents.

"This is my best friend in the world." She spoke to the guy, who leisurely sized me up.

I ignored it and smiled warmly at my friend. Though fashion magazines would label her as plus size, she didn't fit that bill to me at all. Her soft curves filled her dresses out as if they were specifically designed for her body, and it drove guys crazy. Together, we made quite a pair. With my stick-straight blonde hair, and her tight auburn spirals, we looked like copper and gold from behind.

Her voluptuous figure and my lean, athletic build often made us look like the number ten when standing side by side. Even our personalities were opposite. Kay, with her bubbly, outgoing attitude only seemed to shine brighter when paired with my cynical moods and sarcastic tongue. How we ever got along, I'll never know. Hell, it's still a mystery to this day.

Kay settled herself back onto the stool, and introduced me to Blondie, whose name I didn't attempt to remember, nor did I pretend to try.

Tucker meandered his way down the length of the bar, stopping when he came up to me.

"Hi, Edy," he hedged carefully.

"Hey, Tucker," I responded, avoiding direct eye contact.

"It's been awhile," he said.

I pursed my lips, nodded curtly.

"You look great."

No, I groaned silently. *Don't say stuff like that.* I smiled through clenched teeth. "Thanks. You, too." I slid my gaze to Kay, who just smirked back at me.

"Can I get you anything?" he asked.

"Just water."

His expression read confused, which I expected. He's used to me ordering whiskey, not something as lame as water.

He quickly made up a glass of water, fitting the rim with a wedge of lemon. He spread a napkin on the bar and placed the glass in front of me. "Here you go."

I offered a small smile. "Thanks." I straddled the bar stool and sat down.

He leaned his elbows on the bar, and said, "Where you been hiding, Edy?"

"Working," I said into my glass.

"My ass," he said. "You've been avoiding this

place because of me."

I choked on my water.

"I'm sorry for the way I acted," he continued blindly, not even noticing the astonished look on my face. "I just really liked you. I thought things wouldn't change after…" He tossed a quick glance around and lowered his voice. "You know."

I swiped the back of my sleeve across my mouth. "After I fucked your brains out, while drunk off my ass?"

He startled upright.

"Look, Tucker," I said, ignoring the gaping best friend beside me who was dying to pry me apart for details. "You're a nice guy, and you have a smoking hot body and everything, but I don't have time for something steady."

He blushed and shifted uncomfortably on his feet.

I shrugged, and said, "Sorry," as if it was a question. I'm not sure why it came out that way, but it did.

His head bobbed in an eager nod, no doubt restraining tears, which just confirmed my thoughts about him. *He's too delicate for me.* He turned and hurried away, busying himself with something at the far end of the bar.

"What the hell, Edy?" Kay slapped my arm. "You slept with him?"

"It was a long time ago," I answered, turning to her. "I was drunk. I barely remember it." Kay was nursing a tall flute of something bright pink; her lips were stained the same color.

She leaned in close and held her hand up to her mouth, whispering, "He's hot. I want details." Her

93

breath smelled of alcohol. Strong, but also fruity, like berries.

Just the scent of it on my face triggered a need to taste the forbidden drink again. I shut my eyes and mentally recited, *I am in control.*

When I opened them again, I hunted for an out, a way to be alone even for just a minute to collect myself. "I need to go to the bathroom."

"I'll come with you," Kay said, which didn't surprise me. She always tagged along on trips to the bathroom, which I grew to tolerate. She'd yak while we walked, then she'd yak while I peed, and then she'd yak some more while I washed and dried my hands.

We got up, and after she whispered something to Blondie, we made our way to the restroom. There were only two stalls, and both were occupied, so we had to wait. I leaned against the wall, offering a smile and nod here and there as she chatted excitedly about "what's his name."

I shifted my eyes to the cluttered papers that were tacked to a board on the wall. It held an array of advertisements. Local band gig schedules, lost dogs, a disc jockey's business card, and missing persons ads. Usually, there were one or two missing persons posters, but that night I counted fifteen, all crammed and overlapping one another.

Fifteen missing persons? My chest squeezed, and a sinking feeling spread through me, like boiling water. Staring at the innocent faces on the paper, I just *knew* the spike in missing persons had something to do with the vamp murders. *But what?*

Chapter 12

I must have grown pale because Kay gently touched my elbow, and said, "Edy? Are you okay?"

I shook myself from the stupor. "Uh, yeah." I glanced back up at the board.

"Do you need to go? Is it too hard being here?"

I shook my head in protest, but then quickly cursed myself for not taking the offer to split when I had it.

One of the stall doors opened, and a drunk lady stepped out. It was Rita, a regular at the pub. She drank to the point she'd get cut off by the pub owner. Messy, and stumbling, she fell against the sink, and splashed her face with water.

"Time to go home," I said to her.

She lifted her head and looked at me through the mirror. She sneered. "Look whose feeling high and mighty tonight."

I stiffened. "What the hell do you mean by that?"

The other stall door opened, and an older woman poured out. She discreetly washed and dried her hands and exited quietly.

"You don't think a drunk can recognize its own?" Rita said, swaying. "I'd seen you here before."

I narrowed my gaze, my vision blanketing red as I glared at her. "You don't know what you're talking about."

Kay ducked into a free stall and shut the door.

Rita groped at the paper towels, ripping off a clump so big she could have dried her entire body with it.

She sniggered arrogantly, patting her hands with the wad as she replied smugly, "Look at ya. You're craving a taste right now."

"Call yourself a cab and go home."

"Don't tell me what to do," she slurred, tossing the paper towels toward the trash bin but missing.

The toilet flushed, and Kay came out. Her eyes darted between me and Rita. She appeared lost, like she didn't know if she should step in or just leave.

I planted my fists on my hips and stepped up to Rita. "You leave this pub without being in the backseat of cab, and I'll haul your drunk ass in for public intoxication."

She jerked as if slapped. "I don't need to see that asshole judge again," she mumbled more to herself than to me, wobbling on her heels. She wove her way through the space, alcohol clinging to her like a shawl. She shoved open the door and walked out, unsteady on her feet.

I watched her from the opened door. She stumbled about the pub, making her way to the bar. Patrons moved out of her way, some even reaching out to steady her as she swayed on her feet. Once she finally made it the bar, she gripped it as though the world was spinning. For her, it probably was. She rummaged through her purse, looking for money.

Tucker looked as though he was about to tell her something when she pressed a fist full of money into his palm. Sensing me watching, she suddenly whirled, glowering at me through slitted, blurry eyes. I held her stare, my mouth drawn tightly over my lips. Defiant, she flipped me the bird, then staggered out of the pub, not bothering to shut the door behind her.

"What a lush," Kay said, turning the facet on and slipping her hands beneath the water.

I cringed, and she caught it. Her face slackened, and her eyes rounded.

"Oh, I'm so sorry, Edy. I didn't mean—"

I held up my hand. "It's okay." But it wasn't. I regarded her pretty, clueless face, struggling to tamp down my anger. Alcoholism is an illness, much like any other disease. The need consumes you like cancer, and every day it's a struggle to resist its advances.

Kay hastily dried her hands and reached out to touch my shoulder. I backed away. "Don't."

She frowned. "I wasn't thinking when I said that. Besides, I didn't call *you* a lush."

I crossed my arms in front of me defensively. "You might as well have." I fought back the stinging tears.

"You're different, Edy. Rita…well, Rita's a hot mess."

"This was a bad idea." I spoke through choked up emotion, everything suddenly too overwhelming. The potent alcohol drenching the air, the small space of the bathroom, the hunger to extinguish my dry throat with a splash of vodka. I backed out of the room and swung around to dash out of the smoky pub.

"Edy, wait!" she called.

I nearly jogged up the stairs, bursting out of the door, spilling myself out into the chilly night. I took greedy gulps of fresh air, trying to rid myself of the intoxicating atmosphere, and the clawing need to down a drink with that will knock me square on my ass.

97

Kay emerged from the building. "Edy," she cried. "Please, come back. I'm sorry!"

I ran across the parking lot, putting much needed distance between me, and the temptation that lurked inside. When I reached my car, I flung myself against the side of it and gripped my knees. *I am in control. I am in control.*

I repeated this until my breathing steadied, and the blur of tears recessed back into the stupid ducts they came from. I looked around me. I was alone, which meant Kay was wise enough to leave me the hell alone.

I scrubbed at my eyes with the back of my hand and unlocked the car, dropping into the driver's seat like a sack of potatoes. I considered going back to the office to look into those missing persons cases, but I was just too exhausted and too edgy from the night's events. A dangerous combination while on duty.

I thought I was ready to confront my temptations, and up until I ran into Rita, I had precision control over it. It was seeing myself in the aged woman's face that made me falter. Her faraway eyes, revealing a deep depression masked beneath the haze of liquor, and the humiliating way she swayed on her feet. Four years ago, I was Rita.

I sighed and started the car. Flicking a parting glance to the pub door, I slowly drove away. After a while I glimpsed in the rearview mirror, happy to see Alex's Pub getting farther and farther away. That night, my victory was hollow. I didn't cave into temptation, but the need was still there, whispering its nasty, seductive thoughts into my ear. I had hoped those urges had disappeared entirely, but like they teach you in AA, sobriety is an endless struggle.

****

The next morning, I headed into the office early. I wanted to review the recent missing persons cases before meeting Topher. I pulled the files of each report and hunkered down over a mug of piping hot coffee. The victims ranged in ages, ethnicities, and social statuses. Homeless men, teenage girls, retirees, and even an eleven-year-old boy were among the missing. Nothing linked them. I shoved the papers away with a grunt, frustrated.

"Something wrong?" Seth asked from behind me.

I glimpsed over my shoulder, holding my head in my hands. "Dead ends piss me off."

His eyes grazed over the missing persons posters, and files. "What's all this?"

I spun in my chair to face him. "I have a hunch."

He positioned himself on the edge of the desk.

"There's a spike in missing persons," I continued. "and I have a gut feeling it has something to do with the vamp murders."

He folded his arms and looked thoughtful for a moment. "A slew of vampire leaders whacked and a spike in mortals missing." His head moved in a slow nod. "Definitely seems suspicious."

I grabbed a folder and flipped it open. Squinting at the report type, I touched my chin. "Yeah. But I can't make a connection."

"We'll find one," Seth said. "But it will have to wait. We have a Were to interrogate."

I looked at Seth from over the paperwork. "We're not interrogating Topher. I'm just going to ask him a few questions and check out his alibi."

"He has an alibi?" He seemed surprised.

"He's been out of town for a couple days. If that checks out, we're back to square one."

He thinned his lips. That was the first he heard of Topher's alibi, so by his silence, I pretty much guessed he was expecting an easy questioning and a possible arrest.

I checked the clock on the wall and snapped the folder shut. "Topher's place is about a thirty-minute ride. We better get going." I stood and slipped into my jacket.

"*We?*" he asked with a grin.

I pulled my hair loose from my collar and glared a dead-pan stare into his eyes. "Don't get all girly on me, Newbie."

He bent to grab his duffel bag from the floor, and I expelled an annoyed breath.

"You don't need that. We're just asking him a couple routine questions."

He frowned. "You never know. We might need it," he protested.

"You bring that to Topher's property, and he'll get suspicious. He may not even talk to us."

"I'll leave it in the car."

I groaned a "*Fine!*" and off we went.

Chapter 13

Topher's ranch was homey with its window boxes full of pansies, its wrap-around porch, and neatly trimmed bushes in the front yard. Not at all what the movies depict. Usually, Weres are shown lingering deep in the woods, amongst shadows, caves, or bell towers. But the truth is, most Supes live in homes, just like you, and I. They mow lawns, tend to gardens, scrape peeling paint, and hang Christmas lights. Regular Joes who happened to sprout fur from time to time.

Topher was waiting for us on his porch swing. He wore a plain white tee and jeans with worn holes in the knees. He studied us carefully as we approached, mostly sizing up Seth. I couldn't help but wonder if he smelled Princess Peachy Keen on him already.

"Hey there," I called out to Topher, my hand coming to rest lightly on my holster. It was a usual gesture for me, not one that read as challenging or hostile.

"Edy," Topher acknowledged with a nod. His gaze shifted to Seth, the skin pinching slightly at the corner of his eyes.

"This is my...my..." I floundered, the word refusing to form on my lips.

"Partner," Seth provided for me. I scowled at him as he climbed the steps of the porch and stuck his hand out to the Were. "Seth Grooms."

Topher didn't stand. Instead, he eyed Seth's outstretched hand, his nostrils flaring once as he drew in his scent. Weres—like their animal counterparts—used their heightened sense of smell to gather information. They could tell a lot from just a whiff of air.

A mortal's mood, when a female was menstruating, or even which direction you'd come from. Only after he harvested whatever intel Seth's particular scent offered did Topher take Seth's hand into his with a strong grip, no doubt demonstrating the power he possessed.

Seth didn't wince, which not only surprised me, but impressed me. Maybe, he wasn't the dainty flower I thought he was…

My gaze drifted along the length of him. Great fitting jeans hugged his lean legs, and a dark-blue wool jacket rode up around his trimmed waist whenever he reached too high. My mind finally registered he was wearing a pea-coat, and I curled my lip. *A pea-coat? Really?* They reminded me of grinning male models in pricey magazines with seersucker pants and loafers. My throat dried painfully. And we're back to dainty…

"So, what is so important that I had to cut my trip short a few hours?" Topher asked, swinging his eyes to me, and leaning back into the swing.

I rested against the porch support beam, taking care to keep my movements slow and calm, even though my senses were on high alert, aware that he was reading my body language, like an open book.

Topher spread his arms out wide along the top of the bench seat and cocked his head at me, listening, but indifferent.

"Two nights ago, there was a mass murder," I explained, matter-of-factly.

He straightened to look fully at me, a brow arched severely over sharp, almost black eyes.

"Nearly every vamp leader in the surrounding districts was murdered, almost simultaneously."

"Yes, I've heard."

"What do you mean, you've heard," Seth questioned.

Topher turned to him. "I *mean*, I've *heard*," he answered drily. "News like that doesn't stay hidden long. Not in the Supe world."

"So tell me what else you know," I said nonchalantly.

His gaze swung to me. "Why don't we just cut to the chase, Edy." He smiled an insincere smile. "You suspect someone in my pack, or else you wouldn't be here."

I glanced down at my boots. "A print was found at one of the scenes." My gaze raised back to Topher. "It was confirmed to be a Shifter track."

If he was surprised, Topher didn't show it. His frigid posture and impassive stare indicated a wall had been erected between us. He was being extra careful, answering only direct questions and guarding himself with blatant aloofness.

I decided to change tactics. "Do you know Tek Ronboi?"

"Leader of the rural district. Yes, I know of him."

"He was among the dead. Found beheaded in Miss Isabelle's bordello."

"Seems to me," he said, crossing his legs at the ankles. "That's vamp business."

"The print was found there," I added, waiting for a response or subtle twitch to betray his detachment from the whole situation. There was none.

"It's not from a member of my pack."

I shifted on my feet, adjusting my holster. "How do you know?"

His jaw tightened. "I know the whereabouts of my entire pack." He said it with a frightening finality that made his eyes blaze.

Seth looked incredulous. He folded his arms hotly, as if to say, *humph.* "*All* of them? At *all* times?"

The porch swing creaked as Topher moved to stand. His heavy boots clomped as he stepped up to Seth, looking him dead in the eye. "If you have to question that, you know nothing of Were dealings. The ways we can communicate are infinite. Little transpires that does not travel through the ranks."

Seth was unfazed, he just squinted at Topher, dissecting each word and gesture, like a human lie detector. "Would you mind if we cast each member's track?" he asked, raising his eyebrows as he read the jump in Topher's muscles.

Topher's hands balled into fists. "You will not."

"Something to hide, Alpha?" Seth didn't bother to mask his confident smirk.

Topher practically growled.

I stepped in, putting myself between the fuming Were and Seth. "We don't need casts. We just need answers. The print wasn't able to be traced, so we're at a dead end. All we know for sure is, it's from a canine Shifter."

Topher glared at me. "There are more canine species than just the wolf." His chest was beginning to heave, signaling his struggle to control his anger. If he allowed it any free rein, he'd Shift on impulse, and his wolf form would go wild, possibly tearing me and Seth into bloody ribbons.

I smoothed my voice, trying to diffuse the mounting tension. "Topher. You know how I work. I wouldn't be wasting your time or mine if the clue wasn't solid. But the specialists at PCI ID'd it as wolf." I paused, allowing him to ingest that information at his own speed.

His nostrils flared a few times, but other than that, he remained silent as stone.

"Will you at least grant us permission to question your pack?" I asked as politely as I could.

He stared down at me, quiet for a few tense moments. Then, his jaw ticked. "That track does not belong to any of my pack mates." His tone was deliberately steady, marking his displease for having to repeat himself.

"Then let us eliminate all suspicion."

"Why were you out of town? Was it to lay low?" Seth threw the question over my shoulder like an assault.

I turned and hissed, "Shut up!"

His brows reached up to his hairline, silently asking, *What?*

I whipped my head back to Topher.

His eyes were venom as he gritted his teeth, the swelling of gums filling his mouth as his teeth and muscles rippled in anticipation of Shifting. "Pack business is none of your concern, *mortal*."

I leaned into his field of vision. "Topher."

With nowhere else to look, his eyes touched mine,

softening marginally. "Edy," he began, controlling his fevered breathing. "My pack has long held good standing within the community. We adhere to Otherworld Law and even conform to mortal laws. I do not take kindly to speculation and will not allow the PCI to disrespect my authority. *I* will question my pack, and if there is any pertinent information, rest assured, I will do the honorable thing and inform you personally."

I studied him and nodded. "Okay."

"*Okay?*" Seth mirrored disbelievingly.

I pretended not to hear him, keeping my focus on Topher. "Call me anytime with information." I reached out and gripped the banister, turning to leave. Seth followed.

As we descended the porch steps, Topher said, "I am confident I will find nothing. My pack has little dealings with vamps. Our focus is pack affairs and border protection."

My breath snagged at that statement. *Border protection.* I looked up at Topher, the recent incident with an outsider churned wildly in my head. Pieces quickly snapped into proper place, and realization soon dawned on Topher as well.

"The wanderer," he snarled, narrowing his now entirely black and dangerous eyes.

"The wanderer?" Seth asked, bewildered.

"Leo Trevino," I replied, glancing at him. "I'll explain everything on the way back to the precinct." I faced Topher again, who stood over us on the top porch step. His arms were folded so tight his muscles pulsated beneath the thin fabric of his shirt.

"I'll be in contact," he said, before turning and snatching the screen door open. It banged shut behind him, leaving Seth and me alone in the front yard.

"Come on," I said. "We have a wolf to hunt."

Chapter 14

Seth and I spent the next week pulling files on Leo and familiarizing ourselves with his history. We spoke to several relatives, the judge who convicted him of assault, and several other minor acquaintances of Leopold Trevino. All led nowhere.

The case reeked of the wandering Shifter. His past was marred with ugly crimes. Brutal beatings and general mischief. I had a sneaky suspicion he was connected to Tek's murder. I just had to catch that wolf paw of his red-handed.

I was on the verge of flipping my desk over in frustration when my cellphone rang. I frowned, my stomach fisting like a knot when I read the ID. *Mrs. Webber. Why is Kay's mom calling me?* She *never* called me, but I knew she had my phone number written on the dry erase board beside her home phone. It was listed under the "Emergency Numbers column".

"Hello?" I answered with an oddly shaky voice.

"Kennedy?" She was one of the few people who called me by my full name, but I didn't mind. Mrs. Webber was a nice lady, a subdued version of her boisterous daughter, but her smile always seemed warm and natural. Today, her voice was tight and coming out harshly.

I cut right to the chase. "Something wrong, Mrs. Webber?"

"Well, I'm not sure. Have you heard from Kay? I haven't seen her in weeks, and she's not answering her phone. I'm tempted to hail a taxi to her apartment."

Mrs. Webber didn't drive and never had. She married young and always depended on her husband to take her where she needed to go. After Kay's father passed away ten years ago, Kay's been nagging her to learn, but her mother adamantly refused, saying buses, taxis, and feet were created for a purpose, and she intended on using them.

"I saw her a week ago," I said, remembering Kay looking great in her pale blue sweater, flirting, and smiling so carefree.

"Can you try to call her? Maybe she'll answer for you."

"Of course," I replied blankly, gripping the edge of the desk to steady my swimming head. Pessimism seeped through me like it always did, like quicksand eating me slowly. I always assumed the worst and never considered a rational explanation for anything.

I envisioned Kay in a multitude of harrowing positions. Crushed inside her tiny, two-door car at the bottom of a cliff. Barely clinging to life, as she gripped a slippery log, rushing down a ravine. Tied to chair, gagged, and beaten bloody.

"God," Mrs. Webber breathed out in a rush. "I sincerely hope I'm just overreacting, but it's not like Kay not to answer her phone."

I felt like I should say something encouraging, so I muttered, "I'm sure she's fine." I shook the images away and white-knuckled the phone closer to my ear. "I'll find her, okay? I promise."

"Thank you, Kennedy. I'll be waiting for your call,

you hear? And you tan that hide of hers when you find her."

"You know I will."

I said good-bye, then hurried to dial Kay's number. It rang three times, then went to voicemail. *Why didn't I call her earlier?* Guilt clawed at me.

Her sweet voice filtered through the phone. "Hi, it's Kay. Leave me a message."

I hung up, my stomach twisting in dozens of sick little knots. Something didn't feel right. Kay ate, slept, and peed with her phone. *Why was she not answering?*

"Everything all right?" Seth asked.

I blinked and looked over at him, suddenly remembering he was even there. "Oh. Uh…" I frowned, not sure how to answer.

I shoved away from the desk. "Something's come up." I pulled my jacket free from the back of my chair. "I have to go."

"Does it have something to do with the case?"

I shook my head, slipping into my jacket. "It's personal."

"Want some company?" His eyes were darker today, almost absorbing the same deep green from his collared shirt. Concern was written painfully across his face. *God. This guy's emotions might as well be tattooed across his forehead.*

"I can come with," he offered, standing from his seat. "You know, for moral support."

I flashed him an irritated glance.

He raised his palms in surrender. "I was just asking."

I snatched my keys off my desk and whipped through the office like a whirlwind, ignoring everyone who shot me a surprised glance as I stormed past them.

*****

I lifted the fake rock in the flowerpot, turning it over in my hand and pulling out Kay's spare key. My heart had sunk into my toes when I pulled into the apartment complex. Her car was nowhere in sight. Where the hell was she? I placed the key in the lock and took a deep breath as I turned it, hearing the gentle *whisk* as the mechanism freed. I pushed open the door and slipped inside.

"Kay?" I called, walking through the tiny living room. Nothing appeared out of place. The TV remote controller was balanced on the arm of the sofa, and an empty glass rested on a coaster on the end table. I peeked into the kitchen. The countertops were clean, except for a couple envelopes and a roll of stamps.

I moved on to her bedroom but not before glancing inside the bathroom. A hairbrush full of Kay's coppery hair sat on the sink next to a half-empty tube of toothpaste. Her floral shower curtain was shoved all the way open. Her beloved bottles of coconut shampoo and conditioner lined the edged of the tub.

"Kay?" I tried again as I worked my way down the hall. I stopped at her door, which was partially closed. No answer. I rubbed my achy chest, pulling in comforting draws of breath through my nose and expelling them slowly through my mouth. I had seen countless crime scenes in my day.

Bloody, horrible displays of aggression that forever haunt my memories. I didn't want to discover Kay like that. I couldn't bear my last image of her being a slaughtered body or a vacant-eyed victim. But I was already here, and I had to find her, no matter what state she was in. I steeled my nerves and stepped inside.

Chapter 15

The room was empty and entirely intact. I sighed in relief and flopped backward onto Kay's bed, bouncing a little when I hit the mattress. Kay's bed had always been so hard. It killed my back whenever I spent the night, and she always insisted we slept in the same bed. I usually slipped out of the covers and retreated to the couch once she started snoring. My chest cinched painfully at the memory.

I stared up at the ceiling. *Where are you, Kay?* I cursed myself for leaving the pub the way I had. Why had I been so damn sensitive? I pieced together that night. Last time I had seen her was outside the pub doors. I could have kicked my own ass for not remembering Blondie's name because now I had absolutely no leads. *Maybe Tucker knows him?* With that being the only place to start, I pushed myself onto my feet and walked out her room. Giving it one more glance, I turned and left Kay's apartment exactly as I found it. Undisturbed and without Kay.

****

"Sorry, Edy. I didn't catch his name," Tucker said, drying a wide-lipped mug. "That was the first night I'd ever seen him."

I frowned. "Damn." I slammed my fist onto the bar, rattling some guys' beer bottle a few stools down. "Did you see them leave together?"

He thought for a moment. His forehead was creased, as he tried to recall the details. "I don't remember seeing Kay after you left." He tucked the mug beneath the bar. "The guy hung around the pub awhile, saw him chatting with a cute brunette at one point."

I bit my inner cheek, strumming my fingers on the bar. "So Kay didn't come back inside?"

Tucker scrubbed the back of his neck. "I really can't remember. Sorry."

Hearing that Kay might not have come back inside filled my brain with a grating buzzing sound. It rushed at my eardrums and temples, giving me instant vertigo. I spread my hands out on the bar in front of me. I squeezed my eyes shut, willing it to pass. *If Kay didn't leave with Blondie, then where is she?*

I slammed my palm against the bar, muttering a curse. I no longer had a suspect, which meant no fucking starting point. Being yanked from the street meant anyone or any*thing* could have abducted Kay.

I decided not to call Mrs. Webber. Not yet anyway. Even though things looked bleak, I didn't want to confirm her worst suspicions until I had something positive to tell her. That I had a strong lead, and it was a matter of time before I zeroed in on the scum who had her.

Besides, it would break my heart to have to look at missing persons posters all over town with Kay's smiling face splashed across the paper. I didn't know who had Kay, but I was determined to find out.

Her car was still parked at the pub's back lot. Seeing it there nearly crumbled me into the asphalt. I tried to open the driver's side door, but it was locked. I withdrew the mini jimmy I kept stashed in my boot and quickly popped the lock. I scoured the insides of her car, but nothing was amiss. My stomach twisted with dread. *Something is terribly wrong.*

Fighting off a debilitating panic attack, I set out to check the pub's perimeters, desperate to find a fraction of a clue I could use. I walked hunched, scanning the ground. My mind quickly filtered through the litter, discarding the cigarette butts, bottle caps, and other trash as I hunted for any trace of Kay.

I rounded the sidewalk and followed the side of the building as it led me through a narrow alley. It smelled of rotten food, piss, and alcohol. A couple of trash cans sat near the pub's back doors, and a dim security light blinked overhead.

It definitely looked like a place for shady dealings. As I came up on the trash cans, I heard a scratching noise nearby. I froze. My heartbeat picked up and I shifted my gaze quickly around the alley.

When I took a hesitant step, one of the trash cans flung forward, spilling trash onto the asphalt. My nerves leapt on instinct, and I snatched my gun from its holster, aiming it at the trash can. A fat raccoon shrieked and tore off down the alley, disappearing into the shadows.

"Stupid over-grown rat!" I shoved my gun back into the holster and kept on, scanning the ground carefully. I had to muddle through the garbage from the toppled trash can, kicking away dirty cups and empty soda bottles. I was nearing the end of the alley when something silver caught my eye. I narrowed my gaze as I approached it. It was a cellphone. A very familiar cellphone. I knelt down and picked it up with a trembling hand. My heart shattered when I flipped it over in my palm, recognizing the polka dotted case. *Kay's phone.*

I could feel the rapid pounding of my heart in my ears and throat. *No.* I collapsed to the ground. *No.* Kay was all I had left in this world. I couldn't lose her too. I gripped the hair at my temples and folded in two. For the first time in years, I allowed the tears to come. They simmered hotly behind my eyes and poured forth with such might it gave me an instant headache.

Distantly aware my phone was ringing, I ignored it and kept bawling, pathetically at that. I felt lost, like I was trying to grasp a leaf in a whirlwind. I had no idea where to start. No direction and not one possible lead.

The pub door opened, and someone came out. Their footfalls slapped against the pavement as they rushed to me. I blinked my eyes open, but the stinging was too much to bear beneath the glow of the security lights.

"Edy!" Tucker cried, dropping beside me. "Edy, what's wrong?" His arm draped across my back, and he slowly dragged me to a stand. "Edy, say something!"

I lifted Kay's phone. "It's hers," I said through my sobs.

He took it gently from my fingers. His eyes glazed with sympathy, which sobered me up momentarily. I went rigid and shook myself free of him.

"I know what you're thinking," I shouted. "Stop it. I will find her."

He reached his hands out to me. "I know you will, Edy. I don't doubt that for a minute." He glanced back at the pub. "Just come inside. I'll clock out and take you home."

I shook my head angrily. "No, I can't go home." My eyes skipped around the alley wildly. "I have to…I have to find her."

"You will," he assured me.

I dragged my sleeve across my nose. I felt trapped, like a wild animal going stir crazy in a cage.

"Come on inside, Edy." He wrapped a protective arm around my waist. He smelled like the pub, fried foods, smoke, and booze. "Everything will okay."

Suddenly exhausted, I didn't resist as he led me through the back door, and I even allowed him to direct me through the busy kitchen. It was only when he tried to get me to sit in the break room, did I protest. I insisted on going to the restroom. I needed to splash my face with cold water and gather my damn wits about me before anyone else saw me all splotchy and red-eyed.

"I'll be at the bar if you need me," Tucker said just before leaving me at the bathroom door.

I nodded and slipped inside. Thankfully, it was empty. I twisted the facet knob on full blast and shoved both hands beneath it. My body was humming with adrenaline, like my muscles were guitar strings, pulled excruciatingly taut over weary bones. I splashed several handfuls of water on my face, refreshed by the cold sting against my flushed skin.

I lifted my gaze to the mirror. I looked like hell. Like I should be crawling into a bed somewhere and withering away into a coma. But I *felt* edgy and needed to release the pent-up energy somehow. My subconscious warned me that staying in the pub could prove dangerous. That I was a fragile time bomb of bad decisions just ready to denote.

I pushed myself away from the sink and stormed

out of the bathroom. The pub's haze of cigarette smoke and steaming food hit me like a wall. My stomach roiled in protest of the offensive mix of odors, but I pushed through it and slid onto the nearest stool. Tucker noticed me and excused himself from a conversation with a coworker. He hurried over and leaned across the bar.

"You okay?"

I barely nodded, staring, but unseeing down at my hands.

He lowered his voice. "Want me to drive you home?" he asked cautiously because of what happened *last* time he took me home.

I shook my head as if it hurt to hear the offer.

"Can I get you anything?"

I stilled, my mind reeling with bullying thoughts that pummeled me from the inside out. My demons wanted to sooth the hurt with alcohol. To numb it until I no longer felt it. Or felt anything for that matter. I flinched, struggling desperately to keep the urge at bay. But overpowering the craving was like pinning a wild stallion to the ground with nothing but my bare hands.

I thought I was succeeding, but when Tucker laid Kay's cellphone on the bar in front of me, I lost it. I stared at the familiar slender phone and said through gritted teeth, "Whiskey."

Tucker hesitated.

"Whiskey, damn it," I snapped, glaring at him. "Now!"

His mouth twisted into a frown, and he grabbed a bottle from the back wall. He uncapped it and splashed some of the liquid gold into a glass, and my mouth salivated with anticipation. He set the glass in front of me and stepped back, like he didn't want to be privy to the madness.

I snatched the glass hungrily. Tucker just watched me, oblivious he was watching me slowly succumb to my weakness. Submitting to the demons I thought I had long exorcised. I held the glass to my nose, and the odor reached out and cold-cocked me.

What should have knocked me on my ass, took my breath away. My mind went into full on feeding frenzy mode. *God, how I've missed this smell.* The urge to quench my thirst surpassed any sensibility and arrowed straight to satisfying the vicious gnawing in my gut.

Glowering at Kay's cellphone, I placed the glass to my lips. *Don't do this,* I pleaded with myself. *You are in control, remember?* I clamped my eyes shut, ignoring the rational side of me, and tipped my head, downing the glass of whiskey in one hearty chug.

Chapter 16

The liquor burned its way down my throat but effectively extinguished the relentless hunger in my stomach. I pushed the glass toward Tucker.

"Another," I demanded.

For the moment, my head was clear. I propped my elbows on the bar and flipped through the rolodex of facts in my head. One: Kay's been missing for one week. Two: she wasn't seen returning to the pub. Three: her phone puts her in the alley, which was likely where the struggle took place. Four: I have zero suspects.

Tucker set another glass of whiskey in front of me. I grabbed it and tossed it back eagerly, hissing through my teeth as it barreled its way down to my stomach.

My phone rang in my pocket. As I dug it out, I said to Tucker, "Keep 'em coming until I say otherwise."

I glanced down at the caller ID. *Seth.* I wasn't in the mood to talk about the vamp cases, so I pressed *ignore* on my phone and dropped it next to Kay's phone.

I held my head in my hands, thinking about Kay, and the endless possibilities of where she could be…what could be happening to her. *How am I supposed to call her mom and explain that Kay was gone? And that I had no idea where she was?*

Over the next half hour, the pub flowed with

activity around me. Customers came in, drank, and left. At one point a man approached me, offering to buy me a drink. Before I could even think about what I was saying, I responded with my automatic answer that was drilled into me during my AA meetings.

"Thank you for the offer, but I no longer indulge my weaknesses." I didn't even bother looking up. The man scoffed, and said, "Really? Could have fooled me," before walking away. My bleary gaze slid sideways. I squinted hard, trying to melt the two retreating figures of the stranger into one. My head buzzed dully. I was officially drunk.

Soon, I lost count of how many I'd had. My limbs were liquid, and that old familiar feeling was back. The responsible part of me fought against it, balking and cussing myself for giving in to temptation. The other part was like a half-lit frat boy, ready to rip my clothes off and run naked down the streets of Cloverfield.

When my phone rang again, I bobbed my head to the ringtone a few seconds before answering it.

"Yo," I said into the receiver.

"Edy?" The way Seth said my name, stretching it out as if confused, made me chuckle. "Is that you?"

"The one and only," I replied, tipping an ice cube into my mouth.

"You sound different. Are you okay?"

I crunched down on the ice. "Never better." I signaled for Tucker to bring another drink.

"Where are you?"

"Out."

"Out where?"

I cast my eyes around the pub suspiciously. "Shh," I whispered into the phone. "Listen to me, Noogie."

"Noogie? Don't you mean Newbie?"

"My BFF is missing."

"BFF? Edy, are you screwing with me?"

I shushed him again, forcibly this time. "She's gone. Like poof, gone. We need to find her, k? Noogie, you have to help me find her, and then it will be my turn to hide." I giggled through my fingers.

"Edy, you're drunk. I'm coming to get you. Where are you?"

"Sitting on a bar stool." I nodded, like that was the right answer.

"Sitting on a bar stool, *where?*" Seth sounded exasperated but determined. I could practically picture him pinching the bridge of his nose.

"A pub…I think?" I struggled to remember the name but was coming up empty.

"A pub? Okay, you just narrowed it down to about two hundred places. Ask the bartender where you are."

"Aye, you there, barkeep," I hollered to Tucker, swaying on my barstool. He arched a brow and came over, his eyes darting around him like he was expecting someone to pop out and scare him.

"Noogie wants to know where I am." I thrust the phone out toward him. "Tell him."

Tucker eyed the phone before hesitantly taking it and holding it to his ear. "Hello?" His features slackened, and after a pause, he said, "Alex's pub downtown. Sure, I'll keep an eye on her." He handed the phone back with a smirk and walked away.

"Noogie?" I said, watching Tucker serve a blonde girl at the end of the bar. His gaze kept coming back to me, and I felt a flare of anger try to push its way past the stupid high I was on. I scowled into the phone. "I am a big girl, you know."

"I know, Edy," he said gently. "Just stay put, I'm coming to get you."

I put the phone down and took a slow look around the bar. People all around me were having a good time. They were laughing, talking, and drinking. It was an all too familiar scene. I'd seen it thousands of times before. Something deep inside me broke, sobering me for a few fleeting coherent seconds. In those seconds, I hated myself.

Like a blow to the gut, my insides twisted, nearly doubling me over. I thought I might wretch right there at the bar. *Why was I here*? I thought I had this thing beat. A familiar pounding began to build behind my eyes, and I knew it was going to take a few aspirins just to numb it.

Ashamed and ready to go, I was about to hail myself a taxi when I felt a warm hand press against the small of my back.

"Edy," Seth said at my shoulder. I turned. "Come on. Let me take you home." He handed Tucker a wad of cash, then urged me stand as he supported my weight. I slipped off the bar stool. I fell against him, my body like gelatin, boneless and lithe.

He wrapped his arms around me, almost lifting me in the air. "I got you," he said against my temple.

He pocketed both cellphones before guiding me out the pub. I walked on wobbly legs, leaning against him, depending on him to keep me upright. With one hand, he unlocked and opened the door of his hotrod. He arranged me in the seat, then jogged around the hood of the car, and got in himself.

"Okay?" he asked, starting the engine. The rumble

vibrated my teeth, the booze magnifying the sensation to a painful chatter. Any other time, the trembling would have aroused me. The growling of a high-performance engine and a tough metal body style often sent my panties flaming into ashes. But that night, in my inebriated state, the car was too loud, too fast, and way too bouncy.

I directed him the best I could to my apartment complex. We took two wrong turns and missed a road entirely, but we finally got there. He parked the car and watched me for a moment. I kept missing the handle of the door, my fingers slapping lazily against the window and dashboard.

Frustrated and ready to kick the window out, I was relieved when Seth opened the door for me and pulled me out. He lifted me into his arms, carrying me like a child. My head lolled to his shoulder, noticing for the first time his woodsy scent.

"Thank you," I whispered against his neck.

He just smiled. When he found my apartment door, he carefully placed my feet to the ground, sure to keep a firm hold on me as he dug my keys out of my pocket. I giggled as he did.

"Edy." He laughed and shook his head, amused. Unlocking the door, he pushed it open with his foot. "Come on. We're almost there."

I staggered inside, my vision doubled before me. With a strong hand holding fast to my waist, Seth guided me to my bedroom. I broke free of him when I spotted my bed. It called to me like a lover, seducing me with its promise of warmth and a fluffy embrace. I crawled under the comforter fully clothed, sighing with delight as I nestled into the stack of pillows.

"That a girl," Seth said, smiling. "But let's get you comfortable, all right?" He pulled back the comforter and set to work unzipping my boots. Too tired to help or resist, I laid there as he undressed me. He removed my boots gently and placed them side by side on the floor. His obsessive quirk of neatness made me smile.

"Jacket," he instructed, taking my wrist, and pulling me upright. I sagged like a rag doll against him, but he easily slid my jacket from my shoulders, taking it and lying it neatly across the footboard.

"I'll be a gentleman and leave the rest," he said with a small, endearing smile.

I flopped back against the pillows and mumbled something incoherent. Exhaustion swooped in like a villain, cackling and torturing me until finally...I gave in to it.

Chapter 17

I awoke a few hours later with my jeans twisted uncomfortably around my waist, and my shirt bunched halfway up my back. Wishing to strip out of the bothersome clothes, I dragged myself out of bed and stood. I swayed on my feet, my head still swimming with alcohol. I unsnapped my jeans and slid them down, stepping out of them as I grabbed the hem of my shirt.

A voice came from the darkness. "Edy?"

I yelped and turned toward the voice, fumbling to the nightstand, and yanking the chain on the lamp.

Seth squinted against the flood of intrusive light. He was slouched in the armchair stationed in the far corner of my room, an accent pillow crammed behind his neck. He scrubbed his eyes sleepily.

"What the hell are you doing here?" I snapped. I bent and snatched my jeans off the floor.

His gaze slid up my legs, lingering on my lace panties. My cheeks warmed, and I looked away, swallowing hard.

"I was worried about you," he answered, sitting up in the chair. Those words drew my eyes to his. We gazed at one another for a long while. He was simply dressed, his jeans and undershirt looking mighty fine on his frame.

"So you just stayed over? Talk about creepy," I

said, disconnecting our exchange. I strode to my closet with Seth's eyes following me the entire way.

"You were pretty out of it," he responded. "It didn't feel right leaving you alone."

I rested my fingers on the closet doorknob, blinking back the double-vison the alcohol brought on. I rubbed my aching forehead. "Well…thanks," I said, hearing the slushiness of my own voice. Irritated with myself, I yanked the door open wide. The so-called liquid power still coursed through me. It weighed my feet down, as though I was dragging myself through wet sand. Unbidden giggles bubbled just beneath the surface in this inebriated state I was in. I pursed my lips tight to keep them from escaping. Of all the versions of drunk Edy, I hated silly Edy the most.

I changed behind my closet door, choosing a simple cotton nightie with spaghetti straps. Even with Seth there, I opted to go commando, since I knew all too well the hassle of underwear while drunk.

Stepping back out from behind the door, I noticed he was gone. For a flash of a second, I was disappointed. *Why?* I remember thinking. *Why are you disappointed? It's Seth, for Christ's sake. The newbie.*

I had just sat down on the edge of my bed when he walked through my bedroom door. He was barefoot and carrying a glass of water. He padded across the floor, stopping right in front of me. His legs brushed against my knees, sending a surge of awareness through me. I flushed and looked away.

He held out a fist to me. Slowly, I inclined my head to stare up at him and held my palm beneath his. He opened his fingers, and two aspirins dropped into my hand. He smiled and offered me the water.

I took it and downed the pills in one swallow. I half wished I had tossed back a shot, rather than water, needing something to take the edge off my hypersensitive body.

"What time is it?" I asked, trying to fill the blaring silence.

"Quarter past three," he answered, taking the glass from me, and setting it on the nightstand. He yawned, covering his mouth with a fist. "Well past my bedtime." He winked down at me.

I gave a tight smile. He seemed so comfortable in a stranger's house. It was as if he had visited me a thousand times before. Perhaps, that was just him— easy going Seth—whose obliviousness to his own awkwardness only heightened his appeal.

Or maybe it was my dampened state. Or maybe, it was fact that I haven't had sex in two months—which let me tell you, is a lifetime for ole Edy James. Or maybe, it was because no matter how much I pretended Seth annoyed me, he really piqued my curiosity and made me second guess my usual choice in men.

Typically, I went for bad boys who'd rather polish their sports cars than rub me down right. Seth seemed different. Attentive. Unselfish. I was sure he'd be a giving lover in bed, more focused on his partner than himself.

Let me rephrase that. He didn't seem different. He *was* different. He was boring to the point of intriguing. Bland as a sack of flour. And I dreamed of messing that all up. Even his perfectly groomed hair had me yearning to do nasty things to him. Like digging my nails into his scalp and mussing it up, or jumping his bones so feverishly, his hair would be left in sweaty clumps.

I know what you all are thinking. It was too soon to get physical with Seth. In normal circumstances, you'd be right. I *hadn't* known him long, but our relationship was far from normal. The PCI changed everything. Long hours shackled with the sheer weight of knowing the truth about Supes advanced everything ten-fold. It was like counting our time together in dog years.

"Well," he said. "I'll just be over there," he jerked his chin to the chair in the corner. "if you need me."

He turned to leave, and before I could think better of it, I grabbed ahold of him, stopping him instantly. He glanced down at my fingers pressed to his arm. His brows met in question before turning his gaze on me.

I gulped, ignoring the alarms sounding off in my head. *You're too drunk. He's too good for you.*

"Do I do anything for you, Seth?" I asked, instantly regretting it. I bit back a curse, but the words were already gone, unable to be drawn back in. I released my hand from him as if I had touched a scalding pot.

His jeans were slung dangerously low on his hips. And his t-shirt. Damn that t-shirt. It was paper-thin, so I couldn't help but spot the strip of hair that trickled down from his belly button. I tracked the trail hungrily, wishing I could follow it as it disappeared into the top of his pants.

He studied me intently. "Do you *do* anything for me? Hell, Edy, what kind of question is that?"

"An honest one," I said, frowning. My head spun, though I honestly don't know it was from the booze or from his close proximity. Inside, I groaned, digging my nails into the cushy folds of the comforter.

Then, he was touching my face-delicately-like a

priceless antique. "Edy, you do *every*thing for me."

My heart swelled, and I leapt to my feet. I took his cheeks into my hands, smothering him with a kiss. Stunned motionless for a moment, he let me assault him, before his hands finally skimmed up my back, and sank into my hair. A moan of pleasure escaped me.

His touch melted my need for him into a quivering pool of sensitive nerve endings and breathy pants. I ground my hips into his, needing to feel him against me. He groaned into my lips and untangled his fingers from my hair. His palms cupped my ass, a sharp intake of breath hissing through his teeth when he realized I was naked beneath the nightgown.

He lifted me up and into him, cradling my weight effortlessly. I knew he could feel the heat that was coming from the center of my legs against his abdomen, but I didn't care. I was too far gone. When my body needed release, I was all in, not allowing anything to be half-assed. He allowed me to wiggle unabashedly against him, completely unapologetic for my nakedness that stroked greedily against him.

"Edy," he whispered, his voice thick and husky. "Are you sure you want to do this?"

"Take off your pants," I ordered between kisses, half crazed with my building lust.

As he lowered me to my feet, I pawed at his shirt eagerly, the heat in my core becoming unbearable. He seized my wrists and held me at bay.

Pressing his forehead to mine, he murmured, "Edy, please." His breaths came out in rapid successions, heaving his chest against mine with each intake and release. My skin was acutely aware of him, sensitive and heightened until I thought I'd implode with the next barest of touch. "Not like this."

I snapped backward. My blood swiftly alternated its course and rushed up to my neck and cheeks. *Is he really turning me down?*

"I just want to make sure it's not the whiskey talking. I want *you* to want me. Not the booze."

Humiliated, I tugged my wrists free. I glowered at him, adjusting my nightgown back into place. "You're a fucking killjoy, you know that?" Angry, embarrassed tears welled in my eyes. I turned my back to him. I couldn't bear him to see me like that. Vulnerable. Weak. "Get out."

I clambered into the bed, desperate for space. Out of my peripheral vision, I noticed how helpless he looked.

"Edy, don't be mad. Please." Again, I was lured into meeting his gaze. The emotions that man held in his voice was nothing I have ever encountered before in my entire life. Then, my eyes caught sight of his bulging pants, and pride hit me like a Mack truck. *I did that to him.* It pleased me to know I drove him wild.

He dragged a hand down his face and groaned. "I'm doing the right thing here. You just don't realize it yet." He tried to smile, but it was fragile, like he wasn't sure how to handle me.

Though I was desperate for him to make love to me, somewhere deep in my alcohol-soaked sanity, I knew he was right. I sighed heavily, and that seemed to speak volumes to him. He cautiously crawled onto the bed, his eyes never straying from my face. The bed dipped under his weight, and I couldn't push him away even if I wanted to.

"We okay?" he asked quietly.

I nodded, fisting the comforter, and drawing it up near my neck. How could I be mad at him? That boyish charm of his made him damn near irresistible.

"Can I still stay the night?" He hooked a piece of hair behind my ear. I leaned into the touch, delighting in the shiver it sent through me. "I want to take care of you."

I nodded again, and said, "I'd like that."

His lips curved into a sweet smile. He settled beside me, tucking his arm beneath my neck, and pulling me into him. He stretched his frame out comfortably on top of the comforter, his bare feet peeking out of the bottom of his jeans. I felt myself smile as I nestled against his chest, draping my arm across his stomach. His rustic scent enveloped me, and soon, the high from the whiskey and the lusting eased. He stroked the length of my arm in slow, methodical precision, putting me into an easy and contented sleep.

Chapter 18

When I opened my eyes, I was still wrapped up in Seth. His face was turned away from me, his chest rising and falling in even intervals, still knee-deep in peaceful sleep.

The urge to slip quietly out of his embrace and tip toe away pulled at me like an energetic child. It was an automatic reflex to my usual sack sessions, so tamping that instinct down was a struggle. But when I cast my eyes to Seth, I had to remind myself that this time was different. For starters, we didn't even have sex. Plus, *Seth* was the man lying next to me, not some gear-head I picked up at a car show.

As I laid there, my cheek pressed against his shoulder, I retraced the events that led us there. Our bickering, his adorable smile, me busting his balls, our heated kiss, his doting nature when he insisted on picking me up at the pub...My mind hitched on a thought. The pub. *Kay.*

I bolted upright, startling Seth from his sleep.

He roused slowly, blinking a few times to adjust his heavy, sleep-laden eyes. "What's wrong?"

How could I forget about Kay? My stomach clenched painfully as remorse rushed through me, giving me an instant headache. *God, I'm an ass.*

"My friend," I said shakily. "I have to go." I got out of bed and went to my closet to dress.

"What friend?" He sat up, watching me as I stepped into a pair of jeans. "You know, you said something about a friend last night. Something about her being gone."

I pursed my lips and moved my head in an embarrassed nod. Cringing at the thought of what else I might have said. I snatched a blouse from a hanger, fisting the soft fabric to steady my trembling hands.

He pushed himself off the bed. "What did you mean when you said she was gone?"

I felt Seth's presence at my back. My arms felt like lead, and it took concentration to make them work. *Oh God, Kay.* With my throat threatening to collapse at any moment, I finally said her name out loud since I discovered she was gone.

"Kay?" he repeated, clearly confused. Still gripping the blouse to my chest, my shoulders sagged with a repressed sob. Seth touched me, trying to offer comfort, but I flinched and stepped just out of his reach. Taking in a deep breath, I closed my eyes for a beat and groped for control over my emotions.

"Edy. What is it?"

I turned to face him. His sweet mouth was drawn into a tight scowl. His looked worried, likely anxious by my unusual vulnerability. His woodsy scent drifted in the space between us, and I inhaled it deeply. It was then that I realized he had a profound effect on me. Just his closeness soothed me. His natural ability to comfort me with just his very presence was disconcerting. And delightful.

With eyes shining with tenderness, he opened his arms in an offered embrace. I stared at him for a moment, tears welling in my own eyes until he blurred into a puddle of nothingness. I walked blindly forward and stepped into his arms. It felt so good to be held by him. Strong, unyielding arms wrapped around me like a favorite blanket sheltering me, warming me, enfolding me.

"My friend Kay went missing a week ago," I said into his chest. "I was with her that night at the pub, but I got angry with her and left."

I wanted to cry, or scream, or hell, why not do both, but I refused to allow myself the luxury. I deserved to feel every bit of the guilt that haunted me. Seth stroked the length of my back, quiet as I told him everything. Mrs. Webber, Kay's car, and her forgotten cellphone in the parking lot.

"Edy," he said when I was through. "You can't blame yourself."

I made a noise of irritation. "Of course I can! I left her! It is all my fucking fault!" I was still clutching my blouse, I knew because I could feel my fists shaking as I squeezed the life out of it. My entire body shook with those familiar, yet overwhelmingly toxic emotions. Anxiousness, mixed with rage, and bitter desperation. *Release*, I thought. *I need a release.* I learned in AA, that addicts often needed instant gratification or a *release* as they often called it.

Something that immediately took the edge off their panic, curbing it to a controllable level. My releases often came in the form of booze, speed, or sex. Since my head still ached from a hangover, and there wasn't a car in the bedroom, Seth's strapping body would definitely do. Desperate for release, I lifted my chin and pressed delicate kisses along his stubbly jawline.

He reacted almost instantaneously. He groaned and

rolled his head back to give me full access to his neck. I licked at the hollow in his throat, moaning as his pulse fluttered against my tongue. His fisted my hair, shooting delicious pain along my scalp and down to my core. Whirling thoughts, all varying forms of dirty deeds ricocheted in my mind.

Impatient and literally pulsating beneath Seth's touch, I impulsively unsnapped Seth's jeans and slipped my fingers under the denim fabric. He wore nothing underneath, and it drove me wild. His breath hitched, as I pushed his pants down, letting them pool at his feet. My palms slid down his muscular thighs, as I dropped to my knees in front of him.

"Edy." His voice was course, like sandpaper.

"Please, Seth. I need a release. I need…" My voice dropped off, my insides singing with a craving so powerful it nearly suffocated me.

I stared up at him, my eyes pleading for understanding, though I doubt he could offer it. Seth wasn't an addict. He didn't hunger the way I did. He didn't fight invisible battles every damn day like I did. "Please," I begged with unflattering desperation. "I need this. I need you."

My addiction to instant gratification and wrong decisions was too demanding, and my willpower much too weak.

I didn't let him protest. I took him, *all* of him, greedily. Slow and steady at first, teasing him to the point he begged for more. When I nibbled the crown of him, then drove it deep into my throat, his breathing came out in shallow hisses. The primal sound alone made me mindless with power and need. His pelvis began to buck wildly, trying to help me, but I dug my nails into his ass to keep him still. *I'm in control here.* That thought alone was laughable as I was rarely ever in control over anything.

He panted my name over and over, as he wound the length of my hair and fisted it tight. I allowed a moan to rumble its way through me, charging his frantic thrusts.

With his quickened breathing, and almost animalistic grunts, I knew he was getting close. Like me, he was desperate for release. A different release than my own, but a release none-the-less. With a final squeeze to his backside, I finally allowed him to shudder and give in to the ecstasy. His carnal pleasure was…well, *my* pleasure. In good time, I'd let him return the favor. Wiping my mouth, I thought with a sly smile, *Oh boy, will I...*

I rose to back to full height and planted a kiss on his full lips. Drawing back, I smirked at him. With his disheveled hair, and flushed cheeks, he looked unkempt and feral. A stark contrast to the ever polished Seth Grooms. I was helplessly aroused, but just seeing and feeling him come undone beneath my touch was satisfying enough. For now.

I left him in a dumbfounded state, his knees full of jelly as he tried to pull up his pants. Instead, he staggered a little, and had grasp the closet door for support.

"Damn, Edy." His skin shimmered with sweat, and his legs still visibly shook. "That was…"

I lifted onto my toes and quieted him with another kiss.

"Thanks for letting me use you like that," I said, pulling the nightgown off over my head.

He grinned woozily. "Anytime."

I put on my shirt, fastening the buttons hurriedly. "Come on. We have to get to work. Captain is going to go nuclear if I'm late again."

*****

The only reaction we got out of Captain when we walked through the office doors together was a quirked eyebrow. Seth and I took advantage of the good luck and quickly hunkered down at our desks. We poured over the vamp case for several hours, but it was pointless.

With Topher not allowing us to speak to the pack, we were at a standstill. Focusing on the case was difficult. I kept finding myself thinking about Kay. I'd zone out, chewing my nails as I wondered where she was, and if she was okay. Seth began to recognize the moments I drifted into the dark thoughts. He'd run his fingers down my arm or give my neck a little squeeze, drawing me back.

Eventually, I pulled up the missing persons files again, hunting for a clue I might have missed. There weren't any. With elbows propped on the desk, I pulled out my phone and turned it worriedly in my hands.

I did this for a long while, until Seth reached over and covered my hand with his. I shifted my eyes to him.

"Call her."

He was talking about Mrs. Webber. I bit my lip, thinking it over. How do you make a call like that? How do you tell someone their daughter is gone, without a trace?

I breathed a *no* and flung myself back in the chair. "I can't. I don't know what to say."

"She has a right to know," he commented. He

didn't say it in a judgmental tone, which I was grateful for. He was just stating a simple fact. "She should start the process of registering her as a missing person."

I lifted my hand, halting him. "No. Mortal lawmen won't do shit to find her. It's up to me."

He expelled a breath, his face etched with concern as he considered what to say. "Okay," he replied finally. "We'll find her and bring her home." He reached across our distance and threaded his fingers through mine.

I gave him a smile in gratitude. "I think I need to go back to the pub," I said, detangling our fingers, acutely aware of the curious glances we were getting.

Heat snuck its way up my neck, and cheeks. *Am I fucking blushing?* A novelty for me since I don't embarrass easily. I tucked my hair behind my ears, and hastily added, "There could be more clues."

He leaned back in the chair, and steepled his index fingers. His keen eyes directly on my face when he asked, "Didn't you comb that place clean already?"

I averted my gaze, slightly ticked at myself for leaving the scene without completely clearing it first. "I abandoned the search after I found the phone."

His brows raised.

I shielded my eyes from his incredulous gaping. "Stop looking at me like that."

"I'm sorry. I'm just shocked, that's all."

Setting my jaw tight, I rushed to say, "Never had to comb a crime scene that hit so close to home." I shoved the missing persons posters back into their folders.

His chair rolled close to mine, and I felt his breath against my hair as he said, "We'll find her. Together."

Chapter 19

After dragging my gaze back and forth tirelessly across the pub's parking lot and alley for over an hour, I was beginning to lose hope of finding anything. Seth and I canvased the entire alleyway, and neither of us found a speck of anything useful. I muttered a frustrated curse and stomped my boot into the broken stretch of concrete. Then, a voice came out of thin air.

"Hey, blondie. Over here."

I cut my eyes to the far corner of the alley. My surprise quickly ebbed into annoyance when I saw the squat man hovering several feet off the ground. I rolled my eyes and groaned. *Cherubs.* They were almost as grating as mermaids.

I took my time strolling over to him. Cherubs are craftier than they are cute, and they rarely did anything merely in the name of love. Their greed made them hoarders by nature, and their innate passion made them explosive.

This one resembled a burly lumberjack, shrunken down of course, to the size of a small child. Given his stature, I figured all he could saw was twigs. He was outfitted in red flannel and hiking boots, and he even wore one of those winter caps with the fleece ear flaps. Miniscule wings of downy feathers struggled to keep his robust frame afloat.

I flicked my gaze back to Seth, who had lifted his

head to watch me move closer to the cherub. It was reassuring to know he was there with me, helping me with my search and not to mention there for backup if things got sticky.

I kept a shrewd eye on the cherub, my muscles poised and ready to haul off and smack the shit out of him if needed. I halted in front of him, narrowing my glare before saying, "You got something to tell me, little man?"

The cherub's eyes went beady. "I'll show you little," he snarled, reaching for the zipper of his tiny denim pants.

Repulsed, I said, "You whip that thing out, and I'll drop kick your tiny ass into next week."

He scowled through his bushy beard, adjusting his belt buckle back into place. "I have information the PCI would want to hear." His voice was hoarse and rumbly, like a boulder rolling on gravel.

I crossed my arms in front of me. "And that is?"

Mouth twitching and eyes flashing, he circled around me lazily, like he had all the time in the world, or maybe it was because his tiny wings could barely support his weight. The smell of pipe tobacco and fermented grapes followed him like an invisible cloud, reminding me of the pub, which also reminded me of Kay. My ribcage compressed at the thought of her.

Frazzled by the images of Kay, carefree and flirty, I dug my nails into the leather fabric of my jacket. "Spill it," I said, losing my patience.

His wings beat madly as he floated around me in a wide arc. "Tsk, tsk. You must know by now that all information has a price." He moved closer, invading my personal space. By instinct, I stepped away from him.

He grinned at that.

"Fine. What do you want?" I shot a pointed look to his wings. "Some Viagra for those pathetic wings of yours?"

Something evil glowed behind his eyes, and I knew I was pushing my luck. Throughout history, the winged creatures have been depicted as sweet, round-cheeked children, but they weren't that at all. Instead they were often seedy, shifty-eyed beings who got a kick out of wreaking havoc with mortal relationships.

It's true they encouraged love, but it was usually illicit love. Affairs, incest, and other moral-less relations. Looking at the miniature lumberjack, I wondered where the misconception came from. With his thick beard and rough voice, there was no mistaken him for a child, much less a cheery one who plugged unknowing mortals with love-infused arrows.

Just as the cherub's gaze darted over my shoulder, I felt a presence come up behind me.

"Here's half," Seth said at my elbow, thrusting a fifty at the cherub. "You get the other half after you talk."

The cherub smirked like a sly fox, grabbing the money, and shoving it into his pocket greedily.

He licked his lips, as if the information he's about to relay is super juicy. "The Bonded she-vamp is not to be trusted."

Seth and I exchanged a confused look.

"The Bonded she-vamp?" Seth question was more to me, than to the cherub.

"Is there more?" I asked irritably, pinning the cherub with a glare.

His dark eyes settled on Seth, as if Seth was in

charge. That infuriated me. My hands curled into fists at my side, and I had to take steadying breaths to keep from punting the cherub like a football.

"Can you tell us anything else?" Seth inquired. "To help narrow it down perhaps?"

The cherub's eyes seemed to almost disappear among his wrinkles and facial hair. "Bonded vamps are rare," he said, his wings jerking him backward. "The newly Bonded she-vamp is the one you seek."

Newly Bonded she-vamp. I thought hard about that, praying the cherub wasn't giving us the run-around with his stupid ass riddles.

"Thank you," Seth said, stretching out his arm to offer a crisp bill.

The cherub snatched it, almost salivating at the sight of money. His eyes bounced wildly for a moment, staring at the bill, then his gaze lifted back to Seth.

Something foreboding passed over his face. "Here's a tip. Free of charge." His husky voice lowered to a muffled hush as he leaned close to Seth's face and whispered. I couldn't make out what he said.

The cherub spun around and hauled ass away. Well, *tried* to haul ass away. His wings sputtered and protested. It was more like watching a bird who had just slammed, beak-first into a window…trying desperately to recoup by shaking off the impact, but they wind up careening into the ground a few times before flying away in erratic circles.

"Let me know if you change your mind about that Viagra," I called with a mocking grin.

He scowled darkly and flipped me off. I chuckled, watching after him as he slowly put space between us. Though slightly comical, it was actually sort of pathetic. He looked like a fat bumblebee, drunk on nectar.

Seth stepped into my line of vision. "I wonder what he meant by that?" He scratched through his hair with a quizzical look on his face.

Almost forgetting the hushed exchange between them, my heart punched hard against my chest. I prayed it was a lead on Kay. "What did he say?"

"Stay vigilant of those who surround you. Not everyone is what they say." His eyes were wide, clearly curious of the cherub's words.

What the hell does that mean? I shrugged, trying to seem unfazed by the ominous warning. "Who knows? You can't trust cherubs, Seth. They aren't exactly ethical beings. Try not to read too much into anything they say."

He gave a slow, unsure nod.

"So," I said through a sigh. "A newly Bonded she-vamp?"

His wide, interested eyes hardened, switching focus from the strange warning to the potentially useful tip from the cherub. He folded his arms and touched his index finger to his chin. "The cherub was right about them being rare, so this could prove to be a pretty good tip."

I nodded in agreement, flicking my gaze across the desolate alley we stood in. "Come on, let's go. We've exhausted this place." It pained me to say that. Declaring the alley clear meant I still had no clues to Kays' disappearance. She was still out there—alone and terrified. I resigned myself to the fact that I had a lot of work ahead of me, but Kay was worth it. I'd find her. And I'd make the bastard who took her *pay*.

Seth and I rounded the corner of the building, which spilled us back onto the sidewalk that passed in front of the pub. I tossed a glance to the pub entrance. This place was all too familiar. Old brickwork gave Alex's some character. The buildings' huge windows were plastered with band posters, menus, and drink-of-the-day specials.

A waitress taped a piece of paper to the glass. My eyes were drawn to it as there was no denying what it was: a missing persons poster.

Chapter 20

My breath caught at the face looking back at me.

"Oh my God." I stared at Rita's face. The photo of her had to have been old. Before she became an alcoholic. Her hair was neatly piled into a bun, and her eyes were bright.

Seth came up beside me and looked from me to the poster of Rita. "Do you know her?"

"Sort of," I responded, not taking my eyes off the poster. "She's a regular here."

He went silent. He seemed to be calculating something, but I didn't ask what.

"You think whoever took Kay, took her too?"

I cast my gaze to the ground, my mind racing with far too many thoughts to form a feasible theory, but my gut screamed an affirmative *YES*! The deliberate murders of the vampire leaders, the spike in human quotas in the districts, and the surge in missing persons weren't just a coincidence. They *couldn't* be.

I glanced over at Seth. "We have some long hours ahead of us," I told him. "And I'm going to need coffee to get through it." Before stepping off the sidewalk, I glimpsed back at the poster of Rita one last time. Frowning, I added, "Mass quantities of it."

****

After a quick stop at the nearest gas station, Seth and I were armed with hot, black coffee and sticky honey buns. At our desk in the precinct, we hunkered down over our unhealthy lunch and starting picking through the limited clues. We bounced theories off one another, but nothing seemed plausible. Though, with Supes, *anything* is plausible.

Captain stormed in around three o'clock and stalked through the office as though on a terrible mission. His gaze touched on every face in the room as he said, "Does a*ny*one have something to give me yet?" He thrust his arms out wide.

"God damn it, someone throw me a goddamn bone here." It was relatively quiet, save for the fax machine trilling and papers shuffling. He tugged at his collar, which barely fit around his thick neck. "Nothing? What the hell people? I'm paying you to be detectives, not receptionists."

Seth and I exchanged a look. His brows lurched up, quietly urging me to tell Captain about our tip from the cherub. I gave a little shake of my head, and mouthed *no*. He peered at me, perplexed, but I just turned away.

I wasn't telling the Captain shit. Not until I figured out who the newly Bonded she-vamp was anyway. Petty? Sure. Childish? Maybe. Unprofessional? Absolutely. But it was *my* tip dammit, and I wasn't about to let someone else figure out *my* tip.

Vick's gaze sought me out, coming to rest on me with a smugness that made my palm itch to slap him. "What about Topher?" he asked above the tense-laded air of the office. "Wasn't Edy supposed to question him? We haven't heard the status of that meeting."

I scowled.

Captain turned his attention to me. "Yeah." He seemed annoyed that he'd forgot the fact that I volunteered to question the pack leader. "Do tell. What came of it, James?"

I laced my fingers, and leaned my elbows on the arm rests, trying to appear more casual than I felt. My blood surged with adrenaline, aching to be active. To be shifting gears along the highway or stomping my boot heel into the ass of some Supe.

"He refused a pack interrogation," I said. "Which also meant there was no chance of castings of their paws."

Red blanketed Captain's face, and his mouth compressed to a tiny, angry button. "Since when does a suspect get a choice?" Spidery veins bulged in his temples, marking his mounting fury.

"He's not a suspect," I countered, clamping my fingers tighter.

"That print was Shifter," Captain argued. "One of his pack members is our killer. So you go back and tell that damn dog the PCI will interrogate whoever and whatever we damn well please."

I opened my mouth to protest, but Captain whipped around and marched to his office, slamming the door on us all.

My eyes shifted around the room at all the staring faces. A few were kind enough to busy themselves at their desk, but others watched me, like bratty siblings who found amusement in my public scolding. "Fuck off. All of you." Finally, I met Seth's gaze, and he gave me an encouraging smile.

"Drink your coffee, Edy," he said gently, handing me my paper cup from the gas station. It was still warm from the fresh pot of cheap coffee he'd made in the break room an hour ago. "Forget about Captain and ignore the rest of these assholes."

His uneven smile made my heart do funny things, and controlling my anger was one of them. Instead of flipping them all the bird or throwing a stapler at Vick, I just took in a deep draw of breath, allowing the scent of the coffee to smooth over my bristly nerves. I took a big swig and set the cup back down on the desk.

"Thanks," I said and flipped open my file of Tek Ronboi's case. I stared down at the enlarged photo Seth had taken at the scene: Tek's lifeless body sprawled on Isabelle's bed. His head severed neatly, like his skin had been butter, and the murder weapon, a warm knife. My eyes skipped across Tek's profile. *Vampire. Hailed from Zimbabwe. Leader of the western rural district. Bonded to Claudette Klemmings.* I reread that line again. *Bonded to Claudette Klemmings.*

I gripped the armrests of my chair and spun toward Seth. He was kicked back with his feet casually propped on the desk. His brows were furrowed tight as he studied a file in his hand. He didn't look at all annoyed that I interrupted him; he just gazed back me, interested.

"I know who the newly Bonded she-vamp is."

He sat up, tossing the file onto the desk. "Who?"

"Claudette. Tek Ronboi's mate."

Dawning spread across his face, brightening his eyes. He flashed me a toothy smile in approval. "Looks, like we have ourselves a vamp to talk to."

His mood spread quickly to me, and I grinned. Finally! A lead!

He got to his feet and slipped his arms into his coat. I followed suit, zipping myself snug into my jacket, and took one last swig of coffee before we headed out.

Captain bustled out of his office, his eyes quickly lighting on Seth and I packing our gear. His brows pinched, and he wasted no time striding over to us. "Where the hell are you two going?" He planted his hands on his hips, leering over us with those glaring eyes of his.

"Out," I answered with a clipped tone, not wanting to tell him too much.

Seth adjusted the collar of his coat. "Got a tip from a cherub earlier. Going to sniff it out and see if it leads us anywhere."

I groaned inwardly. So much for sitting on the information until I checked it out.

"A *cherub*?" The Captain practically choked on the word. "You're following a lead given by a god-damn *cherub*? Have you lost your minds? You might as well be chasing your own asses in circles."

Seth was unruffled, smoothly gathering his duffel bag and gesturing me to go. "Anything's worth checking out at this point."

I departed without a word to Captain, Seth a few steps behind me. A few people tracked us with curious stares as we went by them. Part of me wanted to turn sharply to them and ask what the hell they were looking at, but instead, I took my cue from Seth, who completely ignored them. I walked proudly with my chin up, and my usual, "I don't give a fuck" mentality.

****

I climbed out of the car first, but Seth wasn't far behind. All around us were rolling, grassy hilltops, and towering pine trees that cast long shadows on the ground. The western rural district was remote with limited luxuries available to the mortals and vamps who lived there. They had the basics, like electricity and running water, but their cellphone service was spotty in most of the region.

Tek and Claudette's home, however, was far from modest. It was a relatively new structure with modern architecture of sharp angles and floor to ceiling windows. I remember thinking they must have specially made curtains that obstruct sunlight because typically vamps and windows weren't a good combination.

A grand mahogany door greeted us. I lifted my knuckles and rapped them hard on the thick wood. After several long, almost purposely drawn out moments, the doorknob twisted.

"Finally," I muttered under my breath.

The door pulled open, and a stately woman stood in the threshold. I had never met Claudette before, as she kept a low profile among the Supe community. She was pretty but in an intimidating sort of way. Flawless, mocha skin flowed like silk over toned muscles, and ebony hair hung in long spirals down her back. She had a prominent, pointed chin with a dimple chiseled in the center. Cunning eyes that made me tense on instinct swept over me from top to bottom.

"Claudette Klemmings?" I asked, hooking my thumbs on my gun belt. Just looking at her with that lithe body and luscious hair, I wanted to declare her ass guilty right then and there.

"Ronboi," she corrected, lifting her chin, and looking down her nose at me. I stifled a scoff. *Right. Ronboi. Like vamps care about taking each other's names.*

"PCI," Seth stated, flashing her a badge. "We'd

like to ask you some questions."

"Of course," she said, gesturing for us to enter. I flashed a hurried glimpse to Seth, before following her inside. The inside of the house was exactly like the outside. Stark and contemporary with mod-inspired lamps with furry shades, and artwork so simplistic they nearly blended into the walls.

She motioned for us to sit. Seth obliged by sinking into the plush red leather couch, squeaking the cushions as he did. I chose to remain standing. Claudette settled her svelte frame in a strange piece of furniture that resembled a curvy footrest.

"So, Detectives," she began, resting her palms on her knees. "What can I do for you?"

"We're handling your mate's case," Seth said. "So far, there hasn't been much prospect in solving it. So we're hoping you could provide us some information that may help with that."

Her features smoothed into an eerily placidness. "I don't understand how I can be assistance, but because I hope to find justice for my beloved mate, I'm willing to try." Her lips curved into an artificial smile.

"Did you love Tek?" I asked. My blunt demand made Seth visibly cringe.

Claudette shot me a vicious glare. "Of course I did."

I held my hands out in surrender. "It's a valid question given the intent of most vamps. You guys tend to Bond for the sake of advancement, not out of love."

Her mouth pressed into a stern line.

"Could you tell us about the night of Tek's death?" Seth interjected, clearly trying to change the subject.

She turned her steely gaze back to him. "I was on

patrol." The stiff set of her shoulders signaled she was guarding her emotions.

"Patrol?" he probed.

She tilted her chin like a fucking high, and mighty queen on a throne. "I am second in command to the Hillside District. It was my night to patrol."

"Don't you have minions around to do the patrolling?" I questioned, starting to stroll leisurely around the living room. I ran my finger along the length of the shiny, marble fireplace mantel. Inspecting the pad of my finger, I noticed it was clean. Not a speck of dirt or dust. Not that this answered anything about the case, but it seemed to irritate Claudette, which was reason enough to do it.

"I am not above patrol work," she said stiffly. "It shows unity in the ranks."

I snorted, and lifted a metal bust of a nude woman. "*Unity*. Right." I examined it for no reason, then purposely chose a different spot on the mantel to return it. I'm a bit of an ass, what can I say?

"Can someone vouch for your whereabouts?" The way Seth presented the question was kind and not at all challenging. I admired the way he framed his words, but it was a tactic I could never pull off. I was too blunt. Too direct. Too in your face.

You could almost see the internal workings of Claudette's mind, strategizing on what to say and how to act. "My leader, Garon Walker." She arranged herself primly on the chair. "He will gladly verify what you need to know."

I compartmentalized the information to confirm her story with Garon Walker, and with as much nonchalance I could manage, I asked, "Did you and Tek have an argument the night he died?"

Her sharp eyes bore into me. "No. Tek and I were perfectly suited. We had a compliant relationship."

Compliant relationship? She made it sound so basic, so businesslike...so *boring.* I ran my gaze across her harsh features, noting her emotionless face as we discussed her dead mate. Vamps were notorious for being deadpan, but something told me their pairing was strategic, not romantic. *No wonder Tek was getting some action on the side,* I remember thinking.

I cocked my head to the side. "Do you know Isabelle Merriweather?" I questioned, fully aware I was about as subtle as a blinking neon sign on a hooker's panties. Seth went rigid, but I didn't care.

Claudette's eyes were black ice, cutting and dangerous. "What are you insinuating, Detective?"

I smirked, clearly hitting a raw nerve. "So you know her?"

"I think I've answered enough questions," she said, standing abruptly and striding briskly to the door. She opened it and stood with one hand on her hip, and the other resting on the knob. "Get out."

Seth got up and went to her. He handed her a business card and said, "Call me if you remember anything that might be helpful." He ducked out the door and disappeared.

I strolled slowly through the room, my hand resting lightly on my holster. I kept my eyes trained on her as I passed through the threshold and said, "I'll send your regards to Isabelle."

Her lips curled upward, revealing her pointy fangs. She may have even hissed, but I was already stomping my way down the driveway to know for sure.

When I slid behind the wheel, Seth was already buckled in, and ready to roll.

"You are a piece of work, Edy," he said, trying to keep a straight face but failing miserably. "The shit you say could get you killed, you know that? I don't know how you aren't dead by now."

I grinned and wiggled my brows. "Twenty percent is luck, and the other eighty percent is pure bad-assery."

We returned to the precinct and after logging in a few more hours of useless paperwork, I decided to call it a night and go home.

Stepping beneath a hot spray of water, I sighed as my overwrought muscles relaxed and unknotted. The past weeks pressed in on me. Captain assigning me a partner. Kay's disappearance. The vampire murders. The spike in quotas. For the first time ever, I could actually say I was overwhelmed.

My leads sucked, and I felt as if I was drifting at sea, unable to cling to anything worth investigating.

I stood in the shower until the water ran cold. Freezing, I clambered out with a curse, wrapping my shivering body in a thick towel.

I padded into my room and halted when I laid eyes on the bed. The other night came crashing in on me like a freight train. I could easily see Seth and I tangled up in each other's arms. Our embrace loving but strictly platonic after he declared he wouldn't take advantage of me while I was drunk.

Well, it was platonic. A pleasant tingling broke loose inside my core. It intensified as I recalled the way his moans rasped thickly in his throat as I ruthlessly devoured him.

I dropped my towel where I stood and crawled into

bed. I curled around Seth's pillow, drawing it closer to my face. His scent still lingered on the pillowcase. The throbbing between my legs was insistent, growing stronger and stronger with each inhale of Seth's delicious smell.

"Damnit," I growled, slipping my hand down to the pulsing ache. I thought of Seth as I let my fingers play upon the slickness, reliving his moans and thrusts as he grew closer to his climax. Before long, I was bucking against my own fingers, the tension in my body like a drawn bow as an orgasm steadily built.

Picturing Seth's hooded gaze and slack-jawed gasps as he came hard inside me had me thrashing against the mattress. Then, as quickly as the orgasm roared up on me, a sudden flood of release overtook my body, wringing me spent and boneless.

Laying there alone in my bed, I stared up at the ceiling—wishing Seth was beside me, rather than inside my head. That was another first for me. Usually I was shoving a man *out* of my bed...not longing for one to be in it. I don't remember drifting off to sleep; I only remembered waking up, satiated, but lonely.

Chapter 21

On my way into work, it came to me. Topher mentioned possibly tagging Leo with a GPS for disobeying Pack Laws. Did he ever do it? A spark of hope ignited within me. If I could locate Leo, then maybe, just maybe...he can lead me to Kay. I quickly dialed Seth's number.

He attempted to greet me, but I dove right in, eager to set my plan into motion. "I'll be at the station in ten. Be ready."

And ready he was. He was waiting for me outside, dressed casually in black jeans and a great fitting jacket, his duffel bag full of weapons at his feet. His choice in clothing had subtly shifted from *Gramps* to *Goddam!* and it was only then that I noticed. *When had that happened?* I wondered.

He shielded his eyes from the sun as I pulled up to the curb. Flashing me a smile, he opened the door and sank into the passenger seat. "So what's this all about?" he asked, clicking the seatbelt into place.

His scent filled the small space of the car, almost drawing me away from my thoughts.

"We need to find Leo," I said as we drove off. "And I know just who can track him for us."

"You don't mean—"

"Yep, Topher. Hell, maybe if we're lucky, we'll be able fit Leo for silver cuffs before the day is over." I smiled wolfishly, shifting the car into the only speed I knew.

****

Lucky for us, Topher was home. He answered the front door wearing just pajama pants, with disheveled hair, and a look of pure irritation on his face.

"What?" he barked through the screen door.

"Hey to you too," I said back, gauging his bristly mood. I gave him a smooth smile. "Sorry to just drop by Topher, but the PCI really needs your help."

He lifted one eyebrow, but other than that, he appeared annoyed we were there. His jaw was set tight, and he made no offer for us to come inside, nor did he come out to the porch to greet us.

When he didn't say anything to that, I said, "We really need you to locate Leo Trevino for us."

He started to close the door.

"Wait," I said, placing a hand on the screen door. "Please, Topher. Do this for me."

He peered at me from behind the door. His ice-blue eyes hovering on mine impatiently as if waiting for me to give him a good enough reason not to slam the door in my face.

"For your sister?" I said, the words tumbling together quickly.

He blanched.

There-I had him. His eyes bore into me, punching through me with restrained anger. After a few drawn out, and very intense seconds, he pulled the door back wide, and stepped up to the screen door. There was a tick in his jaw, and it was a clear warning: *Tread lightly.*

"I know he was properly sentenced according the

Were judgement," I continued. "but as her brother, wouldn't you like to see the scum pay? To the fullest extent? Now that the Weres had their judgement, make him answer to the PCI as well. For her."

Topher crossed his arms, regarding me from down his noble nose, like a king on a throne.

"What's going on," came a soft, feminine voice. A woman slid up beside him. Wearing only the matching top to his pajamas, it became quite clear why he was acting so pissy. We had interrupted them. The woman's ebony hair was piled in a messy bun on the top of her head, and her cheeks were still flushed a bright pink.

I swallowed and looked squarely at Topher. "Well?" I asked. "What do you say?"

The woman snaked an arm through Topher's and clung to him. She must have sensed the tension. Her thick brows knitted as her bright eyes swung from me, to Seth, then up to Topher's scowl, which was set like stone. "What's going on? Why are the PCI here?" Her voice was sharp and filled with alarm.

He covered her hand tenderly with his. "It's okay," he said to her. "They're just here to beg for help."

Anger lanced through me. *Beg*? Before I could rebuff Topher's grating comment, Seth crept forward.

I felt the air shift as the Were swelled his chest and set a scornful glare on him.

"If that's what it will take," Seth said to him through the fine mesh of the screen door. "So be it. But you want to know what I think?"

Topher's jaw clenched.

Either Seth didn't notice, or he simply didn't care about the contempt exuding like a waft of stink off the intimidating Were. He kept going. "I think you already know what you're going to do. It's in your blood to protect family, and by helping us, you know you'll be seeking discreet, but lawful revenge for your sister."

I gaped at him in quiet admiration. *What happened to him?* Last time he was around Topher, he acted like a meager beta-wolf stupidly vying for an alpha status that was unattainable. Now, he was a cool, calculated negotiator. Had he put his petty feud with the Were aside for me? In his willingness to be reasonable and readiness to even beg for assistance, he revealed how important I was to him. And in that moment, the wall around my heart cracked. What was Seth doing to me?

I wanted to scoop him into my arms and kiss him, but given we were standing on a Werewolf's porch, pleading to use his GPS locator on a volatile, human-hating Shifter, it clearly wasn't the right time.

A collection of tense seconds ticked by painfully slow. Seth and I stood on the porch, silent and hopeful. The woman, who I was certain was a Shifter by the way her nose twitched, watched the scene apprehensively. Topher ground his teeth, mulling his options over. I wondered what his thoughts were. *Did he already know his answer? Was he just making an elaborate show of deciding? Did he just enjoy watching us squirm?*

At one point, his nostrils stretched wide, inhaling and filtering through our emotions the way only Shifters could. From me, he sensed anticipation, desperation, and eagerness. From Seth: resolve and submission. All of which were prime emotions for a Were to feel high, and mighty. Normally knowing that would have had me bristling like an angry cat, but with Kay's life *literally* at stake, I was willing to bargain my very soul to get my hands on the one responsible.

"No," Topher said, his tone very final.

"What?" My neck and ears grew flush. "Why?"

"It's against Pack laws. I'm sorry, Edy, but you'll have to find the wanderer on your own."

He slammed the door on us, and I saw red. Beating on the door with a closed fist, I screamed at Topher. "Damn you! All Weres care about are themselves! My friend could be dead! Help us! Help *me*, Goddamn you!" I was disappointed. I thought for sure he would help me. Hot, angry tears streamed down my cheeks. My hand grew sore with each repeated rap on the wooden door.

"Edy," Seth said quietly.

I continued to beat on the door, sobbing with grief. I felt like the last chance of finding Kay had slipped through my fingers.

Seth grabbed my wrist, restraining me. "Edy, let's go. We'll find another way." His eyes found mine, holding there until I calmed. "We will find another way. I promise."

My chest heaved as I stood there on Topher's front porch, Seth's grasp still firmly circling my wrist. Embarrassed and pissed, I snatched my hand away. Grounding out a curse, I pivoted away from him and ran to the car.

He held back, thank God, allowing me some space. I flung myself into the seat and punched the steering wheel. My hand smarted, but I ignored it. All I could think about was Kay. Where the hell was she? And damnit, where was Leo? "Fuck Topher", I said between gritted teeth. A single tear hung from the tip of my nose. I angrily wiped it away. I felt lost. Without Topher's help, I had no direction. Leo could be anywhere. Finding a Were was nearly impossible, especially one that didn't want to be found. I let out a frustrated scream.

From the corner of my eye, I saw Seth slowly making his way to the car. I sniffed, and quickly patted my face dry and collected myself. By the time he was clicking his seat belt into place, I had my shit together and a plan in mind. It was a dumb plan, but I was set on doing it anyway.

"I'm taking you back to precinct," I told him. "I…I need to be alone."

He only nodded.

On the drive back to work, I fumed over Topher's refusal to help. *Why? Just because some bullshit Pack Law?*

I practically shoved Seth out the car, hauling ass as soon as the door swung shut. I shouldn't have looked up into the rearview mirror, but I did. He was standing there watching after me.

Guilt hit me in the gut, but damnit, I was not turning around. I continued to drive, leaving Seth to choke on my exhaust as I went to the very last place I should have: Red's Liquor Store.

****

I drank myself into a dark oblivion that night. You're probably thinking, *"That was your plan?"* Hey. I told you it was a dumb plan, didn't I? I needed to quiet my mind, and drinking was the only way I knew how. At first, I enjoyed the pleasant buzz, and for a little while, it did what it was supposed to do. I forgot all about Kay. And Topher, and his bullshit excuse for not helping me. The booze did its job; my limbs were loose and my mind was deliciously free. But soon, my mind wandered. Unsolicited memories of my parents' accident came back with a wash of grief so raw it felt like a punch in the gut. Curling myself into a ball on the floor, I recalled the doctor's drawn, solemn face, and his words that will haunt me forever: "I'm sorry, Kennedy. Your parents didn't survive the crash."

My chest felt hollow all over again. I rubbed at it, trying to sooth the empty feeling, but when that didn't work, I grabbed the bottle of dark whiskey. Blurry-eyed, I stared at it for a long moment, and then, bottoms up. I drained it in several long chugs. The warm liquid filled that fucking gaping hole within me, and even though I knew deep down, it was just a temporary fix, I didn't care.

To hell with sobriety. To hell with AA. I was gasping for breath as I tossed the empty bottle aside. I glared at it, my chest heaving. Tears pooled behind my eyes, but I shut them tight, refusing to let them fall. I was livid with myself. *How could I be so weak...again?* My head started to feel fuzzy, and my eyelids felt like sandbags. With a mumbled grunt, I slumped into a stinking, drunken heap.

I woke up on the floor the next morning with a vicious hangover but surprisingly clear-headed. I had to quit feeling sorry for myself and get my ass into gear. Kay was still out there somewhere and getting wasted was not helping. I cursed myself for falling off the wagon again. Hell, I didn't just fall off the wagon. I doused it with gas, jumped off, and watched it burn. I glared at my haggard reflection as I furiously brushed my teeth, trying to get rid of the tang of alcohol from my mouth.

I looked like trash. Annoyed, I spit the foamy

toothpaste into the sink, and leaned closer to the mirror. *Correction*: I looked like a rabid raccoon who lived *in* a trash can. Last night's mascara spread like bruises under my eyes, and my hair was as limp as a pre-Viagra penis. I sat the toothbrush down and washed my still puffy face. As I dried myself, I sighed deeply, and decided to forgive myself. Edy James is far from perfect. And she will definitely slip up again. Only next time, I'll do my best to remind myself of this moment. The gnawing feeling of disgrace, and disappointment. And maybe, just maybe, I'll resist the temptation.

****

It was a typical day at the precinct. A few calls came in about some petty crimes, and while some officers worked those cases, others were busy dissecting the vampire murders.

Seth and I spent a few hours following dead leads, which thoroughly pissed me off. We were basically bidding our time until nightfall when we could verify Claudette's alibi with district leader, Garon Walker.

When the conversation about the case finally stalled, Seth asked me, "You want to talk about yesterday?"

I didn't look up from the file on my desk. "Nope."

"You sure?"

I shoved the file away, letting it slide nearly off the desk. Drawing Supe Slayer out of its holster, I checked the magazine. It was fully loaded. "Yup."

"It's okay to be angry, Edy."

"I'm not angry," I retorted, clicking the magazine back into place. I looked squarely at Seth. "I'm fucking pissed." I slid the gun back home. "Now enough talk.

164

Let's go find Garon."

Chapter 22

Garon's territory was just about two hours away, so the ride was unbearably long. When we arrived, dusk was just settling in, smearing the sky a pretty pink and purple. The picturesque sky almost made it easy to forget just where we were headed: vampire domain.

As the car headlights swung across the ornate Victorian house, I caught myself thinking it was far too pretty to be a vamp's home. With its turrets pointing skyward and fancy wrap-around porch, it seemed more suitable for a woman of good breeding and wealth to be parading around the vast property with a mint julep in her gloved fingers rather than providing shelter to a blood-thirsty creature of the night.

I parked atop the sprawling driveway and cocked my head toward Seth.

He lifted a hand. "I know, I know. Let you do the talking." He knew me too well by now to know I wasn't about to let anyone—not even him—grill the vampire who may know something about Kay.

With a shake of his head, he reached for the door handle. I caught him by the sleeve. He paused, waiting for an explanation.

"Back me up?" I said.

His gave me a measured stare before letting out a deep sigh. "Of course. I always got your back, Edy."

I smiled tightly and got out.

The house looked eerie. Vines choked the massive pillars that stabilized the empty porch. Peeling paint flaked and drifted in the cutting Washington wind. Neglected flower boxes reminded me of long-forgotten gravesites. Sprigs of weeds poked through the hardened dirt like tiny hands.

The sun was just a glimmer through the trees now. Darkness would soon be falling, playtime for vampires. You could sense the earth shifting in those moments, as if holding its breath before the coming storm. In the cloak of night, Seth and I could easily become fair game for a hungry vampire within those walls or among these many, many acres of land.

My hand sought out Supe Slayer. Knowing it was close brought me comfort as I climbed the squeaking stairs and rapped the front door with my fist.

The house remained silent. I knocked again, more persistent this time. A crisp call of a wolf in the distance startled me. Was that a Were or a common wolf? It was hard to tell between the two calls as they were so alike.

Something stirred inside the house, then a moment later the front door creaked open. A vampire, barely out of her teens in mortal years, stood framed in the doorway. Her white-blonde upswept hair and big pale eyes made her look almost angelic, despite her miniscule skirt and cropped neon halter-top. She snapped her bubble gum as she sized us up.

"Yeah?" she said, in a very typical teenage tone.

"Where's Garon?" I asked her, my gaze flicking behind her, taking in what I could of the interior of the house. There were a few vamps lounging around various sofas and vintage settees. They spoke amongst themselves, not really paying much attention to me and Seth.

"He hasn't risen yet," the vampire said. "You know the sun just, like, went down, you know?" She rubbed her eyes.

"Get him up," Seth demanded.

The vamp suddenly snarled, the points of her fangs milky white against her pink mouth. "Master doesn't like to be interrupted."

I unclipped my badge and lifted it her. "PCI orders. Bring me Garon. Now."

She blew out a huge, flimsy bubble, before popping it with her fangs. "Fine," she replied with a cool roll of her eyes. "It's your neck. Not mine." She sauntered away, leaving the front door open.

Again, the wolf howled. I cocked my ear, trying to decipher: Supe or common wolf?

Heavy footsteps drew my thoughts away from the wolf call. In the blink of an eye, Garon Walker stood before us. Draped in a silk robe, he filled the doorframe, all thick arms, and wide, masculine shoulders. His black as soot hair was a shocking contrast against his marble skin.

"Agents," he greeted without a smile. "How can I be of service?"

I cut right to the chase. "Can you verify the whereabouts of Claudette Klemmings on November ninth? Roughly eight o'clock?"

The vampire leader lifted his chin. "Of course. She was on duty."

I watched him carefully. There was no hesitation. No falter in his voice.

"Other than your word, is there a way to prove it?"

"Are you questioning me, Agent?" The big vamp puffed up, somehow filling the space even more with his presence. The other vampires were now watching us with curiosity, sensing the mounting tension in the air.

I ignored the tightness in my chest and countered, "Well, no offense, but vamps are notorious liars. Plus, the fact that we can't hook you up to a lie-detector machine, cause you kind of need a heartbeat and a pulse for it to be accurate. You suckers, pun *intended*, are master manipulators. Your damn genes have made it virtually impossible for your bodies to betray the bullshit that comes out of your mouths."

Seth was silent beside me. Even the vampires inside the house had grown quiet, all waiting with bated breath for their leader's reaction.

Garon's dark eyes studied me, then he threw back his head and laughed heartily. The group of vamps inside laughed as well, but theirs seemed unsure—fragile almost—as if any second Garon could change his mind and snap the nearest neck.

I was fully aware the nearest neck was mine.

The intimidating leader stopped laughing and looked me squarely in the eye. "Worry not, Agent. My word is law around here. I assure you. Claudette was performing duties required of her by her coven that night."

I cocked an eyebrow and resigned myself to the fact that Claudette had an alibi. Whether I believed it or not was another story. "What do you make of her relationship with Tek Ronboi?"

Garon remained stone-faced. I envisioned kicking him in the balls just to get a reaction. Have I mentioned how infuriating vamps could be with their cold, impassive eyes, and their unflinching muscles?

"They were Bonded," Garon stated simply.

"Yeah. I already knew that. I'm asking you what you thought about that so-called *union*. Level with me here, Garon. Tek was banging Isabelle. Surely Claudette didn't approve?"

"I care not about the pleasure of the skin unless it consists of my own. Just as I do not interfere in the dealings of others, so long as it does not intercept my personal gains."

I grunted. Time for a new tactic. "If Claudette and Tek were Bonded, why is she still working for you in the Hillside district and not overseeing Tek's western rural district?"

"She has loyalties here."

I tapped my chin, thinking, refusing to take my eyes off Garon.

"Edy," Seth edged quietly. "We got what we came for. Let's go."

I ignored him, not even bothering to acknowledge him with a reply. Instead, I pushed on. "What about you, Garon? Where were you November ninth? Are you aware of the mass murders on your fellow leaders that night?"

"Of course," Garon replied. "All of our kind knows of the tragedy. However, Agent, you know how my people can be."

"Blood-thirsty?" Seth offered.

Garon's eyes alighted on Seth for a heartbeat, and he grunted, almost amused. "I was going to say, fickle."

I folded my arms, ready to gain something useful from this night. "You were spared. Why do you think that is?"

"My district is heavily patrolled. Plus, I don't keep typical vamp hours, as you can see." He spread his arms out, indicating his silk pajama pants and bare feet. "You rudely rose me from my slumber, dear Agent." He smiled, but it was more shark-like than kind. "I don't usually rise until well into the morning hours."

Though he appeared to be no older than thirty-five, Garon was an ancient vampire, Turned a millennium ago somewhere in a time-forgotten village in Europe. Vamps with that kind of time stamp are often referred to as *Epochs*, often rising for only a few hours of darkness each night.

Who cared about things like "sleeping your life away" when eternity was a sure thing? Plus, with their advanced age came their vulnerability to withstand even a hint of sunlight. The older a vampire is, the less radiation they can tolerate. By Garon's standards, even just the warmth of a sunbeam through a curtain could fry him up like bacon.

Still, I fished for some sort of intel—no matter how insignificant. "May I ask where you slumber?"

The blonde vampire slunk her way toward her leader. Several other vampires closed in as well. From their pinched faces and glaring, contempt-filled eyes, it was obvious I was overstaying my welcome. Garon lifted a hand, and each vampire responded by halting...except the blonde. She took position beside Garon, hunched and ready to pounce, her chin splashed a vivid red.

Garon slid his gaze to her. "It's okay, Angelica. The Agents have a job to do. I'm merely answering questions."

Her eyes remained fixed on me.

"I slumber beneath the house," Garon stated, turning his attention back to me.

"In the cellar?" I prodded.

"That's right." The district leader was the picture of perfect composure. Nothing I asked seemed to rattle him in the slightest.

"Who has access to the cellar?"

The stale stench of vampire drew stronger as the vampires gathered closer. A rumbling was beginning to pass through the group.

"I slumber long, and deep. Interruptions are *rarely* tolerated." His eyes were black ice now. The prickly sense of unease crawling along my scalp reminded me to tread lightly. I was in vampire territory, surrounded by a clan that would kill for their leader without thinking. "Very few have the privilege of seeing my slumber quarters."

"Why not sleep in a bedroom?"

Angelica rolled her eyes. Garon gave me a wicked smile. "I choose to lie as far away from God's hellfire as possible."

Angelica snapped her bubble gum and gave me a bored but hateful stare. "He's an Epoch, duh."

"Right," I said with a nod. "An Epoch." I felt like I was chasing my own tail at that point. Garon had nothing else to offer, though I was trying to wring him dry just in case.

"Come on, Edy," Seth said. "There's nothing else here."

He was right. This was officially a dead end.

"Thanks for the information," Seth told Garon. "If you learn anything that may help the case, contact us at the precinct."

Garon gave a slight bow of his head, his ink-black hair looking polished under the moonlight.

Seth and retreated to my car and locked ourselves safely inside before we spoke.

"Well, tonight wasn't a total loss." I cranked up the car and put it in drive. "We learned Garon wasn't one of the victims of the mass murder because of his crypt beneath the mansion."

I gave a parting glance to Garon's mansion on the hill. The vamps were spilling out of the front door, disappearing into the night, like dark ghosts.

Seth withdrew a pad of paper and a pen. "And we confirmed Claudette's whereabouts."

After turning out of Garon's long driveway, I leaned into the gas and shifted gears. "If you believe that alibi, Newbie, you're as naïve as you look."

Chapter 23

With the western rural district over a mile behind us, my phone started dinging with voicemail messages I had missed while I was out of range at Garon's place.

I slipped my phone from my pocket and scanned the screen. One missed call from Mrs. Webber. I hit delete and moved on. I still wasn't ready to face Kay's mom. Not yet. I needed a concrete lead. A ray of hope. Not to mention, less shake in my voice. I kept scrolling. There were four more missed calls, all from an unknown number, and one voicemail.

My heartrate kicked up. *What if it has something to do with Kay? What if it was Kay?* I chewed at my bottom lip anxiously.

"Something wrong?" Seth asked.

"Not sure yet." I mashed a few buttons on the phone screen, opening up my voicemail options. Hitting the speaker button, I glanced at Seth. "But we're about to find out." With my stomach churning violently, I pressed PLAY. The voicemail began with a light crackle, like wind blowing across the receiver. Then a familiar, bass-soaked voice spoke.

"Edy. This is Topher. Meet me at my ranch, tomorrow at nightfall." The call ended, and the cab was stone silent for a beat.

"He's no stranger to giving orders, is he?" Seth said with an aggravated snort.

I didn't respond. I just shifted into another gear and floored it. Seth scrambled to grab the handles on the ceiling and dashboard, gnashing his teeth as the car sped faster.

"How do you not get pulled over daily?" he asked.

"Used to," I answered, not taking my eyes off the road. A dark spot emerged in steamy horizon of the highway. I watched grow into a green minivan, and I quickly changed lines to avoid slowing down.

"But…?"

I flicked my gaze to Seth, who was peeking through one eyelid at the road ahead.

"There should be a '*but*' somewhere at the end of that sentence," he said.

My lip twitched into a wry smile. "Let's just say I have a no-fail fuzz buster."

He opened his other eye and turned his piercing gaze on me. "What does that mean?"

I looked back at the road. "Nothing. Forget about it."

"No way. Now you have me intrigued." He started searching the cab, his eyes finally lighting on the after-market switch near the stereo. He pointed and looked to me. "That's it, isn't it? What's it hooked to?"

I kept my profile to him and abruptly switched lanes, jerking him sideways.

"I'll figure it out you know. I'm good with cars. I'll just check beneath the hood—"

"The hell you will," I snapped. "Looking under my car's hood without my permission was a lot like lifting my skirt without an invite. It could cost you a broken finger or two." I shifted in my seat. "Besides, I only use it when I need it."

"What is it?"

"Mind scrambler." I drew in my lips, waiting for his guaranteed response. *That will get you suspended,* I mocked to myself in Seth's voice.

"You know they'll suspend you if they find you using that. It's only supposed to be used for major crime scenes or world disasters. Using the mind scrambler without the authority of—"

"I know, I know," I interrupted, throwing my hand up. "Jeesh. Do you always quote the PCI handbook?" I tried to sound snarky, but I nearly laughed out loud at how well I knew him.

I *knew* he was going to recite the rules to me. The guy was a stickler for protocols and conciseness. I, on the other hand, often flew by the seat of my pants or by whatever flew out of my mouth…

"What do you do? Just turn it on whenever you speed?" He reached for it, but I slapped away his hand.

"Haven't you ever used one before?" I asked.

"No. I've read about them, and heard people talk about them, but I've never seen one in action."

Mind scramblers were exactly what they were called: mind scramblers. The device uses special sonar waves to cause confusion in human brains. It was developed to treat crowds of witnesses at once, disrupting normal thinking patterns. It stirs up a murky, confused state that's often described as just waking up from a deep sleep when the mind is coherent but not exactly focused or alert. Neither damaging nor permanent, I never understood why the PCI didn't incorporate them more into daily procedures.

"You're seeing it action now," I told him as I glanced back in the rearview mirror.

"It's on now?" He turned his head to look out the window, as if he could see the sonar waves rippling outward from the vehicle.

"You think I'd be able to do one-ten without it?"

He whipped around sharply, his gaze darting to the speedometer. "You're going one-ten?" He looked pale. His hand moved to his seat belt, tugging the strap to ensure it was in place.

In the distance, I noticed the shiny silver car of a state trooper sitting in the median. Before I could even mention it, we flew past it, leaving it nothing but a blur and a memory.

Seth turned as much as his seat belt would allow and stared back through the rear glass. "Nothing," he half muttered, half chuckled.

The scrambler jumbled up the mortal lawmen's thoughts enough he never even noticed my car zooming past him, much less registered my speed on his radar.

"That's incredible," Seth said, smiling. "But Edy, can I ask you something?"

I spared a quick glance at him. "What?"

His smile dropped. "Why the hell are we going one-ten!"

"It calms my nerves," I answered, focusing back on the road ahead.

"Great," he muttered, gripping his seat. "What ever happened to bath salts and Yoga?"

Hiding a smile, I settled into the drive. With each mile marker I blew past, the stress of the day lightened, relaxing the tension in my neck. Hey, don't judge me; everyone has a vice. Mine just happen to be reckless…

"Hey," Seth said suddenly. "Let's go play some pool."

"What?" I shot him a puzzled sideways look.

"Come on. It will be fun. The case is on pause while we wait for Topher anyway. What do you say?"

My stomach knotted. A bar? I learned the hard way that I'm not strong enough to resist my urges. "I don't know."

He touched my knee. "I'll make sure you don't do anything stupid." He winked, and that uneven smile slowly broke across his face.

Against my better judgement, I relented, only because I believed Seth when he said he wouldn't let me do anything stupid. I don't know why he had that effect on me so early on. Maybe it was the honesty in his eyes. Or the way my insides tingled whenever he looked at me. Whatever it was, it was a foreign feeling, and I wasn't sure what to make of it.

The moon disappeared behind the clouds during our drive, and somewhere in the distance thunder rumbled like a belly ache. The parking lot to Taps was full, indicating that there must be a tournament of sorts going on inside. Whether it was pool, darts, or karaoke, I didn't know. I prayed it wasn't karaoke. There was no way I was going to sit through drunk renditions of Love Shack, Purple Rain, or Baby Got Back. A light rain started to beat against the windshield as I swung my car into the only empty spot left.

"Got an umbrella?" Seth asked, unclicking his seatbelt. I shot him an '*Oh please*' face and got out of the car. The clouds had crowded out the moon, making the sky an endless blanket of gray. The rain picked up, and I cursed. It felt like a bad omen. My eyes flicked to the neon signs blinking *Ice Cold Beer* and *Cocktails* in Taps' window. *Self-control,* I told myself. *You have to have self-control.* Cold rain slipped down my neck, sending a shiver through me.

Seth jogged ahead, his shoes slapping against the asphalt as he ran. He held the door open for me. When I ducked under the awning, I wiped the rain from my face and stepped inside the pool hall. It was a familiar sight. The haze of smoke and gaudy alcohol advertisements plastered to the walls. The clink of glasses and laughter from strangers.

A dry lump in my throat suddenly cropped up. I swallowed it down and took a measured look around. All the pool sharks in town were placing bets and pulling out all their best trick shots that night. We had to wait for a table, so Seth and I made our way to the bar to pass the time. I straddled a bar stool and slipped out of my jacket.

"What can I get you?" The bartender, a cute girl in her early twenties asked. She smiled at me, but her question was pointed more toward Seth, than me. Seth leaned on his elbows. "Beer. Ladies choice." He glanced at me. "What about you, Edy?"

"Just a water."

"Well, that's easy enough," the girl said, setting out a bottle of German beer for Seth and a bottled water for me. She popped the lid of the beer bottle with a *crack* and handed it to Seth with a flirty smile.

"Thanks," he said, and lifted the bottle to his lips. I tried not to notice his neck moving as he drank, and I tried to ignore the shadow of stubble that covered his jawline, but as the heat crept up my cheeks, I had to force myself to look away.

The bartender was off tending to someone else by then. She had left my water in front of me, the cap still on. *Guess she only opens drinks for the men,* I thought as I took in the rest of the room. For once, they were all strangers to me.

Not too long ago, I would have known many of these faces. I would frequent this place every night until I knew the staff and regulars by name. I would have drunk most of them under the table at some point and probably would have gone home with more than I'd like to admit.

"So." Seth put his beer down. "Where did you do your beat before PCI?"

"Cloverfield."

He looked surprised. "Cloverfield?" He took another swig of beer. "Really? I'm surprised they recruit so close to home. Nobody questions what you do?"

I thought of Kay. She knew I was a cop, but to her, I was a regular beat cop, doing regular things, like traffic detail and responding to 911 dispatch calls. Of course, it's not because she wasn't interested in what I did. She did her fair share of prying but after doling out enough vague answers, people eventually quit pushing you for details.

"Nope," I said before I took a long sip of water. It was bland on my tongue, but it quenched the fire burning within my stomach. The smell of alcohol around me had ignited the need to drink, but I refused to give into the greedy bastard. *Self-control*, I told myself again.

Seth nodded. "You must keep a pretty low profile."

"Yep." I drank again.

He turned his body toward me. "What's going on with you?" With a tilt of his head, he squinted at me, searching my face for something.

My eyes skipped around the bar, which was a mistake. It was all the answer he needed.

He laid a hand on my shoulder. "We can leave if you want."

I shook him off, the pity in his voice angered me, but I bit my tongue. Seth meant well and didn't deserve to be on the receiving end of one of my rants. Nodding past him, I said, "There's an empty table. Let's get it before someone else does."

We claimed the table, and I let Seth rack it up. He did it swiftly, indicating his familiarity with the game. When he was through, he grabbed a pool stick from the wall and handed it to me. "I'll let you break them."

I took the stick from him with a smirk, sizing up the rack as I framed up my stance. He may know the game of pool well, but he doesn't know that I do too. The old Edy often paid her bar tabs with her wins. And let me tell you, the old Edy could rack up a hefty bar tab. I closed one eye to steady the pool stick, taking care to balance it carefully between my fingers.

CRACK! The balls spread across the table. The yellow solid sank into the far pocket, and the blue stripe teetered at the mouth of the side pocket. *Damn. So close.*

"Nice," Seth said appreciatively. He chalked the tip of his pool stick and studied the table. He crouched to be eye-level with it, his eye skipping to each ball before he rose and took position. "Pool is nothing but geometry and physics." When he leaned over the table, the small of his back played peek-a-boo with me when his shirt rode up. I longed to rake my nails over it, so I clutched the pool stick in my hand even tighter.

He ran his stick through the motion several times, the action fluid and graceful before finally taking the shot. It was a good shot too. The red stripe knocked my blue stripe into the hole just before it too sank into the pocket.

He bent again, this time at the far end of the table and squared up his play. "Once you find the right angle, all that's left is finding the right speed." He jabbed the pool stick and sent the green and red solid home. He strutted around the table like a proud peacock, all grins and glory before reaching around me for the chalk.

"Solid sex advice," I quipped dryly. "Now, how about a pool tip?"

He laughed, tossing me the caulk. I caught it easily, finding myself enjoying the banter between us. He was like a one-man demolition team. Slowly but surely, he was breaking me down. I hated it, yet I loved it. He took another shot, but this time the ball bounced off the pool table wall, then rolled across the tabletop until it stopped just short of the pocket. He swore but took his place against the wall while I took my turn.

I didn't study the table like he did. I just went for it, like I did everything else in life. Act first, think later. For pool, I didn't rely on physics and math like Seth did. Instead, I prowled for what made the most sense. Which scenario would sink the most balls?

I meandered to where Seth was standing, honing in on the best place to take my shot. From here, I could sink at least three balls. I bent and readied my stick into position. I glanced back at him. I needed to ensure I wouldn't crack the wrong set of balls, if you know what I mean. Unbidden, the memory of our late-night foray stirred within me. The musky scent of him. The welling, throbbing need deep within me that ebbed away to pure satisfaction at his undoing. The pure thrill of seducing Seth and hearing those damned husky moans of his turned me on then, and they were turning me on again.

Seth must have been recalling that night too. His gaze slowly swept up my legs and across my backside. When our eyes met, there was no denying what he was thinking. The old Edy would have dragged him into a bathroom stall right then and there, but sober Edy had a little more self-control. Good old self-control. *Sometimes I hate sober Edy,* I thought with a groan.

I wet my lips and went back to my play, though it was hard to concentrate. Taking aim, I took my shot and sank only one of the three balls. *Damn, I'm too distracted.* Biting my lip, I took a deep breath and strategized my next move. *Crack!* I put away the solid orange and striped yellow.

"Should we put a wager on the game?" Seth asked from behind me. I took aim, sighting the pool stick in on the center of the ball.

"What have you got in mind?" My voice was a rasp, and I hated myself for it. Feeling betrayed by my own body, I cleared my throat and focused on the eight ball.

"If I win, you stop calling me Newbie."

My mouth twitched. "And when I win?" With a sweep of my arm, I sent the eight ball into the pocket with a *sploosh.* I rose and glanced over at Seth.

He didn't miss my sly comment. With a laugh, he replied, "*If* you win, we re-visit the other night." His hazel eyes darkened. "Only this time, you're on the receiving end."

"Oh?" I leaned on the pool stick to steady my wobbly knees. My heart was a horny rabbit humping wildly away within my chest. *Get it together, Edy.* Envisioning all the sweaty, blanket fisting, writhing I'd be doing, I swallowed hard and looked him square in the eye. "Deal."

From that moment, it was on. Seth and I took turns sinking balls, neither of us spoke much, except to gloat now and then. Finally, with only two balls left, I held my breath as I steadied my pool stick. The game was heated as the stakes were high for me, but I wondered if he was secretly going easy on me.

That night, I didn't care. There would be other games where I could kick his ass fair and square. With one fluid motion, I sent the cue ball soaring exactly where I wanted to. I smiled as the final two balls dropped into the pocket.

I strolled toward Seth. "So, Newbie. When can I cash in my win?" I wrapped my hand around his pool stick and glided it up and down seductively.

His eyes watched the movement hungrily. "Whenever you want."

I gazed at his lips, leaning in close. "Tonight is as good a night as any," I whispered.

*****

The next morning, I left Seth spent and snoring in my bed as I rose to make us some coffee. He had been a surprisingly excellent lover. I figured he'd be adequate enough, but when that boy got on his knees before me, he did things with his tongue that made me nearly tear the bed sheets to shreds.

As the coffee brewed, I rummaged through my cupboards for something edible. *When was the last time*

I'd been grocery shopping? I pulled a box of cereal from the shelf. Who am I kidding? I don't go grocery shopping. My fuel is caffeine and greasy fast food. Reaching for a bowl, I felt Seth come up behind me. He nuzzled my neck, wrapping his arms around my waist.

"Good morning," he purred against my ear.

I smiled despite myself. "Last night was better."

He chuckled, planting tender kisses down my neck and across my right shoulder.

I closed my eyes and gave into his worshipping kisses. My body was reacting with wanton desire, but my mind stubbornly rebelled, trying desperately to slap some sense into me. *What am I doing? What if things go wrong with us? How in the hell would I be able to work with him? I should have known better than to fuck my partner.*

I frowned. *Self-control,* my mind countered. *Where's your self-control?* I turned abruptly, startling Seth back onto his heels. I grabbed him by the waistband of his boxers and pull him into me, capturing his lips with my own. *Fuck self-control,* I thought. I could feel his excitement grow against me, and I was ready to take him, right there, right then. He felt it too because he lifted me up and sat me on the counter.

Slipping my panties off, he pushed into me without warning, and I gasped at the delicious sensation. Forgetting about the cereal, the coffee, and my annoying conscience, I let Seth take me right there on the counter. And then again in my bed. It wasn't the first time I ignored my better judgement, and it sure as hell wouldn't be the last.

Chapter 24

We still had hours to kill before we could meet with Topher, and though we could have easily passed that time with more love-making, I thought it would be best if we hit the weapon range to sate another of my favorite thrills.

Blowing some targets into shreds was good for my soul and it tamped my patience. I have to admit, I mostly envisioned Leo and Topher as I fired away at the paper targets, but the crotch shots happened whenever Vick's smug face came to mind.

We were cleaning our gear when the range's door cracked open, and Vick (of all people) popped his head in.

He glanced down range at the torn-up targets. "Damn, Edy. You shot his dick off. That's fucking harsh." He shook his head and looked back at me. "Franco's on the phone for you."

I continued polishing the barrel of the heavy revolver sitting in my palm. "Tell him I'm busy."

"As much as I'd really love to tell Franco you're neutering targets, I think you really need to take this call."

Sighing, I sat the revolver down, and followed Vick out, my mind swimming with questions. *What's this about? Was it Carl?* My heart compressed in my chest. I was fond of the big guy. I prayed he was okay.

I snatched the nearest phone from its cradle and jabbed the blinking HOLD button. "Agent James."

"Edy." Franco's voice came through the receiver. "I have some intel on the Greater Demon."

The Greater Demon. My throat shrank, drying like a desert at the mention of it. I nearly forgotten about it. With Kay's disappearance, the vampire district murders, plus the pleasant distraction of Seth, the Greater Demon fell off my radar. I silently cursed myself for letting that happen. Pubes infiltrated the PCI under the command of someone. And for what purpose? My hand impulsively clenched, as if I was strangling the being, though I had smoked its evil ass weeks ago.

"He was summoned by an unidentified being." Franco certainly lived up to his name because his tone was exactly that—frank.

However, this wasn't exactly news. Most demons are brought into the Earth realm by a summoning. From there, the demons are mandated to do the summoner's bidding. Often times, demons went rogue on their otherworldly obligations, usually killing whoever was foolish enough to summon them. Whoever summoned the Greater Demon was powerful enough to not have been slain on the spot but also for having enough clout to keep the demon on its payroll for so long.

"We have a location," Franco said.

For some reason, I knew this mattered. That his next words would rattle everything, and possibly complicate matters even further. My pulse throbbed painfully against my temples, giving me a headache. I swallowed. "Where?"

"St. Hoover."

I stilled. *St. Hoover? That's Topher's territory.*

"I have exact coordinates," Franco offered. "It's a long shot, but if you can find the conjuring ring that brought the bastard here, you just might be able to track down the summoner."

In a daze, I jotted down the coordinates and thanked Franco for the information.

"Good luck, Edy," he told me, just before hanging up.

"Everything okay?" Seth asked, coming up behind me.

"Change of plans." I sat the phone back in its cradle. "We're searching Topher's place." I strode to my desk, snatching my jacket from the chair and reaching into the pocket.

"What?" Seth followed behind me. "Why?"

I pulled out a can of Were mace. "I'll explain on the way." I tossed it to Seth. He caught it, glancing down at the can with a look of question on his face.

"Just in case things get hairy."

"Not funny, Edy."

****

Seth and I drove to Topher's place in silence. Seth was clinging to the seat beneath him, probably praying the entire way, while I was lost in thought, muddling through wave after wave of questions. *What the fuck did Topher want? Why are we meeting at nightfall, and why is there a conjuring ring on his property?*

When the exit came into view for Topher's ranch, my stomach churned violently. We were moments away from answers, *thank God*. Tightening my grip on the steering wheel, my knuckles paled as the car slipped off the highway and onto a secluded street.

Towering trees filled in nearly every available space. The old-fashioned full service gas station in the center of town was practically a landmark This part of town seemed far removed from the hubbub of Cloverfield, and I could easily see why the pack favored it.

I eased the car into a thicket of overgrown vines.

"How in the hell are we going to find the conjuring ring?" Seth asked, looking out at the vast woods around us. "This place is easily fifty acres."

I got out of the car and walked around to the trunk. The air was crisp, much colder for this time of year than usual. My nose grew numb as I flipped the trunk open and searched through the various PCI supplies I kept stored there. Shoving aside a bundle of rope, and some bottles of holy water, I found what I was looking for: a warding stone. Hexed by warlocks, warding stones act as a sort of a metal detector, except for demon energy.

I held the stone in the air. "This."

Seth studied it. "Warding stone?" His hazel eyes lifted from the stone in my hand to meet my gaze. I nodded in answer. He stared again at the round object nestled in my palm. Heavier than it looked, the stone was milk-white. As if made from chalk itself, it left behind a fine dusting of silky white powder on your fingertips. "Amazing. I've heard of them, but never actually used one. How exactly does it work?"

I rolled the stone in my palm. "It grows warm when near demon energy. Even residual energy." Seth gave a slow nod of understanding, his face full of wonder at the stone. I glanced upward.

The sun was still high in the sky over our heads, which was good because we had a lot of ground to cover before dusk.

Fisting the warding stone, I locked eyes with Seth and said, "Let's go."

****

I'm not sure how many acres we tread, but my feet were aching by the time the stone flickered against my palm. It was a good thing too, because the sun was sinking low in the distance, but it was still glimmering defiantly through the leaf-less tree branches. The forest was becoming a more shadowed and ominous place with each passing minute.

"I've got something," I said as I opened my hand, continuing my path through the underbrush. My boots crunched along the leaves as I followed the stone's quiet direction. Seth kept a few paces behind me, scanning the wide forest around us.

The stone grew warmer and warmer.

A small clearing opened up before us, and that was when the stone flared an angry white-hot. With a gasp, I let it drop to the ground at my feet.

"You did it," Seth said, stepping up to the blackened pentagram burnt into the clearing's dried grass. "You found it."

The ring was not like normal conjuring rings. Typically, conjuring rings were drawn with artful precision, usually by a witch or warlock or another spell caster. This ring was crude, unpolished, and surrounded by strange herbs, not the standard holy salt.

Seth paced its perimeter, while I crouched down and sifted through the dirt, identifying sage and rosemary amongst a half a dozen unrecognizable herbs spread about the ground.

"I don't think this was made by a regular spell

caster." I lifted my head to look at Seth.

He cocked his head inquisitively. "Then who made it?"

"Tek."

Chapter 25

"Tek? Tek Ronboi? The dead vampire?"

I stood, my adrenaline slowly up-ticking through my veins as everything started falling into place. "Remember when Isabelle said she thought Claudette was using Tek for his black magic?"

Seth gave an agreeing nod. "Tek was a witch doctor. That explains the herbs."

Slipping on a leather glove, I walked over to the warding stone and lifted it from the grass. It was still blazing hot from the residual demon energy.

Seth's footfalls crunched along the leaves. "What next?" he asked, shaking his head in disbelief. "Voodoo, demons, vamps, Weres, and a crazy-ass cherub all in the same case."

"Yeah," I agreed. "Even for the PCI, it's a bit strange."

"You think they're all in it together?"

"If they are—then we're in a whole lot of trouble."

*****

The road leading to Topher's house was unpaved, so I let off the gas and carefully maneuvered the car around the potholes that scattered the street. The ranch stretched out wide across the lawn, its chimney puffing out wisps of airy smoke across a star-filled sky.

Topher was already outside, but he wasn't waiting on the porch swing like last time. He was on the front lawn, talking to two other men and a fierce looking woman. One of the men I identified as Haddicus Raine, the pack's lieutenant.

"Do you know them?" Seth questioned, gazing out the window at the intimating group of Weres.

"One is Topher's lieutenant," I answered, easing the car up Topher's driveway and parking. "I'm guessing the rest are pack officials too."

The Weres stopped chatting, and each turned to watch as we climbed out of the car. The weight of the pack's stare was crushing, like hungry wolves lying in wait as their prey drew closer and closer. Out of habit, I touched my coat pocket, ensuring the Were mace was still there.

"Evening," Topher called to us.

We stepped onto the cobblestone path that wound through Topher's manicured front lawn, following it as it neatly deposited us directly in front of the pack members. The men made quick work of appraising us, each smiling graciously at me when I glanced at them.

The woman, however, was brutal with her sharp eyes, raking over Seth and me with open disgust. She wore a flattering turtleneck sweater, with slim leggings that were tucked into tall, badass, fur-lined boots. Her choice in footwear was the only reason I bit back a cutting remark.

"Topher," Seth said, crossing his arms over his puffed chest.

"Edy," Topher greeted, turning his steel blue eyes on me.

I just nodded an acknowledgment, struggling to contain the string of curses running through my head. I was still highly pissed off at him for not helping me locate Leo.

"These are my pack officials," Topher explained, shifting his gaze to the members. "Haddicus Raine, my first lieutenant." Haddicus dipped his chin, a smile playing at his lips when our eyes touched. I had met Haddicus a few times before. The first was during a routine traffic stop near a motorcycle club, which was heavily populated by Weres.

At the time, I was a regular beat cop, who happened to notice the brake light on his motorcycle wasn't working. I didn't know he was a werewolf at the time, and he gave no indication of being anything but a normal, well-mannered man. He was polite as I informed him of his tail-light and offered him a written warning.

It wasn't until our next meeting, which was here at Topher's ranch, when Haddicus was officially named lieutenant did I find out he was a werewolf. I was a member of the PCI then, but it was my first Were ceremony, so I was a little green to what was about to happen.

Whenever a Supe is named as a prominent leader in their society, a PCI team-member has to bear witness to the ceremony. We have to be aware of all authority figures in order to properly uphold Otherworld Laws. How the pack ultimately chose their officials was still a bit of mystery.

Rumor has it they must prove themselves in battle or devote loyalty to the pack by some grand act of sacrifice. I never questioned how Haddicus rose through the ranks, but looking at him here, with his broad shoulders and clever eyes, I never doubted he wasn't equipped for the job.

I remember standing on the outskirts of the tree line, leaning against a tall pine as the Were ceremony began. I watched with fascination as a noble looking black wolf took position in the center of the ceremonial stage. The Were words of honor were being spoken by the pack officials, almost in a chant. The wolf gazed out across the field at the pack members, most in their human form, a few in their wolf.

The chanting stopped, and Topher stepped up to the wolf, his attention cast to the crowd. "Today, let it be known that Haddicus Raine is now lieutenant of the Wexenburg Pack, which spans across Cloverfield to Seattle. Man and wolf of arms whether in battle, or in plan, Haddicus will defend our pack's honor, and offer guidance until the last beat of his heart." He looked down at the wolf beside him and lifted his fist in the air. "To Haddicus!"

The crowd cheered.

Haddicus threw his head back and let out a mighty howl. I rubbed the goosebumps on my arms, watching the whole thing, transfixed. His coarse fur began to retract; the odd crackling sounds, like bones snapping beneath pressure, encouraged the pack into a frenzy. Like with other animals, excitement was catching, triggering some to transition into their wolf form.

Haddicus' muzzle absorbed into his face, and the sharp canines that filled his mouth were replaced with blunt teeth. Haddicus rose to full height, completely naked and glorious. I gaped at him appreciatively for a few seconds. The man was hot. Tanned and well-toned, I found myself wondering if doggy style was his preferred position...

Tonight, Haddicus wore a plaid flannel shirt and

great fitting jeans. His chiseled features were handsome, and well composed. Thick black brows hovered above piercing green eyes. With his shoulders pushed back and his strong set jaw, he fit the image of a master of war. A strategist. A fighter. An advisor.

"Edy." Haddicus' deep, rumbly voice spurred a memory of his nude body standing proudly above the throng of pack members.

Topher thankfully kept up with the introductions, pulling my attention back to the other officials. The other man was Floyd Harker, the pack's Major, and the woman, Stephanie Diller, was a Sergeant. She apparently couldn't be bothered to speak, and given her snooty demeanor, it was clear she thought mortals were a subpar species.

"So," I said at the first available opening. "What's this all about?" I looked around the group. "Why are we here?"

Topher's thin lips worked into a fragile smirk. "The wanderer did you a favor by crossing into my territory."

I turned to Seth. His face was scrunched in thought. Looking back at Topher, I shook my head. "I don't understand."

His eyes were chunks of hard ice. "You will."

Chapter 26

"Whoa whoa whoa," I said, holding up my hands. "Hold the fuck up. Yesterday you weren't willing to help us locate Leo, but tonight you are? What kind of fucking game are you playing here, Topher?" I glowered at him, the rush of angry heat rising up through me from my toes.

"It's against Pack Laws to meddle in the affairs of the PCI, unless…"

"Unless it benefits the Pack," I cut in.

Floyd shifted uncomfortably. Stephanie tensed beside Topher, glaring at me with raging eyes. Haddicus merely looked amused by my outburst.

"The wanderer has found allies," Topher said. "Yesterday he was an army of one." He cut a glance to the pack officials. "Today…he leads an army."

I swallowed, not liking the direction this going. "What do you mean?"

"Packless Weres are packless for a reason. They're disloyal to their blood and can't be trusted. Mark my words, he's up to something.

Get in your car and follow me until the main road," Topher explained. "Then you will have to travel on foot. The perimeter is heavily guarded, so don't go getting any crazy ideas, thinking you can rush the place."

"Place? What place?"

"You have to see it with your own eyes, ma'am," Floyd said solemnly, glancing down to his bolo tie. He thumbed the turquoise stone in the center as if it brought him comfort. His paunchy stomach hung over an enormous, shiny belt buckle, and a pair of worn cowboy boots covered his feet. I was willing to bet his Were form resembled more of an old hound dog, than a frightening wolf.

Floyd lifted his gaze, his bushy eyebrows forming a solid line over his eyes. "Explaining it with words is a gravely injustice to the unthinkable carnage taking place inside those perimeters."

My stomach knotted viciously.

"Just where in the hell are you taking us?" Seth demanded angrily, directing most of it toward Topher. "If it's as awful as you say, why the hell should we allow you to lead us straight into it without reinforcements?"

"Because it's the only way to properly assess the situation," Topher growled, cutting a glaring gaze to Seth, who only jutted his chin forward defiantly. "I know how the PCI works. They'll have a legion of lawmen storming the grounds before even getting the layout of the land."

Seth bristled. "What's wrong with that?"

Topher narrowed his gaze, letting the tension in the air to build before saying, "A cunning fox captures more prey than the mighty lion pride."

Seth laughed, though he was clearly unamused. He turned to me and pointed at Topher. "Do you believe this guy?"

Before I could say anything, Stephanie stepped protectively between Topher and Seth, her innate sense to guard her leader taking over all her instincts. She broadened her shoulders and settled into a stance that read: *Back the fuck up.*

The way she fluffed up like an angry hen at Seth irked me. I put myself at Seth's side, flashing her a glimpse of Supe Slayer. I quirked a brow at her, daring her to move.

"Enough," Topher commanded. "We must go. We have miles to cover."

Stephanie and I continued to stare each other down. Her face remained a mask of indignant loathing. It wasn't a secret some Weres despised mortals. Viewing us as a weak species, unworthy of being at the top of the food chain.

In fact, this was a sentiment shared by a lot of Supes. I wasn't entirely sure if that was how Stephanie felt, or if she was just fanatically defensive of her leader. Either way, the chick rubbed me the wrong way.

"Stephanie," Topher spat.

"Heel, girl," I added with a wink and a smile.

Her lip curled into a snarl, but she backed away.

"Floyd and I will scout out first; ensure their watch hasn't changed," Haddicus said. "If all is the same, I'll signal the go-ahead." When he gave commands, he seemed to grow six inches taller.

Masterful and dominant, he was impressive but not showy. The aura surrounding him read: *I'll take care of you. All you have to do is trust me and follow my lead.*

No one moved, all waiting instruction from the pack leader. With just a dip of Topher's head, Haddicus broke from the group first. Stepping away, he shrugged out of his motorcycle jacket and dropped it to the lawn. Toeing out of his boots, he began working on the buttons of his pants.

I quickly turned my head. Sure, Haddicus was hot, but Seth was so much more. Seth was…perfection. His willowy frame was sculpted with lean muscles, and chiseled jawline gave him a strong profile. Hazel eyes that changed as often as a kaleidoscope, and a touch of dorkiness that oddly had my internal engine purring like a cat in heat.

Topher took the hem of his shirt into his hand. Looking at me, he said, "When the main road ends, park there. It will be over four miles of foot work." He finished removing his shirt, letting it drop into a pile near his feet.

"Four miles?" Seth breathed, scrubbing a hand down his face.

Topher looked at him pointedly. "Feet too tender to make the trek, Detective?"

Seth's hazel eyes hardened. "Fuck, no."

Topher's smile was as toothy as a shark's. "You sure? You smell a lot like pussy. And not in the good way…"

A blanket of red washed across Seth's face. "What the fuck did you just say?" The muscles in his neck tensed, and he took a step toward the Were.

I touched Seth's shoulder.

His gaze jerked to me, and I implored him to stop with a subtle shake of my head. After what seemed like forever, his clenched fists eventually loosened, and he turned his back on Topher with a grim scowl.

The Were looked triumphant but didn't say anything else. He just finished stepping out of his jeans with a smug look on his face. He transitioned into wolf form with just a few thrusts of his limbs, and a shudder-inducing crack in his neck. It was awesome to see a Were turn fluidly into their second body, and it was obvious Topher was just as comfortable in his wolf skin, as he was in his human.

Stephanie quickly stripped out of her clothes, but shifted slowly, like she had to have complete focus to do so. Her back arched violently, causing a shudder to ripple through me. She gritted her teeth in pain, nearly weeping as her bones snapped and contorted. Her slim human figure took the shape of an equally slim she-wolf. Her coat was reddish-brown, which gave her a foxlike appearance. Her golden eyes glowed in the moonlight. Topher was an impressive animal, tall and stately with fierce blue eyes and daggered canines dripping from his muzzle. He threw back his massive head and let out a haunting howl that vibrated ones bones and bowels.

"Come on," I said to Seth as I hurried back down the path, my boots crunching along the stones as I jogged my way back to the car.

"I don't like this," he replied apprehensively.

I bit back my impatience. "We're just going to check it out." I snatched the door open and flung myself into the driver's seat. Seth sat down a second later and pulled the seat belt over him.

As the engine roared to life, Topher stood tall before us, his eyes shining eerily, like two full moons in the headlights. He barked, then together, the four wolves bounded toward the road.

They dashed effortlessly, hugging the tree line as much as possible but keeping within our sight.

After a while, they slowed their pace, indicating we were drawing close to our rendezvous point. I pulled off the side of the road and eased the car between two trees casting a long black shadow on the grass.

"I'm going to say this again," Seth said unclipping his safety belt. "I don't like this."

"We have no other choice. It's Topher's way or no way."

He grumbled at that.

"He's the one who located Leo, so he gets to call the shots on this one. Just let it go."

He blew a deep breath out, tilting his head back against the headrest. "I just don't like the secrets. Why not just come out and tell us?"

"You can trust Topher," I said, surprising myself when I reached out and touched his knee. This was foreign to me, being comforting. And on top of that, comforting a *guy*. Seth could do that to me. Nudging something unknown and strange from me.

That was how I knew Seth was different from the rest. I cared enough about him to *want* to comfort him. He wasn't just a convenient lay or a drunken one-night stand. He was the real deal, and I had no fucking clue what to do with him.

His gaze shifted from the ceiling to me, and he gave me crooked smile. "I trust you." He slid his fingers through mine, laying his hand on top of mine. My palm still rested lightly on his knee.

My heart squeezed.

"I trust *you*," he repeated. "And that's enough." He winked and popped the car door open.

He was already uncomfortable around Weres, and yet here he was, trusting me. Following four werewolves blindly into what so far had only been described to us as unthinkable carnage and doing so only because of his trust in me. *Me*. Kennedy James. Master fuck-up artist and professional dodger of meaningful relationships.

For cops, especially PCI cops, trusting someone was difficult. Supes routinely used mortal feelings, twisting, and manipulating them for their own selfish needs. As a PCI detective, to be trusted was the equivalent of being loved. My insides tingled with the prospect of it.

He'd practically bared his heart openly on his sleeve to me. I couldn't allow it to bleed for me, so I decided I had two options. To run before I fell too deep or to finally give into the allure of Seth Grooms. Shoving myself out of the car, I gazed across the roof of the car at him.

His profile was basked in a silvery glow from the moonlight; his eyes focused hard at the space ahead of him. I could tell his brain was working like a frenzied command center before a shuttle launch by the way he chewed his bottom lip. His hair was mussed and dangling over his forehead making him look down-right delectable.

He caught me staring and offered me his lop-sided smile.

"I trust you too," I whispered quietly in the dark.

Chapter 27

Haddicus and Floyd cleared the perimeter and signaled it safe for us to move forward. Topher and Stephanie led us through the thickly forested area. Every so often they'd pause, waiting for us to catch up. They could maneuver over fallen logs far easier than Seth and me, each leaping gracefully and landing on silent paws.

By the time we met up with Haddicus and Floyd at the edge of the property, my feet ached with fatigue, throbbing painfully with each step I took. Seth was slightly winded at first, but after a moment of rest, seemed ready to tackle another four miles of hiking.

A little breathless, I looked to Topher. "So? What now?"

He jerked his wolf head in the direction behind him, before turning to traipse off into the depths of the forest. Seth and I followed him the best we could in the darkness, though the tangled thicket made it tricky.

We picked our way around stagnant standing pools of water and through dense, nearly black forest. Without the keen night vision of the Weres, I kept walking face-first into low-hanging branches, scraping my cheeks and forehead on thorny vines.

A twig snapped, and I heard Seth mutter a curse behind me.

"You okay?" I asked in a half whisper.

"I can't see shit out here." His tone was drenched with so much scorn, I could almost read his mind. Dark musings about Topher no doubt, and his bright idea to drag us through the forest at night. I partly agreed with that sentiment.

Taking two mortals out into the middle of the woods after sundown seemed pretty stupid, but I knew Topher had to have a good reason. Wherever we were going had to be dangerous for him to take such extreme measures. Thinking of the possibilities dried my throat to an uncomfortable scrape each time I breathed.

Topher padded silently ahead of us. Every so often he'd lift his nose in the air whenever the wind blew or cocked an ear, listening to sounds my human ears couldn't pick up. Stephanie pranced at his right flank, her steps light and nimble. Floyd and Haddicus were patrolling the forest somewhere. I couldn't see them, their wolf forms completely concealed in the shadows.

We trailed behind Topher mostly in silence. The evening air grew colder, and I zipped my jacket higher, wishing I wore my gloves as my fingertips grew numb and tingled uncomfortably.

Finally, the great wolf stopped. My gaze swung around, desperate to see where we were. Moonlight trickled in like tiny pinpoints of light onto the forest floor. The trees thinned just behind the two wolves, but I still couldn't make out our location.

Topher began to transition; the popping, and snapping sounds magnified in the quiet forest. As he elongated his bones back into his human form, his back twisted and jerked until his spine was upright. His gray fur retracted inward as though his internal organs had sucked them inside.

Stephanie stayed in her Were form, keeping vigil of the tight space we occupied.

With a final adjusting of his neck, Topher turned toward us. "This is as far as I go," he said, shaking out his hands, the claws recessing back into human fingers.

A cloud passed over the moon, plunging us all in complete darkness. I concentrated on remaining still, not wanting to wander off alone or to trip on a downed limb.

"Really?" Seth asked through a huff of annoyance. "You lead us out into the middle of nowhere and then have the balls to tell us, this is as far you'll go?" I didn't need to see him to know the veins that ran across his neck were pulsating, or that his hands were probably clenched into tight fists.

"Seth," I whispered, blindly reaching out to him, my fingertips grazing his waist. "Don't." Taunting a werewolf was stupid and incredibly dangerous. Especially when said wolf just led us into the thick of an unknown forest.

"I could be detected," Topher said stiffly, seemingly restraining his anger. "I've traced the wanderer to this area. If he's there tonight, he will surely catch my scent. This is as far as I can lead you. I will await you here. Follow the fence line but do not touch it. It's hot."

"Hot?" I asked.

"Electric fence," Topher explained. "Used on cattle ranches and farms."

"So we're on farmland?" Seth questioned.

"Something like that," he answered grimly.

The moon cleared, illuminating the darkness just enough to outline Seth and Topher's bodies against the black trees. Stephanie kept pacing tight circles behind her leader, never allowing their distance to be more than a few feet apart. Her anxiousness sent a crop of goose bumps along my skin and up my scalp. Watching her maintain this practice tirelessly, with ears pricked high and alert, made me wonder, *What in the hell lies past these trees?*

I wet my painfully dry lips and turned toward Seth. "Follow my lead?"

"Don't I always?"

I would have smiled at that, but since my hackles were raised, rightfully so out in the unknown darkness, I could only muster a feeble nod.

Topher guided me to the fence line. It was a normal pasture grade fence with wooden posts, the typical fencing you'd see holding in cattle on farmland. Six lines of thin wire stretched along the rows of fencing, the top starting at chest height, the last running close to the ground.

"Get your visual, but then get the hell out of there," Topher muttered in a commanding tone. It wasn't a suggestion—it was a demand. He backed away and disappeared into the shadows.

"Six rows of hot wire?" Seth said.

"What?" I asked. "Is that not typical?"

"No. In fact, it seems…" He paused. "Excessive. Most farmers only run a few strands. Animals typically aren't desperate enough to escape to warrant more."

My nerves leapt. *This is bad,* I thought. *Really. Really bad.* "So whatever is being held inside this fence," I hesitated, waiting for my chest to stop constricting. "Really wants to get out."

We continued on, treading the cleared perimeter

before us. The black forest was to our right, the fence to our left. Every so often we'd hear the gentle popping of the electric fence, a reminder that the wire was buzzing with powerful volts of electricity. I took great care to steer clear of the wire, not wanting to experience the pain associated with it.

Been there, done that. You see, last year, I was electrocuted by a stupid water nymph. Hurt like hell too. I broke up her ring of nymph goons who'd been pestering and looting naval ships in and around the California bay area. I had her subdued on the shoreline, knee deep in the Pacific Ocean. She was compliant for the most part. She wasn't struggling against her non-corrosive metal wrist cuffs, and she remained quiet as I read her her rights.

Before I could shove her into the holding tank, she turned and whistled. A huge, leathery electric eel emerged out of nowhere, cutting through the water like a blade. It was headed straight for me, summoned by the nymph. I kicked at it frantically, trying to keep a firm grip on the nymph's bound wrists. The eel lunged and sank its needle-like teeth into my calf. Pain exploded through my body, and I cried out, convulsing until I collapsed into the water with a stiff thud. The eel slipped away, leaving me lying flat on my back. Water lapped over my ears, drowning out the sounds around me.

"Mother fucker," I ground out, unable to do anything as my muscles quivered, leaving my limbs useless and unresponsive for several minutes. The nymph tried to make a break for it while I was incapacitated, but thankfully I called for backup just before I ventured out into the water.

After my first experience with the mermaid, I always ensured backup was on standby whenever I dealt with a water Supe…just in case things got out of hand. The nymph was captured that same day by members of my unit and taken into custody. She was found guilty of the looting ring and also had a charge of assaulting an officer added to her laundry list of petty crimes.

I remember attending her sentencing with bubbling blisters on my palms from where her metal cuffs seared my skin. Stupid nymph.

In the distance, I could see the silhouette of an old silo, and just beyond it stood a newly renovated farmhouse. Security lights flooded the grounds around it, and my heart grew heavy in my chest. The farm wasn't still, as it should in the middle of the night. Instead, it was busy, like a functioning farm that worked opposite daylight hours. There were people milling around, some chatting, while others went in and out of the huge barn adjacent to the house.

"What the hell?" Seth murmured at my shoulder.

I flicked my eyes to him. He gaped at the activity, mouth askew as he processed the scene before us. I turned my attention back to the farm. The pasture was empty.

"I have a bad feeling about this," I whispered, ducking beneath a branch to move closer.

"I have *lots* of bad feelings about this," he replied, pushing thorny vines, and leaf-less branches back to follow me. We only took a couple steps when a twig snapped beneath my boot heel. The sound echoed against the trees. Seth and I both halted mid-step, too scared to flinch a single muscle for fear someone had heard us.

Several faces, pale as ghosts under the security lights, turned toward the noise. They were searching the forest line. *Shit!* I held my breath, my veins humming as adrenaline and fear pulsated through me. My temples throbbed, spreading a deep ache behind my eyes.

Something about the farm was off. All of my instincts were nudging me to leave, to walk away and never look back…but I *couldn't*. My feet stood rooted to the ground. There were answers beyond this fence line, and I wasn't leaving until I got them.

After a few panic-filled moments, the faces finally turned away. I heard Seth exhale shakily from behind me, and I gulped, feeling my frazzled nerves vibrate, like the charged hotwire running beside me.

"Should we continue?" he asked quietly.

"We still don't know what this place is," I answered.

"So that's a yes," he replied, more to himself than to me. "Because walking through the woods at night is a *great* idea."

I ignored him, and carefully sidestepped a downed limb. I noticed we both moved more warily, being overly cautious of where we placed each footstep. The barn soon came into better view.

I scanned the area, noticing a collection of people stirring around the barn. It was like they were waiting for something. *But what?*

A dinner bell chimed loudly. The sound dug into my already aching head with a wincing clatter. I held my temples, squinting. *Jesus! Who uses dinner bells anymore?*

Two men, farmhands I figured, strolled to the barn,

and each took a handle of the great wooden doors. They yanked them apart, opening the doors of the barn, like a gruesome, gaping maw. Surprise and horror snatched my breath away as dozens of people poured out of the barn, scrambling like terrified rats released from a trap. They rushed against each other, pushing and shoving, each trying to get away as fast as they could. They flooded the pasture, some desperate enough to test the hotwire on the fence, which sent them screeching in agony as they convulsed and writhed on the ground. Others hunkered down in the far corners of the pasture, covering their ears as they screamed and cried for mercy.

What the fuck? I stood transfixed as dawning filled my gut with a lump of dread so heavy, I sagged against a tree. The bark bit into my palms, but the discomfort was easy to ignore over the chaos ensuing before me.

The farmhands were vampires, and the people in the pasture were their prey...

Chapter 28

My heart leapt, stealing my breath away. I watched helplessly as the vampires swooped in, scattering the frightened people into chase, which only seemed to thrill them further. The security lights flooded over the vamps, basking their already pallid skin into blinding flashes as they plunged into the crowd of charging people. Their chins and throats were drenched scarlet, a bone-chilling warning that they intended to quench their thirst.

Screams rang out in the night, and after the initial shock wore off, my next instinct was to grab Supe Slayer from my holster and dash straight into the fight with guns blazing. I bit my lip, pondering what to do.

More screams.

I brought my hand up to my gun.

"Edy, no." The pleading in Seth's voice caused me to pull my gaze from the carnage long enough to look at him. The angles in his face were deeply shadowed, but there was no mistaking his desperation. "We can't take them all on," he said. "There's at least twenty vamps out there."

I felt torn in two. The innate feeling to protect those innocent people was overwhelming, but the rational part of me knew it would be suicidal to try. Who were these people? Something within me knew the answer. They were the missing people. All the recently missing people from Cloverfield and surrounding areas. This explained the spike in quotas.

My stomach tightened like a noose with a thought. *Kay.* She could be out there, among the screaming horde of mortals. Among the hunted. My hand twitched over Supe Slayer for half a heartbeat, before going to my cellphone. "I'm going to call it in." I dialed Captain, impatient as it rang over and over. Finally, his gruff, "What?" thundered at the other end.

"Captain. We need backup. We located an active crime scene. We need vamp gear and garlic restraints, now."

"Where the hell are you James?"

"Outskirts of Topher's territory." The line suddenly went dead. "Captain? Captain?" I shoved my phone into my pocket and tossed a worried look to Seth.

"Come on," he said, taking my wrist. His fingers were warm despite the cool weather, and for a fraction of time, I was comforted by his touch. "We need to get the hell out of here." He yanked at me, urging me to go. To look away—to *save* ourselves—but I moved reluctantly, my feet weighted with guilt.

"Captain is coming."

"They'll never make in time."

"We can't just leave them to die," I said, looking over my shoulder as he tried to lead me away. My voice was strangled with indecision. My heart felt like a lead ball in my chest. "Kay could be out there! I won't leave her!"

"Damn it, Edy," he hissed, fisting my sleeve. He flexed his arm, snapping me forward. I gasped, and my nose bumped his as he whispered in my face, "There is *nothing* we can do for them now. We have to get out of here and wait for the unit. They won't know where we are. With their help, we can save some, but we *cannot* save them all."

He was right. We couldn't save them all. If I plundered in, trying to save the day single-handedly, I'd end up being liquid nourishment for the vamps too. I looked up at him through my lashes, and swallowed, nodding woodenly in unwilling agreement.

We pushed our way back through the forest, the screams fading the further we went. The branches seemed to pull at us, snagging on our clothes and tangling in our hair like it didn't want us to leave.

During the entire trek back, my mind was off kilter. Like a pottery wheel slinging thoughts madly around my head. *Who did this to them? Who are those people? How did they end up on the farm? What was Leo's role in all of this?*

Topher was waiting for us back in the small clearing where we had left him. He was alone, or so it seemed, though I knew Stephanie lurked in the shadows somewhere. Patrolling and guarding or doing whatever the hell pack Sergeants do.

The Were regarded us with cool but curious eyes. He stood motionless, patiently waiting for our report. I stared at the ground, speechless, hugging my elbows to stifle the nausea that roiled in my stomach.

"A slaughterhouse," Seth said, breaking the silence. "That's a fucking, *human* slaughterhouse back there." He threw his arm out, gesturing toward the farmhouse. "How long have you known about it?" His tone was challenging, daring Topher to say the wrong thing or make a wrong move.

Topher's eyes turned to slits. "Tread lightly,

Detective," he warned. "I have no qualms about maiming you and calling it an Act of Blind Rage."

The low chorus of growling rumbled through the darkness drove Topher's statement home.

Seth's chest deflated, and he averted his indignant glare to the ground. Sputtering a curse, he turned his back to Topher. The muscles ticked in his jaw as he worked through his thoughts.

Seth rightfully backed down. Acts of Blind Rage are volatile fractions of time when a Were shifts. It's the fraction of time when their beastly nature overrules their brain, replacing all rational, human traits with nothing but pure instinct. In the court of Otherworld Laws, Acts of Blind Rage often acquitted Weres of crimes committed during that brief moment of change.

Seth's gaze swung to me, his eyes helpless but bright with ideas. "Did Captain say they were coming?"

I opened my mouth to answer, but my tongue felt heavy and too dry to speak. I shook my head. Seth's brows lifted high. I flicked my tongue over my lips, and swallowed, trying desperately to get my mouth in working order. I felt transfixed in a surreal moment. A moment of complete horror and bloodshed. Just when you think you've seen everything working for the PCI, something like this slaps you across the face to remind you of just how dangerous Supes can be.

Seth was watching me, waiting for an explanation. I test my voice. "The line." My voice was shaky, but I continued anyway. "It went dead. I must have lost connection."

"What exactly did you see?" Topher asked, directing his question to me.

My eyes lifted to his. I ground my teeth, taking in

several breathes before I felt calm enough to say, "You know exactly what we saw."

"Were they feasting?"

My skin crawled as if thousands of ants were marching along the length of my spine. *Feasting.*

I shook my head, trying to rid the image of the people tearing out of the barn, screaming in terror. Fleeing like panicked bees in a disturb hive, pleading for their lives through their sobs.

"Hunting," I answered. My voice was like a drop in a bucket, hollow and echoing.

"The wanderer is involved in that carnage, but I don't understand why," Topher said, his brows pinching in deep thought over his intense eyes. "What is he getting out of it?"

With an ache in my chest, I said, "An army."

Topher looked to me, his mouth set in a grim line. He didn't say anything, but I knew he agreed.

"Where are they?" Seth stared down the empty road.

I chewed my lip, straining to hear the sound of approaching cars. There was only silence. I called Captain again, but this time his gruff tone was merely his voicemail picking up. I ended the call, frustrated. "Captain isn't answering. Maybe I should call Vick?"

Seth looked back at me, over his shoulder. His furrowed brow only heightened my anxiety. Somehow I knew what he was thinking, but I refused to believe it. "They aren't coming. They know they'll get here too late." He divided his gaze between Topher, and me.

I could tell he was shaken by this. From the way he paced back and forth, and the way he hooked his fingers behind his neck, squeezing, and digging his nails into his skin. It was as though he had to remind himself this was really happening. That subconscious pinch that ensured that it was indeed reality and not some horrific dream.

"But I called for backup," I protested, not understanding why Captain would abandon us. "He wouldn't just leave us out here." We need him. We need the PCI. *They wouldn't leave their own out here, helpless and begging for help. Would they?*

"Come," Topher said, breaking into my thoughts. "There are still a few hours before sunrise. We should go." He walked away, leaving us hesitating. Our inherent compulsion as former beat cops to rescue the innocent blared in our heads, insisting we turn around and *do* something. *Anything.* But we were two against dozens of hungry vampires.

Without the PCI, we didn't stand a chance. We looked at one another, sharing a quiet understanding that although it was hard to walk away…we had to. We had no choice.

Topher did not wait for us. He wove through the trees just as gracefully in his human body as he did in his wolf skin. The three pack officials finally emerged from the shadows, looking impressive, not to mention, intimidating in their wolf forms. Each fell into formation around him, flanking their leader like a living chain.

Just before the wolf pack drifted out of sight, Seth decided to follow them. I lingered a moment longer, glancing back in the direction of the farmhouse. Shame consumed me, filling my legs with sand, making it difficult to pick up my feet.

"Edy," Seth called, rousing me from the stupor

long enough to see through the gut-churning guilt and determine the only way to help those people was to gather back-up from the PCI and raid the farmhouse.

I commanded my legs into motion and shouldered past Seth, finding newfound determination to help them the only way I knew how. My ears burned, and my palm twitched with the urge to unleash Supe Slayer, but I quelled that impulse. I was going have to be patient, but in due time, I was *going* stomp some serious vampire ass.

No one spoke until we got back to the main road. I was too busy creating a plan of attack. Plotting the best strategy and deciding on optimal strike points. Seth was lost in his own thoughts, his jaw clenching and unclenching as he watched the ground pass beneath his feet.

"I have no interest in the Wanderer should you seize him," Topher declared. He lingered near the shadows, still completely nude from transitioning earlier. "The pack already dealt its justice. Whatever his involvement with the vamps does not pertain to the pack, nor does it interest me."

He was so matter-of-fact about it all, I wanted to scream. *How could he remain so calm, knowing the carnage that was taking place through those trees?*

The pack officials lurked nearby, awaiting orders from Topher. Their sharp, reflective eyes measured us keenly, ensuring we keep a respectable distance from their leader.

I leaned against the hood of my car, folding my arms in front of me. Still shaken from the night, I clamped my fingers into my sleeves. Why hadn't Captain come? The vamps were farming humans for fucks sake. A shudder snaked its way up my spine. A blood farm. How fucking twisted was that? The farm had to be connected to the spike of missing persons across town. *That must be how the vamps collect their victims*, I thought. But still I had questions for Topher.

I settled my gaze on him. "What happened that night? After you took Leo back to your territory?" I studied the Were, waiting for a flinch or some subtle indication that he was connected to the human slaughterhouse. Topher's reaction wasn't guarded, or his usual manufactured indifference. Whatever he was about to say was going to be the truth, I just knew it.

"I cannot share all of the details of his trial and judgement," Topher answered honestly, "but part of his punishment was to be fitted with a GPS. The Pack agreed that he needed to be watched."

Seth's head snapped up. "GPS? How? Where's the chip?"

"It's inserted underneath the skin, usually in the neck," Topher explained. "It allows us to monitor his location at all times. Because he infringed on known pack territory, his anonymity has been revoked until we deem it fit to return it."

Gaping, Seth said, "You tracked him through an injectable GPS?" He gave a low whistle. "I hate to admit it, but that's genius. Mortal lawmen should do that to repeat offenders." His enthusiasm for the pack's law practices was evident in his wide, shining eyes.

Topher and I stared at him.

"What?" He looked sheepish and crammed his hands into his pockets. "Never heard a compliment before, dog breath?"

Topher let that dig slide, offering Seth a gloating

smile.

I couldn't help but wonder if it was standard Were protocol to fit territory offenders with a GPS device, or was this commonplace with just the Wexenburg pack?

"Where is he now?" I asked.

"I am not sure," Topher replied. "The tracking monitor is back at the ranch. I'll run his chip when I return, but I suspect his coordinates will lead us back here."

"Will you share those coordinates with PCI?" Seth asked.

"When our kind does dealings with the undead, they then become dead to the Pack." Topher shifted his seemingly unnatural blue eyes onto me. "Meet me back at the ranch and the Wanderer's whereabouts are yours."

"Great," I scoffed, the sarcasm escaping before I had time to think. "You're agreeing to help us now that it's convenient."

Topher's eyes flashed. "Take the offer while it stands, Detective, for it will not be available long."

I held his stare. *Fuck him*, I thought, refusing to be intimidated.

Seth spoke up. "We will be there."

"Just one more thing," I added, unfolding my arms and dropping my hands to my gun belt. "What was Tek Ronboi doing on your land?"

Topher stared at me, aghast. "Tek Ronboi? The vampire has never stepped foot on my territory."

"Oh, yeah?" I shoved myself away from the car hood and strolled up to him. Taking the scrap paper that held the jotted coordinates from my pocket and offering it to him, I said, "Then why is there a conjuring ring at this location?"

He snatched the paper from me and glared down at the numbers upon it. "I know nothing of a conjuring ring."

"It was drawn by a witch doctor. Tek apparently studied the craft. So putting two and two together, I'm guessing it was him."

Topher looked up from the paper. "Why on my land?"

"I was hoping you could answer that," I said.

Topher held my gaze, then said, "I swear on my Pack, I know nothing of this."

I nodded, wanting badly to believe him.

"We might need to canvas your entire territory," Seth told Topher. "See if there are others. Would you be opposed to that?"

Topher's eyes tightened, leveling a heated stare at Seth. "My Pack will search the grounds. I'll be in touch if they find anything." His gaze flicked to the wolves at his heels. "Let's go." He lunged, transitioning gracefully back into a fierce, gray wolf with startling blue eyes.

The other wolves burst into a sprint, kicking up dust as they ran in the direction of Topher's property. The Pack leader paused to look back at us, then broke loose again, reclaiming the front line.

Seth and I watched the wolves disappear into the last hours of the night. Moonlight poured across the grass, basking it in a silvery, almost metallic glow. It was like looking across a blades edge. It would have been pretty if I wasn't so damn exhausted.

I had been awake for more hours than I'd care to count, and the miles of hiking wore me out. But Seth and I still had many hours ahead of us. We had to meet Topher at his place, plus we still had get back to the precinct and find out what the hell happened. Where was our backup?

I walked to the driver's side of the car, glancing at Seth from over the roof. Dark shadows smudged his tired eyes, and he kept covering gaping yawns with a fist.

"Want to stop for some coffee?" I asked, popping the car door open.

He gazed at me sleepily. "Yeah. Even machines like us need fuel from time to time."

Chapter 29

On the drive to Topher's, Seth and I considered the best way to approach Captain. Accusing him of negligence seemed like a death wish, even if it was valid. The guy oozed contempt and prodding him was a lot like tossing a firecracker in a sleeping bears' den.

By now, the vamps had probably already retreated inside their lairs. That gave us time to create a plan of attack. Acting during daylight hours would make it easier for us to creep up on them, and with any luck, we might even be able to free the hostages before the vamps woke. The hairs on the back of my neck slowly stood on end as I considered just how many victims were trapped inside the barn. And just how many victims were already dead.

Plus, we still had to meet Topher at the ranch and hopefully get a location on Leo. I still wondered what the Shifter's role was in all of this. Why was the Were working with the vamps? Recalling Topher's ominous tone when he said, '*When our kind does dealings with the undead, they then become dead to the Pack.*' I knew whatever the reason, it wasn't good for mortals.

With stomachs full of hot, sloshing coffee, we knocked on Topher's screen door. He answered without greeting. He wore a faded Mötely Crue t-shirt and torn jeans. His feet were bare. He may have been dressed casually, but his stern features were all-business. He jerked his chin toward us as he said, "Come in."

The living room was spacious and possessed an old-fashioned cabin vibe. A fireplace crackled with dying embers, and the sweet smell of candied yams clung to the air. A collection of framed photographs was arranged in a neat row along the mantel, and an oblong mirror hung just above them, reminding me of a silver serving tray. Inviting furniture with plump cushions filled much of the space.

He gestured for us to take a seat with a flick of his hand. We did, choosing to sit side by side on the sofa. Seth took in the room, but I was too anxious to look past my own fingers. I fiddled with a hangnail, picking at it neurotically until it bled.

Seth's hand suddenly reached over and clasped mine. When I looked up, his face was kind, full of understanding. "It's okay," he mouthed, squeezing my fingers gently.

The sound of padding feet came from the hallway adjacent to the living room. The woman from yesterday appeared with a small electronic device. She handed it to Topher and retreated quietly from the room. He powered it on. The tiny screen blinked to life and radiated a dull electric green across Topher's face. He pressed a series of buttons, and the screen flashed a few times. His faced hardened like drying cement.

My stomach churned viciously, and I exchanged a worried glance with Seth.

Topher typed in what looked to be a code, his fingers moving urgently this time. The device blinked back at him, and he frowned.

"Something's not right," he said, his brows pinching into an angry furrow.

Seth scooted forward on the cushion, trying to get a better view of the device. "What is it?"

Topher glanced up. "No reading."

"What do you mean, no reading?" Seth questioned further.

He turned the device toward us. The screen was blank other than a meaningless garble of numbers and letters. He pointed to the code. "That's the wanderer's ID chip code. His coordinates should be indicated, but it's blank."

"Malfunction?" Seth asked, though he didn't seem to believe the theory as soon as it left his mouth.

Topher's frown deepened. "No. He removed the fucking chip." With a growl, he flung the device against the wall, shattering the small machine into broken fragments of plastic and tangled wires.

Topher jumped to his feet, knocking his chair backward. It fell to the floor with a *THUNK,* and on instinct I withered back against the sofa cushions, making myself smaller. Something inside me begged me to stay still, to stay quiet. If he Shifted out of anger, Seth and I would be easy prey.

He clenched his fingers into fists as he paced the floor, looking like a caged animal. He shook out his hands, reminding me of a paid fighter preparing for a match. "He broke Were Laws," he said through his teeth. "His judgment was lenient in my eyes, but the Pack had spoken, so I held my tongue. But now…"

He caught his reflection in the mirror above the mantel. He stared at himself for second, the hard angles of his features shadowed and frightening. "*Now*, I care not of Were Laws and accountability. He not only disobeyed Pack orders, but he disrespected me in the process." He slammed his fist on the mantel. The frames shook, some even pitching forward and crashing to the floor. Glass smashed like sheets of thin ice, nicking Topher's bare feet.

The mirror had slid into a crooked slant. I held my breath, waiting for it to break free from the wall, but it hung defiantly in the midst of his outburst.

My muscled tensed when Seth pushed upright to a stand. I lashed my hand out and gripped his shirt. *Don't move.* He glanced back at me, but thankfully didn't make a move toward the raging Were.

Topher sensed our movement and whipped his head to glare at Seth. His chest heaved, and he was practically frothing at the mouth when he sneered, "If you don't get him, I will. And when that day comes, there will be nothing left of him to question."

After Topher stalked out of the living room, my heart finally ratcheted back to a steady rhythm. Were tempers are terrifying and can strike as quick and as dangerous as lightning.

With the passing of just one look, Seth and I both shared the same thought: *Let's get the hell out of here.* We wasted no time flinging ourselves out the house and down the porch steps. I didn't breathe one relaxed breath until I was locked safely inside my car and half a mile away from Topher's place.

"Topher's beyond pissed," Seth said, looking at me. "I've never seen a Were snap like that."

"It's little scary, huh?" I replied.

"Hell, yeah! You ever see a Were lose his shit like that before?"

I could feel his eyes on me, wide and interested. "Well, yeah." My tone was a bit sharp, and instantly I felt guilty for it. I'd forgotten how new he was to the force. He probably hadn't witnessed a Were's nasty temperament yet. I tried to make light of the topic, lifting my shoulder in a shrug. "Just part of the job, I guess."

It was true. Being a part of the PCI unit meant you'd see all sorts of weird shit. And since Weres were notorious for their bad attitudes, seeing one throw a temper tantrum would definitely be one of them.

"Why are you here?" I asked suddenly, generally interested. "I mean, what made you want to be a part of the PCI?"

"Same reason as you." He looked ahead. "To protect people."

"You got me all wrong, Newbie." I scoffed. "That's *not* at all why I'm here."

He glanced at me.

"Well, not at first anyway." I gripped the steering wheel tighter, realizing my palms were dampening. "Mortal law wasn't dangerous enough anymore," I explained. "I needed that next high." I flicked my eyes over to him and then back on the road again. "That seems to be all my life is anymore. Searching for that next high." I shifted in my seat, growing uncomfortable with this conversation.

He didn't press me for more. He just sat back in his seat and stared out his window for the rest of the drive.

The sun was just beginning to wink over the horizon as we pulled into the station. The parking lot was spotted with squad cars and personal vehicles, but the Captain's SUV wasn't among them.

Damn, I thought, throwing the car into park. Although my body was objecting to every move I made, my head was ready for more. Ready for some resolution. Ready to help those poor people. Ready to imprison or even kill the vampires responsible. Ready to do *something*.

Seth tipped his head back, downing the last swallow of his black coffee. He made a quiet sound of pleasure as returned his cup to the holder.

"Was it good?" I asked with a smile, ready to shake the dark cloud that's been hovering over us since I asked him why he joined the PCI.

"Not really. I'd rather have an omelet. Oh, and fried sausage and hash browns smothered with ketchup." He clutched at his stomach. "Can you tell I'm starving?"

"Hash browns with ketchup?" I wrinkled my nose. "Who does that?"

"I do!" He chuckled. "What's wrong with it?"

"Yuck." I lifted my coffee cup and took a sip. It warmed my throat going down but sloshed into my empty stomach like tumbling rocks. *When did I last eat?* I thought about it, retracing the day's events. *The forest...Topher's place...the precinct.* I recalled sitting at my desk, working through the hours with just a can of soda. *Did I really go all day without eating?* My stomach answered with a grumble.

"Why did you say yuck?" Seth insisted, turning his entire body in the seat. Apparently, he was ready to argue his point until I conceded. *Endearing quality number three hundred and six...*

"Hash browns are potatoes," he continued. "Just like French fries. Right?"

I glanced at him skeptically. "Yeah."

"So then, why is it okay to put ketchup on fries but

not hash browns? Total double standard."

A feeling that I forgotten something nudged at me dully, but I couldn't lasso the thought in enough to remember what it was. Seth was still talking as I tried to recall it, and a tiny flare of annoyance spiked through me. *What the hell am I missing?*

Needing a moment of peace so I could think, I pushed the car door open and stepped out. My body was amplified, ready to pounce, ready to react, ready to fight. I hated how everything was on pause while we waited for orders from Captain. Of course, I could go rogue. It wouldn't be the first time but considering the number of vamps we were up against, it would be suicidal.

Deciding whatever it was that was hovering just out of reach would have to stay there, I looked over at him and did my best to soften my face. It was endearing how he could be so passionate about something as simple as hash browns.

"When all this is over, I'm taking you out for hash browns and ketchup," he said, his eyes twinkling, like a happy child. His stupid, lopsided grin had me smiling in return. The sun was directly behind him, the rays spangling around him like a golden aura. In that moment, he looked like an angel. A beautiful angel that needed a wet kiss placed squarely on the lips.

"Okay," I conceded. It was such a lame response, but it was the only one I could come up with his glinting eyes gazing back at me.

We crossed the parking lot, and he stepped in front of me to grab the door handle first. He jerked it open, pausing to let me pass. It was a simple gesture, but it still made my stomach quiver and pool into a puddle of warm, syrupy goo.

Gah! I was becoming everything I hated! Lovesick, and tender. *If I start doodling "Seth" across my post-it notes, I'm going to shoot myself.*

He ducked into the restroom, and I took up residence outside Captain's office. My boots thudded across the tiled floor as I paced tight circles in front of his door almost robotically. My thoughts were all awhirl. *How many people were being held at the farm? How many were already dead? How long has this been going on?*

The doors across the room swung open, and Captain burst inside. He was always *bursting* into things. Rooms, conversations, rage…

His eyes quickly lighted on me, his brows tugging into severe arches. He knew something was wrong. I wasn't a pacer. Normally, I could be found draped lazily across my chair with my feet kicked up on the desk. He'd often slap my boot heels or shove them off with an elbow as he walked by.

He bustled in, like an untrained gorilla. All broad shoulders and thick, long arms sweeping at his sides. "What is it, James?" he demanded, crushing his fist tighter on the handle of his leather briefcase. He didn't bother to stop walking; instead, he brushed past me hastily. He smelled of coffee and aftershave. He unlocked his office door and shoved it open.

"What happened last night? I responded, following behind him. I slammed the door shut behind me.

"Where the hell were you? I called for backup. I could have been killed!"

He tossed the briefcase onto the desk. It slid and crashed into a framed picture of his wife. Either he didn't notice, or he didn't care. He left the frame overturned and turned to me. Deep frown creases permanently marked his face. "And yet you're still here," he said gruffly.

His necktie was crooked and already hanging loose at his throat. I never understood why he even bothered wearing a tie. It was *always* askew, and he perpetually tugged at it irritably.

The office door opened. Captain's eyes skipped over my shoulder just as I sensed Seth's presence. I glanced back, glad to have him with me.

Seth gave me a small but encouraging smile. I took a deep breath, hoping to still my rattling nerves, but it didn't help. My legs trembled with either nervous energy or fatigue, but I couldn't tell which. Actually, it didn't really matter which. Either way, if I didn't find a release soon, I was liable to lose it completely.

I faced Captain, fists on my hips. "Well?"

"I think you've forgotten, James. I give orders; I don't take them, especially from you. And apparently, you don't follow orders either. Why the hell are you colluding with the Weres?"

"Colluding? I was following a lead—"

He lifted a hand to cut me off. "A lead you never cleared with me."

I huffed, throwing my arm into the air. Seth stepped around me. "Sir. We never had the opportunity to. The Weres were elusive. It wasn't until we were upon the scene that we knew exactly what we facing."

"Which was what exactly?" Captain folded his thick arms over his chest.

Together, Seth and I told him everything. The conjuring ring, the farm, the screaming hostages, the vampires. His eyes, usually sharp and squinty went round as I spoke. He collapsed against the edge of his desk and dragged a hand over his bald spot and through his remaining, thinning hair.

"Jesus Christ," he muttered, his skin taking on a sick green color. He clumsily scrambled to his desk chair and sank heavily into it.

"I believe that's the reason for the sudden spike in missing persons," I went on. I felt nauseous as I pictured Kay with a tear-streaked face, racing through the trees, trying her best to evade the vamps. "And the spike in district allotment quotas as well."

Captain's gray eyes settled on me, his lips almost disappearing in his face as he considered that. Slowly, his head moved into a nod.

There was an odd stretch of empty quiet. My toe began tapping, and my fingers fumbled against the seams of my jeans. My skin practically vibrated with the need to *do* something. What, I wasn't sure, but sitting there in silence, waiting for Captain to form a plan was maddening, not to mention rendering me useless for several long minutes.

Finally, I couldn't take the stillness a second longer. "Captain?"

His jaw tensed, and he looked up. "We'll need all hands on deck for this one." He shoved himself to edge of his seat and leaned forward. "I'll call the local precincts to see how many folks they can spare."

He lifted the phone from its cradle and glanced at Seth. "I want everyone in the squad room in one hour." With the phone pressed to ear, he glared at me and ground out, "And don't be late, god-damn it."

My heart felt as though it was trying to punch its

way out of my chest. Finally a plan. My blood thrummed hard in my veins, the adrenaline still coursing through them like chipped ice. It was an odd sensation since my body was entirely spent. Not just from lack of sleep, but from the mental draining events of the past weeks.

Seth was at my elbow. I glanced sideways at him. His lean body close to mine as we walked. So close I could reach out and take his hand if I wanted to. And I wanted to. I just couldn't bring myself to do it in front of the entire squad.

Even though I knew he would have smiled and squeezed my fingers in return, I chose to keep my hands clenched at my thighs. Kennedy James had never needed the comfort of a man before, and I sure as hell wasn't trying to backpedal now.

Once at my desk, I flopped into a chair, and pinched the bridge of my nose. I wanted one hour of sleep. Just one hour. I kicked my feet up to the desktop.

"What are you doing?" Seth asked, slapping the sole of my boot. "We need to go load up."

"In a minute," I muttered, closing my eyes.

"I'll give you five."

I made a groaning noise, which he must have took as a response, because his footfalls carried him away a few steps before he called back, "Meet me in the weapons room."

I gave a thumbs up but didn't open my eyes. Settling into my seat, I was just about ready to enjoy the stolen moment of peace when my cellphone rang. Surprised by the chiming ringtone, I startled upright. I figured the battery had died by now. I slid it out my pocket and glimpsed the screen. *Mrs. Webber.*

A cold, iron hand slid around my heart.

I stared at the phone as it trilled three more times. The battery light blinked at me, a warning it was almost depleted. Finally, it went silent. I exhaled a sigh of relief, fisting the phone in my hand. *Not ready,* I thought. *Still not ready.*

A moment later, it chimed with a voicemail. I tried to swallow, but my mouth was uncomfortably dry. I punched a few buttons on the keypad and lifted the phone to my ear. I shut my eyes when Mrs. Webber's voice filtered through the speaker.

"Kennedy. This is Mrs. Webber. I still haven't heard from Kay. It's not like her to not call her mama. I'm reporting her to missing persons. I…" Her voice choked, and I could tell she was trying not to cry.

My stomach lurched, and I wished I could comfort her somehow. Wished I could tell her I knew exactly where Kay was, and that I was about to save her. But the truth was, I was only speculating Kay was a hostage on the vamp's property. Speculating she was being harvested for blood.

Farmed, like a fucking animal, and worst of all…I was *speculating* she was even still alive. Vertigo hit me hard, and I had to clamp my eyes tighter. "I…I don't know what else to do," Mrs. Webber continued. "Call me if you hear anything. Stay safe, hon."

There was a click, and the voicemail ended. I dropped the phone to the desk, allowing it land with a clatter. I dug my palms into my eye sockets. Reporting Kay to missing persons made it everything real. *Too real.*

Tears burned and welled behind my eyes, but I held them at bay. *Now is not the time,* I scolded myself.

Crying for Kay wasn't an option. It was a waste of energy, and I needed every last ounce of it for what was coming next...

Chapter 30

I was slumped over my desk, my head resting heavily in my hands, when Captain burst into the room. *Had it been an hour already?* I hadn't noticed the time passing at all, lost in a fog of guilt and body-numbing fear for Kay.

"Listen up people," he bellowed. "By now, you all should have read the report, so you all know what we're up against." He crossed his arms tightly over his barrel of a chest and regarded the room with a level gaze. The usual contempt in his eyes was now smothered, instead replaced by a placid, almost restrained look of unease.

My skin prickled as a wave of nervousness washed over me. I had never seen him so rattled before. Sure, he was always angry about something or another, but now I saw a raging storm. A raging storm who knew exactly what course it was treading. Its target clear.

The voices ceased, everyone stone silent as all faces turned toward him.

"We're on the cusp of a major bust here," Captain announced. "One that we cannot handle on our own."

Everyone took a collective gasp. Hearing that there was a situation that we couldn't handle on our own was something my squad was *not* used to hearing.

"I've called in reinforcements from several precincts along the west coast," Captain went on to say. "It will take at least fourteen hours for those reinforcements to get here since most are traveling from southern California."

My spine went rigid. "Fourteen hours?" I blurted out.

His gaze swung to me, piercing me like a serrated barb. I almost flinched. However, annoyance wouldn't allow it. I leveled my stare at him, and, without thinking further, I pressed further.

"You're going to leave those people there *another* night? They'll be slaughtered."

The room broke into frenzied murmurs.

He glowered at me, his lips yanked tight in a frown. "I have reinforcements coming in from as far south as San Diego and as far north as Calgary. Just how in the hell do you propose they get here any damn faster? *We* are merely humans, James, which means *we* are incapable of the magical voodoo we see on a daily basis. Fourteen hours will have to do. There is no other choice."

"There is another choice," I argued. "We can storm the place right now. In broad daylight. Take the vamps by surprise."

His neck flushed red. His eyes flared angrily as stomped his way toward me like a vicious T-Rex ready to gobble me whole.

I jerked to my feet, ready to face him eye to eye. He was a few paces away when Seth emerged from somewhere in the room. He planted himself firmly on Captain's war path, blocking his way.

"Captain, please," he said calmly, his hands spread out in front of him as if in surrender. "Let's be civil here."

Captain glared at Seth, his chest heaving the way it

always did when his blood pressure skyrocketed.

"Civil?" he hissed. "She has the balls to call me out in front of the entire squad, and you're telling *me* to be *civil*?" His gaze slid to me. "I ought to yank you from the case," he shouted, wagging a pointed finger at me.

"For offering an alternative?" I shot back. "Fuck that." I folded my arms crossly over my chest.

Again, his eyes blazed. If it wasn't for Seth, I think the man would've tore my arms off and clubbed me with them right there in front of everyone.

"Captain, hear me out," Seth interjected. "What Edy is trying..." He glanced back over his shoulder at me and gave me a pleading look. "...to say, is..." He faced Captain again. "There are dozens of innocent people on that property. They are being hunted, like animals, every single night. If we sit on this...more will surely die."

Captain chewed on that for a moment. It was a tense moment, almost alive with palpable activity. I held my breath as I waited. Then, his wide shoulders finally hunched as if in defeat. He flicked his gaze down to the floor. "There aren't enough of us. If I give the clearance on this...it is *us* who will surely die."

He whirled brusquely around and strode back to his office. Not one person spoke, all shocked in place. I watched him cross the space of the room, his usual thunderous steps now more like tired shuffles now. When he reached the door, he hesitated. Addressing us solemnly he said, "We wait for reinforcements."

Then, he slammed the door on us all.

I actually *shook* with rage. The anger was so consuming, even my vision tilted from it. I wanted to hurl myself through Captain's office door and scratch his eyes out. I could almost feel his skin under my nails and hear his cries as I shredded his face into ribbons.

I thought of Kay and her kind, green eyes. The way they'd twinkle with mirth whenever she was up to something. I imagined her coconut scent and the silly way she always stuck her tongue out me whenever I acted too grouchy. I even thought of Rita. Not the drunken Rita who slurred the words of karaoke songs but the youthful, vibrant Rita in the Missing Persons photo.

They were out there, trapped on the farmland, caged in like barnyard animals. And tonight, they would be hunted by ravenous vampires.

I made a move toward Captain's office when Seth caught my arm, mooring me back into abrupt reality. I blinked at him several times as the fantasy of murdering Captain ebbed and faded away completely.

"Don't," he murmured.

I stared at him blankly, unable to verbalize the wide arc of emotions I was experiencing. *Anger. Despair. Hopelessness.* I sat there, searching his eyes, wishing he understood how deeply unnerved I was by all of this.

My best friend—hell, who were we kidding, my *only* friend—was possibly being held captive in a slaughterhouse. With my parents dead, Kay was all I had left in the world.

"We'll save her," he said, leveling his gaze as if to prove his commitment to his words.

"How?" I whispered, noticing the heat rising in my blood. My anger was returning. The addict in me needed release. The need was growing and gnawing and soon it would be impossible to ignore. I needed to squelch it soon, or I was liable to do something stupid.

"I don't know yet," he answered honestly. "But you and I will figure that out." He grabbed both of my shoulders and leaned his face closer to mine. "Together."

His calm, reasonable attitude only infuriated me further. *Why does he have to be so damn rational?* "Oh, is that so?" I knocked his hands from my shoulders. His eyes rounded, a look of surprise coloring across his features. I snatched my keys off the desk. "Just how in the hell is that supposed to happen, when we're stuck here with our thumbs in our asses?"

Suddenly aware I was the center of everyone's attention, I lifted my chin and cast my gaze outward. "Tonight…I hope you all sleep well, knowing those damn vamps are feasting on innocent people!" I took off in an angry sprint and didn't stop until I was outside. The sun was high in the sky that day, shining down mercilessly, blinding me as I ran.

Through teary-eyed vision, I somehow located my car and threw myself against it. I slid down the length of the driver's door until I was squatting on the asphalt.

All at once, I crumbled into a weak, paper doll. My emotions had ran so thin it was like a dam bursting over. I cried into my palms, the sobs coming out ugly and gulpy.

The sound of hurried footsteps across pavement caught me off guard. Wiping at my eyes, I sniffed and tried to collect myself. I pressed my back into the car door as if I could disappear into it. I held my breath, waiting and praying whoever it was wouldn't find me.

Seth appeared.

I adverted my gaze to keep him seeing my red,

swollen eyes. "I want to be alone."

"I can't do that."

I closed my eyes for a beat. "Please, Seth. I need a quiet moment."

"I can be quiet." He jammed his hands into his pockets and looked off somewhere. "Take your moment. You won't even know I'm here."

"Damn it, Seth." I spoke to my boots. "Just go, okay?"

He strolled over and sank down to his haunches in front of me. His woodsy scent filled in the space between us. "Drop the tough girl act already. Just let me do this." He touched a hooked finger beneath my chin, and gently tilted upward, encouraging me to look up at him. "Let me be here for you."

He regarded me with gut-wrenching pity. I jerked my chin away, and he let me. "I'm fine, okay? You did your good deed for the day. Now go." I wiped my cheeks angrily.

He didn't respond. He just regarded me quietly. Before I could stop myself, I gave him a hard shove. He fell backward, his ass hitting the asphalt with a hard thud. Thankfully, he only appeared stunned, not hurt.

I climbed to my feet. "I told you to go." From the hard crying, my eyes throbbed, and my head felt full of helium. I reached out and laid my hand on the car's cool metal for grounding.

He gazed up at me, total unfazed that he was sitting in the middle of the parking lot. His features were soft but entirely serious.

"I just noticed something." Getting to his feet, he gave me an odd little smile. His shoes crunched on the loose gravel of the asphalt as he took a step toward me.

I felt my brows knit. "What?"

"You're crossing into a dangerous territory, Edy." His eyes shone, like twin kaleidoscopes, the colors changing swiftly in the bright sun.

I pressed back further into the car door. "What?" I repeated, confused.

I glanced around the empty parking lot. We were alone. I fixed my eyes firmly onto his as he drew even closer. *What is happening?* I thought about taking a sideways step, but I couldn't bring myself to move. The cherub's words suddenly slammed to the forefront of my mind. *"Stay vigilant of those who surround you. Not everyone is what they say.'* There it was. The nagging memory that refused to surface earlier. Looking at Seth, and the unnatural hardness in his eyes, I-for one shame-filled moment-thought about running.

No! I told myself vehemently. *I trust him.*

As he slowly advanced on me like a stalking predator, I reasoned with myself: *You have good gut instincts. Seth has never given you any red flags. The cherub was wrong.*

Another step, another crushing of rocks beneath his feet.

I pressed myself against the car, not sure what to do.

Then, there was nowhere to go.

He stood before me. His gaze swept lazily over me, surely registering the way my chest heaved as I inhaled and exhaled, frantic, emotion-charged breaths. "Your walls are crumbling," he murmured. His hands came up to frame my cheeks, his palms warm and inviting.

Then, I did something I don't normally do. I relented. I let down my guard. Putting complete trust in

Seth, I stifled the cherub's cautioning, and nestled further into his hands. Who knew who the cherub was referring to, or even if he was telling the truth for that matter. Like Captain said, you can't trust a cherub.

"Seth," I whispered. "I don't know what I'm doing here. None of this is me."

"That's not true," he responded. "*This* is the real you. Without the badass armor." He smiled.

I choked back a sob and brought my hands to his wrists. I looked away, and admitted, "I'm not sure I like it."

"You're scared, that's all." He shifted closer, and I could feel the length of his body aligning with my own. "Edy, you are the toughest, smartest woman I've—"

I scoffed, cutting him off. "I'm coming undone here, Seth. And not just with you. Knowing Kay is out there…it's killing me inside. I can't seem to function anymore." Hot tears started piling up behind my eyes. "I have to find her. No matter what. Alive or dead." With that, my emotions broke loose again.

He touched the pads of his thumbs to my eyes, wiping the tears away. "This is all normal, Edy. This is the way you're supposed to feel whenever you care for somebody."

I rolled my eyes. "Love is so stupid. It's easier to be alone. That way no one gets hurt."

"But don't you see, Edy? Love is that next high." My gaze rose to meet his, my heart hammering away within my chest. He stroked his thumbs across my cheeks, looking deep into my eyes. "There is nothing higher."

Not knowing what to say, I captured his lips and gave him a slow, meaningful kiss. He took me into his arms, and I curled into him. I laid my ear against his chest. The rhythm of his steady heartbeat was calming.

I was content to listen to it all afternoon. He stroked the length of me, from the crown of my head to the curve of my ass, before pressing a kiss against my hair. I smiled at the gesture.

He was still breathless as he said, "When I fall, I fall hard. Remember that."

Chapter 31

After a few more unhurried kisses and whispered affections, Seth and I decided it was time to be productive.

"I just can't sit around here and do nothing," I said, starting to pace the parking lot. "Waiting around is not my style."

"So what do you want to do?"

I gave him a leveled look.

He withered slightly. "Never mind. I know what you want to do, but you're crazy if you think I'm going to let you do it."

I sighed. "I know I can't fight them all myself. If I could, I'd do it in a heartbeat."

He took my hand. "I know," he whispered. "We have to find something useful, but *practical* to do."

In silence, we deliberated for a few minutes. The only sound came from the two-lane streets that ran vertically before the precinct's office.

Suddenly an idea came rushing to me. "Wait," I said, patting myself down in search of my keys.

His brows darted up.

"The hotwire," I breathed with relief. "If we can turn it off, they might just have a shot of escaping." I slid in behind the steering wheel. "Come on, come on!" He ran around to the passenger side and got in just as I was slamming the key into the ignition.

Clicking his seatbelt into place, he said, "I can't believe I'm about to say this…but floor it!"

Pressing my foot to the gas, I swung the car onto the busy street of Cloverfield. Finally, I had a solid plan. A plan to set into action right now, not fourteen fucking hours from now!

Once we hit the interstate, I punched it, the outside world becoming nothing but a blur as I maneuvered the vehicle easily into fourth gear. As we flew down the highway, I held onto the hope that Kay was somewhere safe. Somewhere close.

Flipping on the mind scrambler, I shifted into fifth gear and did just what Seth told me to…I floored it.

****

Thanks to my lead foot, it didn't take us too long to get to Topher's, but without him leading us, it took several more hours to find the farmhouse. After a few wrong turns and losing over a half hour due to walking in circles, we finally saw the farm's looming silo up ahead. My chest cranked tighter knowing we were so close.

Seth's gaze swept over me. His features bore clear reservations, but he didn't express them. "What's the plan?" he asked, casting his eyes toward the farm.

I sucked in a deep breath, following his track of vision. "We sneak up, locate the control boxes, and destroy them."

"Simple."

I veered around him and started following the pasture's fence line, not bothering to look back to see if he was following me. I tried to keep my footsteps light, carefully picking across branches. The hotwire buzzed menacingly beside me, ready to pump me full of deadly voltage the moment I brushed against it.

The barn soon came into view. In the daytime, it was easier to see the upgrades that had been made to it. The doors were solid wood, equipped with heavy metal hinges and solid hardware. They were draped with thick chains, securely locking the hostages inside. My eyes darted all around the property, searching for activity. It was unsettling quiet, a drastic contrast from last night's horrific slaughter.

A thought came to mind: *could we break the lock? Could we save the people inside?* I hesitated, developing a new plan of action.

"Look," Seth whispered from behind me, pointing to a man in the distance.

The man strolled toward the barn. I squinted at him, and a bad feeling emerged. He called out to someone. A woman materialized from the long shadow of the silo. They spoke for a few seconds, then she walked away.

"It's guarded," I breathed out, my chest tightening uncomfortably. "They have the fucking place guarded!"

"What do we do now?"

I closed my eyes, reliving the carnage I witnessed last night. The screams of terror. The whooping and cheering of the vamps. I swallowed back the bile that burned in my throat, shoving the gruesome images away. I couldn't allow myself to be distracted. I had to find a way to help them.

"We can still disarm the hotwire," I said. "When we get to the house, cover me."

"Wait, shouldn't we have…I don't know…a *plan*, or something?"

"We do." I crept forward. "The plan is for me to disarm the hotwire. Yours is to cover me."

Seth muttered something under his breath, but I wasn't paying him much attention. My vision was singular now. Disarm the hotwire and then get the fuck out of there.

Each window of the house was dark, covered with what I assumed were thick curtains to block out the sun. I wondered if the vamps were asleep inside or were they awake milling around the shadowed rooms, just waiting for the sun to set so they resume their cruel game of cat and mouse.

The dinner bell swung in the breeze, the metal glimmering like gold whenever the sunlight hit it. My gut told me the control box was near the house. The vamps wouldn't be naïve enough to keep it close to the barn, where the hostages could possibly disarm it themselves.

If the vampires were awake, how could I get close enough to disable it? I bit my lip as my mind tore through possible scenarios. All seemed bleak.

"The control boxes are probably near the porch." Seth whispered. I glimpsed over my shoulder. His gaze held steadfast to the house, scanning the length of it with concentration.

"How do you know?" I asked.

Seth let out a shallow huff of amusement and shook his head. "City girls."

I scowled.

"The control box is what keeps the wire electrified, and it has to be plugged into an electrical outlet to do that," he explained. "Some are solar powered but given the amount of wire they have here, I'm willing to bet it's completely run off electricity."

I turned back around. My vision narrowed as I searched for the boxes. *There. On the porch.* Just beyond the dinner bell, hung four small boxes in a cluster. They were plugged into an electrical outlet, just like he described.

It wouldn't be enough to just unplug them. I had to destroy them. *Can I shoot them from here?* I wondered. I quickly ruled that out; the gunfire would surely rouse the vampires, and besides, there were other Supes on the property.

I was going to have to sneak up to the porch, destroy them, and then get the hell out of there as fast as possible.

Seth dropped the duffel bag to the ground, the leaves crunched lightly beneath its weight. He crouched beside it, and unzipped it, rifling around the contents a few seconds before withdrawing a small pair of wire clippers. He glanced up at me.

"Unplug the boxes, then snip the wires. It would be difficult for the vamps to rewrap the wires, but it can be done. Our best bet is, after we cut the wire, we yank the boxes too. We can bring them back with us.

I nodded, taking the wire clippers from him.

He reached back into the bag and pulled out a chest holster. He stood and fitted himself with it, the leather straps crisscrossing around his shoulder and back.

For a lightning quick moment, I forgot we were on enemy territory, ready to ambush a vampire lair. He looked amazing. Tough, rugged, and undeniably sexy. He shoved a thick-barreled handgun into the holster and then gave me a curt nod.

"Ready?"

Chapter 32

I'm not sure why I hesitated, but I did.

Seth frowned and took my shoulders into his strong hands. "You sure you can handle this?"

I wet my dry lips, avoiding his intense gaze. If I allowed him to look into my eyes, he'd see the desperation—the raw fear—disguised as manic determination. He'd see that I was fragile. That I was so close to my breaking point that I could feel the fissures creeping across my skin, like cracking ice.

"Edy," he demanded, giving me a little shake. I still refused to make eye contact, stubbornly fixing my gaze to the trees behind him. "If Kay is in there, we are going to get her out."

Kay. My eyes jumped to his, clinging to them as if they were the only thing strong enough to tether me to this moment. Who was I kidding? They were. Those damn eyes, glimmering gold, jade, and every shade of brown in creation, had the power to immobilize me like a tranquilizer.

His cellphone vibrated from within his pocket. He drew it out and glanced at the screen. "It's Captain." He steeled himself before answering it. "Captain," he greeted before hitting the speaker button, so I could hear.

"Where the hell are you and James?"

Seth looked at me. "Uh, we're at the farmhouse."

For a heartbeat, there was nothing but tense silence. I could almost feel Captain's anger flooding through the phone.

"What the hell are you two doing?" he growled.

"Disarming the farm's electrical fence. If the raid isn't successful, it could help the hostages escape. Call it a backup plan."

Captain cursed and began shouting something. Seth cut him off by saying, "You're breaking up, Captain. Service sucks out here. See you back at the precinct." He hung up and with a sigh, he said to me, "You know we probably just earned ourselves a massive ass-chewing for this."

"If you're going to be my partner, you better get used to it. Come on, let's do this." I tightened my grip on the wire clippers and set my sights on the control boxes.

I hurried in a half crouch, half run along the final stretch of fence line, following it around the side of the house, and then to the back. I paused below a window, straining to listen. It was virtually silent. No obvious activity was stirring inside, but then, vamps were notoriously stealthy.

The porch ran the entire length of the back of the house and was elevated with just a few shallow steps. I was almost there. The boxes were twenty, maybe thirty, feet away. Seth rode my back like a shadow, never allowing me to stray too far ahead.

We charged the steps, taking two at time, the aged wood creaking and groaning beneath our feet. With my chest heaving, I slid to a stop at the electric boxes. Yellow lights blinked intermittently, and the electric pulse hummed as if alive with energy. I reached down

251

and yanked the plugs from the outlets, instantly extinguishing the currents running through the metal wire.

I breathed a sigh of relief, then lifted the wire clippers with shaky hands, positioning them over the first set of wires. I snipped them cleanly before moving on to the second row. I had one box completely disabled when I heard movement behind me.

My chest compressed uncomfortably, stealing my breath. I turned to find Leo standing a few feet away. My mouth twitched into a snarl. There he was—the son of a bitch. For half a heartbeat, I considered tossing the wire clippers aside so I could reach for Supe Slayer.

"Keep working," Seth whispered. "I'll take care of the mutt."

With great effort, I dragged my glare away from the Shifter's smug face and turned back to my work of dismantling the second control box.

"Well, well," Leo said in a husky voice. "What's going on here?"

"Funny," Seth replied coolly. "I was going to ask you the same question. It's rare for a Were to mingle with vamps. Where's your loyalty, Leo?"

Leo let out a crisp, unamused laugh. "I don't swear loyalty to anyone. Not even my own."

"So why are you working with the vampires then? They must be paying you pretty well to switch sides like that."

I cut the wires of the third box. Perspiration beaded my lip and along my hairline. I felt like I was dismembering a ticking time bomb. My palms were so slick with sweat, the clippers slipped from my grip. They landed with a thump on the wooden porch planks.

I scrambled to retrieve them.

"I wouldn't do that," Leo said to me. "Boss man will be pretty pissed. Trust me, he's not someone you want to piss off."

I ignored him, wiping my hands on my pant legs before reaching to cut the final boxes wires. I heard his heavy footsteps shift closer, and I stiffened clutching the clippers that hung balanced over the wires.

The familiar sound of a gun being drawn from a holster rustled, and I didn't need to turn around to know Seth stood ready, the barrel of his gun aimed between Leo's eyes.

"Don't move," Seth instructed, his voice almost feral.

I squeezed the clipper handles, but before the blades could slice the wire, a blur reared up on me, moving so fast I barely registered what was happening. My body collided with the porch railing, knocking the wind out of me.

I collapsed against the wooden planks of the porch, wheezing. My ribs were screaming, but I knew danger was slinking closer, so I had push through the pain. I rolled over, gasping for air.

"Edy!" Seth called a few feet away, panic in his voice.

I drew Supe Slayer, leveling it to Claudette's chest. My vision swam, her image warbling, like a mirage, before me. I squinted, blinking away the vertigo.

"What's the matter, Detective?" Claudette mocked. "Aren't you used to seeing double?"

"Fuck you."

Claudette stalked me from the shadows, her chin drenched blood-red. I made sure to stay in the bright sunlight, just out of her reach.

"This human farming racket you got going," I told her. "It's *over*."

Leo chuckled, but I didn't dare look away from Claudette.

"Shut up," Seth shouted to Leo.

As the vamp continued her prowl, my finger itched to pull the trigger and smoke her ass right there, but my instincts told me Claudette was acting reckless for a reason. She was protecting someone. But who? Just being outside during the daylight hours proved she'd do anything to ensure their safety, or she'd die trying.

"Who are you protecting?" I demanded. "Who's in the house, Claudette?" Exhaustion was beginning to set in. The barrel of my gun wavered, but I quickly recovered, centering it squarely at her heart. "Let me ask you something. Before you willingly turn your hide into pork rinds, are you certain they'd do the same for you?"

She snarled at me, baring her fangs as she charged, plowing straight into me, sending me crashing back onto the porch. I landed hard on my back, and distantly I heard Seth call for me. Then, a blaring pop of a gunshot went off.

Chapter 33

When I came to, Seth was kneeling over me, his eyes wide with worry. I touched my aching forehead, groaning in pain.

"What happened?"

"Are you all right?" Seth smoothed my hair away from my face. "Jesus, Edy, I thought I'd lost you."

"What happened?"

"You blacked out after Claudette bit you."

"That bitch bit me?" I felt around my neck, easily finding two puncture marks. I withdrew my hand to find bloody fingers. "I'm going to kill her! Where is she?"

"Gone," Seth replied with a tremble in his voice. "After she jumped you, I...I don't know, Edy. I just saw red. I shot her."

Something sizzled nearby. I turned my head to find a pile of ash smoking in the sun. So much for taking her in for more questioning. My neck throbbed as I turned back to Seth. His eyes were wide and his breathing quick.

"What about Leo?"

"He got away." Seth's eyes shifted to my neck, lingering there when he said, "Edy. I've never been more scared in my entire life."

"Then you're in the wrong field," I told him, sitting up. I touched my fingers to my neck, wincing when a stab of pain shot through me. "Shit," I groaned.

"No…Edy." He took my hands, squeezing them gently. "You don't get it. It wasn't the damn vampire or the Were. It was you." His eyes held such tenderness in that moment that I was shocked into silence. "I thought she was going to tear your throat open," he continued. "I don't know what I would have done if she had. All I remember feeling was fear. Fear, and then anger. So I reacted. And I'm not afraid to say I'd do it again if I had to. I'll kill anyone who tries to hurt you. *Anyone*."

"Seth-"

A shrill screech interrupted me. Seth and I released our hold on one another. With palms pressed against our heads we tried desperately to protect our ears as we lurched to our feet. The sound was nothing I'd ever experienced before. It was like a siren had been blasted directly against the crown of my head. My brain was liquefying in my skull, and it was hard not to drop to my knees.

This had to be the woman we had seen earlier, patrolling the barn. I squinted through slitted eyes, trying to focus. Her wild hair rose from her head as if it were alive, whipping in the wind as she ran. She wore the same simple clothes as the woman we'd seen, a black dress with a flowy, billowing skirt, which now flapped behind her like the Jolly Roger. Eyes with no pupils, the woman was now Satan's voice: a banshee. With her jawbones unhinged, her mouth was free to hang like a gaping maw, her scream like living blades, piercing my eardrums.

"Jesus Christ!" I cried, ripping Supe Slayer from the holster. "Shut the fuck up!" I aimed and fired, blowing a hole through the Banshee's chest, quietening her.

With my ears still ringing, we were given no respite. A great whooshing sound came overhead. I raised Supe Slayer, lining up my sights on the creature flying over us. It locked its eerie glowing eyes on us, circling closer and closer. With each beat of its wings, Seth and I were blasted with a rush of wind, nearly unfooting us.

"Get the boxes!" Seth shouted above the noise.

I nodded and ran to them, my boots thumping hard on the wooden boards of the porch. I reached for the first one I came upon. I yanked hard, but it wouldn't budge. With a curse, I withdrew Supe Slayer and opened fire on the boxes. They blew apart, spewing wires and electrical boards. So much for doing things quietly.

There was movement inside the house, but with the sun still blazing hot, the vamps didn't dare to come out.

I turned around in time to see Seth shoot the humanoid out of the sky. It landed hard on the ground, the sound fatal and very definite.

"Mothman," I muttered, coming up on the body. Seth kicked at it, ensuring it was indeed dead. "Haven't seen this guy in *years*."

"So why is he in Washington? And why is he guarding the farm?"

I opened my mouth to speak, but a horrific scream cut me off. I startled and whirled. I felt the color drain from my face. Seth sucked in a sharp breath.

The hybrid standing behind me was a fucked-up collection of goat, bat, and some sort of demon. The beast lowered its curling horns and pawed at the dirt with thick hooves, ready to charge. I pulled the trigger on Supe Slayer, but it only clicked. My hands shook as I reached for more bullets. Without Supe Slayer, I was a helpless target.

"It's a Jersey Devil," Seth called. "We need something sanctified!"

I had holy water in the car, not that that would do me any good right now. The Jersey Devil let out another horrible yell, sending a wave of panic over me.

"Run!" I cried, tearing off for the surrounding forest. With Seth on my heels, we ran, dodging trees and hurtling over fallen limbs.

The Jersey Devil happily gave chase. Beating its leathery wings a few times, the creature easily caught up to us. I reached for more bullets, quickly reloading Supe Slayer as I ran.

Seth fired off several rounds from over his shoulder, but all missed. I slammed the magazine back into place and turned around long enough to take aim. The creature screeched and recoiled from the blast its left wing took. It whirled around drunkenly, unable to fly in a straight path. Its glowing eyes flared angrily, still determined to pursue us.

Seth and I dashed past the tall pines, soon coming upon the clearing that held my parked car. My heart was ready to burst, but I pushed harder. I had to get the holy water!

Seth shot again, covering me as I ran up the trunk and flung it open. I frantically tore through the items, snatching the bottle and unscrewing the lid as I turned around.

The creature was close, but not close enough. I stood ready, waiting for the right moment.

The Jersey Devil screamed, the sound echoing in

the dense forest. It was coming straight at me, its hooves chewing up the ground as it drew closer.

It was thirty feet away. Though my heart raced, I braced myself, willing my nerves to remain calm. I had one shot at this. I couldn't afford to waste it.

Twenty feet away.

Seth fired off several rounds, the bullets slicing through its fur, leaving gaping wounds behind. The creature's cry was thunderous as it thrashed wildly, but it did not relent. Folding its wings, the creature ran faster, its curled horns squarely aimed for me.

Ten feet away.

"I'm out of ammo! Do it now," Seth urged, his voice shrill.

I stared down the Jersey Devil, clutching the bottle tighter. "Come to mama, mother fucker."

It was so close now that when it let out another blood-curdling scream, its halitosis hit me like a sucker punch. It smelled like death and sardines rolled into one. I ignored the urge to gag and swung the bottle in a wide arc, slinging the holy water across the face of the Jersey Devil.

Skin and fur bubbled and burned off right in front of me. The horns fell off, disintegrating as soon as they hit the earth. The creature folded in on itself, crumbling into a pile of bones and slick ichor.

The whole thing took under sixty seconds. It was amazing to see just how quickly a demonic being can evaporate into nothing more than a memory with just a splash of blessed water. Then again, thinking about how fast I flip my living room blinds closed and scramble beneath my covers whenever Mormons knock on my front door, I guess it's not that unimaginable.

I let out a sigh of relief, letting the bottle slip from my fingers. I leaned against the trunk of the car, instantly weary on my feet.

Seth laid a hand on my shoulder. "You okay?"

I closed my eyes for a beat. "Yeah." My body ached from head to toe. The stress and long nights were beginning to catch up with me, but I wasn't going to tell him that. I looked up at Seth. "You?"

"Yeah, I'm good." He leaned against the car beside me and stared out at the trees around us. "Looks like we have yet another mystery to solve."

I grunted. "Just when we think we're some gaining ground, more crazy shit happens." I hung my head, exhausted. "Why would a Banshee, the Mothman, and the Jersey Devil all be here at once? Why are they protecting the farm?"

"I don't know," Seth replied with a sigh. "But somewhere out there, somebody has all the answers. We just have to find them."

Seth and I had to get our asses off that farmland before dusk. Two PCI agents against a swarm of vamps is not very good odds. In fact, it's a guaranteed death. We clambered our beaten, and thoroughly wrung-out bodies into the car, and I fired it up, thankful to still be in one piece. Slamming the pedal to the floor, the car tires tore up the dirt road, stirring up a cloud of dust in their wake.

I took a quick glimpse at the rear-view mirror for good measure. I don't know what I was expecting, but with everything we'd seen recently, I was prepared for anything. I struggled to make sense of the Jersey Devil, Mothman, *and* a Banshee guarding the vampire's property. *Supernatural beings don't work together.*

Unless. *Unless they are building an army.*

I recalled Topher's words: *Yesterday he was an army of one. Today...today he leads an army.*

I shuddered and focused back to the road ahead of me. "We need to find Leo."

"Do you want to call the squad together? We could spread out. Cover more ground."

"No," I said heatedly. "They need to prepare for tonight. I'm going to find that piece of shit and make him talk. *Today*." I shifted gears and flicked my gaze sideways.

Seth was watching the tree line rush past his window. He seemed distracted. Worried even.

"Hey," I said. "You okay?"

Seth remained quiet for a moment. I wondered what he was thinking.

"You want me to take you back to the precinct? I can look for Leo alone."

He looked to me sharply, his eyes blown wide. "Are you crazy?" he shot. "There's no way in hell I'm letting you go alone. We're partners. Where you go, I go."

Seth looked down at his lap. "Edy, I need to tell you something. In case something happens, I want you to know the truth."

My stomach dropped. *Oh shit, Here we go. The beautiful bubble that is Seth is about to burst. I knew it. He was too good to be true.*

"I didn't join the PCI to protect people either."

My heart beat a little faster. Suspicion started to slither its way through me. *What if Seth isn't who I thought he was? My instincts were usually infallible. What did I miss?* I unfurled my fingers on the steering wheel, readying myself to withdraw Supe Slayer should I need to.

I willed myself to remain calm and listen to my gut. My instincts had never failed me before. Looking over at Seth, and his twitchy behavior, I needed to remember that more than ever.

"I wanted revenge."

My hands slipped and the car swerved. Seth's hand lashed out, straightening the wheel before the tires ran off the side of the road.

I blinked at him with surprise. His eyes were hardened slate, no longer the soft, ever-changing hazel. Shakily, I took back control over the car. After hesitating a split second, Seth withdrew his hand.

"My mother was murdered by a Were." He took a deep breath, readying himself. "We were camping. Something we did every year before my dad died." His mouth twitched into something wistful for just a heartbeat before he continued. "Then even after he passed, Mom and I continued to go. Without him." His voice trailed off for a moment as he seemed to reliving something. "I was about half a mile from our campsite, fishing. When I returned…" He inhaled deeply, trying to steady his quavering voice. "There was so much blood."

"How do you know it was a Were?"

"She told me." He ran his palms over his knees. "I don't know how, but she was still alive when I found her. Before she died, she told me she saw a man change into a wolf before he attacked her."

"And you believed her?"

"At first I didn't. I mean, it sounded ridiculous. A werewolf? I thought she was going into shock and was hallucinating or something. I wouldn't listen to her. I kept telling her to be quiet and to be still." Seth clamped his eyes shut. "I wish I had told her I believed her."

Intrigued, I pressed him further. "How did you…"

"Walk away with the memories?" He opened his eyes and looked over at me. His cheeks were wet with tears.

"The park ranger who responded to my call knew us. We had been camping at that site for years and years. He knew my father was dead, and that Mom and I were continuing the tradition without him. He was always there to help us. He knew I had recently graduated from the Academy."

Park rangers across the globe are briefed and sworn to secrecy about the PCI and our dealings. Since a lot of paranormal sightings happen in nature preserves, state parks, and national parks, it's imperative that they stay in the know.

He grunted. "I'm guessing once he learned I was officially an orphan, he thought I'd make the perfect recruit for the PCI. He must have made a call to Boddax that very night."

I reached over and touched his knee. I knew he was in pain. The memories of my parents' car crash were still fresh. I missed them every single day. I had to fight back my own tears as he spoke.

"When Boddax showed up at my door, asking me to join the PCI, I didn't even hesitate. I wanted to hunt down the bastard who killed my mom. Boddax knew that." Seth covered my hand with his.

"He told me about Acts of Blind Rage. I had to resign myself to the fact that my mom would never get the justice she deserved, but I was still determined to join. If I couldn't bring justice to my mother, then I would at least bring justice to others who are hurt by Weres."

"They're not all the same," I told him. "You know that, right?"

"I'm slowly learning that."

We were both quiet. Still holding hands, we sat in a comfortable silence.

"Hey," I said after a while. "Thanks for sharing that with me."

Seth shrugged. "You deserved to know. And besides, you're more than just a partner to me, Edy."

"What do you mean?"

He withdrew his hand and raked his fingers through his hair, giving a clipped, unamused chuckle. "For Christ's sake, Edy, I think I'm falling for you. Can't you tell?"

My body went on autopilot. I continued to shift gears, engage the proper blinkers, and veer around traffic, all while my mind spun. The "l" word. Is he about to say the "l" word. *Oh shit, what do I do now?*

"Say something," Seth pleaded, interrupting my thoughts.

There was so much running through my head, I didn't know which to pluck out, and actually *say*. Something was brewing between Seth and I, but we hadn't put it into words yet. Hell, to be honest, I wasn't sure it could be. Not yet anyway. I shifted nervously in my seat, keeping my eyes forward on the road.

"I know," I managed say.

"You know?" he replied dubiously. His brows went up as if intrigued, but doubtful. He folded his arms crossly in front of him.

I looked over at him. He was watching me expectantly. A fist-like pressure pressed against my heart. I wanted to tell him I loved him, but I just wasn't ready to say it out loud. Not yet.

His eyebrows lifted higher. The cab of the car was virtually silent aside from the roar of the engine.

"I feel the same way," I half-whispered. I wanted to say more. Like how a flurry of butterflies take flight in my stomach whenever he looks at me. Or how his touch can spark not only a tender moment but also ignites a fevered need that takes on a life of its own, demanding to be satiated, refusing to cower, or be ignored. Of course, I could never *say* those things. That would be too much. Too frilly. Too poetic. Too lame.

Feeling shy, and exposed all of a sudden, I pursed my lips together to keep from saying anything too gooey.

That seemed to be enough for him. His eyes went soft, and he took my hand. With a grin, he pressed a kiss to the back of my fingers. My insides warmed, making it hard to stay focused on anything else but the pulsating heat coming from my core. Irritated at my body's wanton reaction, I shifted in my seat again and cleared my throat.

He didn't seem to notice my discomfort. In fact, he seemed quite content with my answer, happily burrowing his face in my palm, like a cat insisting to be petted. I smiled a little, lost in the quiet joy of the moment.

Still though, I watched him suspiciously, waiting for him to demand more. Men usually did—at least the men I was used to.

There always seemed to be two types of men in my life. The needy men and the greedy men. The *needy* men were naive enough to think the terms of our "relationship" meant more than ONE NIGHT ONLY. Those men asked for my phone number. They'd try to take me on actual dates. They'd often request commitments and sacrifices I wasn't willing to make. By far, those men made me cringe.

However, the *greedy* men understood they were simply scratching an itch for me and were eager to do just that. Those men were easier to deal with. They became mere ghosts come morning, and they never, *ever* called the next day.

They don't harass me to give them things like *devotion, effort,* or *time.* Those men I could deal with. Those men were easy, uncomplicated creatures who existed for one reason, and one reason only: a quick fix for my need.

Why was Seth different? Why he was more than just an easy lay? My eyes roamed across his handsome face and down the creamy column of his neck. Suddenly it struck me how I was looking at him the same way Mom used to gaze at Dad. My stomach flipped. *What did that mean?*

I eased the car to a slower pace and took the exit that led into Cloverfield's downtown area. It was well past dusk now, so the city lights were shining brightly throughout the town.

Cloverfield wasn't as urbanized as Seattle, but it's pretty close. Towering, bricked buildings reached high into the city's skyline. Businesses ranging from law firms, to locally owned restaurants and boutiques crammed every available space. A tiny patch of greenspace sat in the center of town.

It served as a city park, where residents could walk their dog, jog, or let their kids run wild. Cloverfield was more than my home, it was my turf. It was up to me to keep it safe from Supes. I glanced at Seth. And it was up to him. We were partners after all.

As Seth rubbed my knuckles back and forth across his lips, a quiet calm came over me. A resolution, I suppose, that this was in fact okay. That having honest-to-goodness real feelings for him was okay. I didn't have to be prisoner to my addiction anymore. I was more than just an alcoholic. More than a borderline sex-addict, and an adrenaline junkie.

Edy James was capable of love.

Chapter 34

Seth and I needed more ammo before we started our hunt for Leo, so we had to stop by the precinct to load up. It was buzzing with activity, so much so that it was hard to believe it was nearing midnight. Agents fluttered in and out of the building, all with one mission weighing heavily on their minds. Solve the damn case. Human lives were at stake, so there was no time to waste.

Agents were trained to tackle the *Who, What, When,* and *Whys*. The Whys in this case were particularly difficult to answer. Nothing made sense. Who would want all the Vamp leaders dead? Who was crazy enough to do it? Who was responsible for the blood farm? As a unit, we tried to piece together the evidence, allowing the leads to direct us.

I was becoming impatient. There were too many opinions, too many voices, and too many useless idle bodies. Finally, it proved to be too much. I went back to packing our gear. Enough talk. It was time for action.

I had just clicked the Supe Slayer's full barrel back into place when a powerful presence filled the squad room. I turned to find Garon Walker. His head was lifted high, his expression smug.

"Agent James," he said, his deep voice rumbling like a freight train.

"Garon," I countered, my curiosity heightened.

"I have something that may prove useful to you, and your case."

"Oh?" My thoughts leapt to Kay. Did he find her?

His eyes flinted to the gun I was holding, and I didn't miss the slight curve of his full lips. *Is he daring me to use it?* I swallowed and reluctantly slipped Supe Slayer into its holster as smoothly as possible. I kept my face carefully placid, refusing to look over-eager. Needy. Weak.

My outside may have reflected an icy detachment, but inside, my reflexes were on high alert, the blood pulsating painfully in my temples. Garon's steely eyes moved to meet my gaze, now devoid of any emotion. Supe Slayer suddenly felt too far, though it was snuggly strapped against my leg. I could feel its weight pressing against me, warm as though it was as alive as I was, ready to be drawn.

With his gaze held firmly to me, Garon whistled, and through the precinct doors, came the Were Shifter, Leo Trevino.

****

The hunt for Leo was over. I locked eyes with the asshole responsible for all the hell I'd been through the past several weeks. The Were snarled, his stare dark and dangerous.

He wasn't coming willingly. Escorted by a massive vamp with a bright blue Mohawk, Leo struggled against him, the chains embracing him rattling as he was dragged through the room.

Seth went rigid beside me.

Garon raised his hand, motioning the vampire to halt. "I believe this is the Were you seek?"

Leo practically frothed at the mouth, spitting and

spouting off expletives.

Touching my hand to Supe Slayer, I nodded. "Yes," I answered. "Where'd you find him?"

"That's not important," Garon replied coolly. "All that matters is he's here now, and he's yours." He signaled to the vampire, who shoved Leo toward Seth and me.

It was then that I noticed the dried blood clinging to Leo's thermal shirt, running dark, almost black trails down his back.

"You do that to yourself?" I circled Leo, finding a bloody gash on the back of his neck. It was a messy wound, all shredded skin and exposed muscle. It was hard to tell what did it. It could have been claws...or hell, even fangs.

I looked over to Garon, his back was all I saw as he and the Mohawked vamp strode out of the precinct and back into the night.

I turned my attention back to Leo. "You remove the GPS chip on your own, or did someone do it for you?"

Leo just grunted.

"Either way, Topher is pissed. If I was you, I'd steer clear of him unless you want your ass handed to you again."

The Were glowered at me, his eyes flashing hatefully.

I smiled. "Well, let's have a chat, shall we?" I tossed a glance to Seth, who was already reaching for his silver handcuffs. Though Leo was already bound by thick silver chains, it was best to secure him with PCI restraints rather than Garon's crude bindings. An agent handed me a pair of bolt cutters.

I waited until I heard the familiar clink of locked cuffs, then stepped up with tool in hand. "So, tell me. Where did Garon find you?" With some effort from me, the bolt cutters snapped through the silver links.

Leo remained quiet.

I unwound the chains from his wrists. The silver had chewed deep wounds into his skin.

"How'd you let a vampire catch you anyway?" With the chains in one hand and the bolt cutters in the other, I angled my head in question. "Off your game tonight, Leo? Must be pretty humiliating to have been captured by a vamp, am I right?"

Leo's mouth twitched, his nostrils flaring wide.

"Edy," Seth warned.

The other agents tensed around me. The room was as silent as a tomb.

"Guess that answers the age-old question: who's stronger? A vampire or a Were?"

With a roar, Leo lunged at me, raising his tethered hands toward my neck. I scrambled backward, though I didn't need to. Seth was already between us, shoving Leo back with all the strength he could muster. A couple of agents stepped in, restraining Leo, forcing him to his knees.

Captain burst in the room. "What the hell is going on here?" His eyes lit on Leo, growing round and wild. "Somebody speak to me!"

"A gift from Garon Walker, district leader," I answered, letting the chains drop to the floor with a clatter.

"This douchebag is responsible for killing all those innocent humans," Seth said, seething.

"Innocent?" Leo shouted, pitching forward in an

effort to get to Seth. "No human is innocent!"

Seth punched him square in the face. There was a nasty crunch and blood trickled from Leo's nose. Captain swore.

Shaking out his hand, Seth got in Leo's face. "I can't wait to throw you behind silver bars."

Leo struggled against his shackles. "You're weak. All of you! Weak and pathetic!"

Seth circled his arm around Leo's neck, restraining him further. "Shut up!"

"What do you mean no human is innocent?" I questioned.

"Get that son of bitch out of here," Captain cut in, his face an angry shade of red.

Leo began to laugh.

Seth tightened his grip, cutting off Leo's air supply, causing him to choke and gag.

"Let him talk," I said, interested in what he had to say.

Seth released his grip just enough to allow Leo to take a few gasps of breath. "Humans serve no purpose," Leo said hoarsely. "They ought to be wiped from the Earth, like pests. It's time for Weres to rise to the top of the food chain."

"Are you fucking kidding me?" I demanded. "That's what all this is about?"

Leo's gaze was dark and singular as he turned his attention on me.

"You're the epitome of every single movie villain." I made a sound of disgust. "A fucking cliché."

Captain cleared his throat, but I charged on, of course. "Even down to the fucking speech." I gave him a mocking clap. "Way to go."

"Edy," Seth said, adjusting his hold on Leo.

"So tell me, Leo. Was it worth it? Were all those lives worth your own? 'Cause one of three things are going to happen. You're going to rot in a silver cell, the vamps will bleed you dry for the district murders, *or* Topher's going to stomp your ass into the ground when he finds you. Either way, life for you is going to be hella shitty."

Leo sneered at me, almost amused.

"Enough," Captain said, bustling forward. "Get this asshole booked."

****

After Leo was booked, he sat alone in the interrogation room for over an hour. Lengthy bookings, and marathon interrogations could sometimes weed out the hard criminals from the petty ones. Seasoned felons could wait for hours without batting an eye, where the novice offenders cracked from sheer boredom.

Leo sat, unmoved, in the wooden chair, his wrists still bound in silver handcuffs. He blinked lazily, and his head sometimes lolled as if drifting off to sleep. Leo Trevino was obviously hardened to the system, completely unaffected by the situation.

Seth and I watched him beyond the two-way glass.

"There has to be more to his story," Seth said, his arms crossed over his chest. "Why kill off district leaders if he's pissed at humans? It doesn't make any sense."

I unhitched myself from the wall and strode up to the panel of glass that dominated the small space.

Leo must have sensed me. He lifted his chin and sought me out. Looking blindly at us, he called out, "I ain't telling you shit." He spat on the floor.

I cut my eyes to Seth. "He's ready to talk."

Seth startled. "Excuse me? Are we hearing the same thing?"

I brushed past him and entered the interrogation room with Leo. A small table in the center of the room is all that divided us. His dark eyes tracked me; a small smirk played at his lips.

"Agent," he greeted.

"Who are you working with, Leo?"

His brow lifted.

"Answer me."

Seth walked into the room. Leo's gaze slid over to him, watching him approach.

"Nobody," he answered simply.

"Don't fuck with me. There is no way you acted alone." I leaned over the desk, planting my palms flat on the woodgrain desktop before him. "*Eleven* district leaders dead in one night? No one is *that* good. Especially not a Were. Those vamps can smell you a mile away."

Leo's eyes iced over. "Fuck off."

I steeled myself, preparing for the possibility he might lunge at me or, worse, shift into a werewolf. I straightened, bringing my hand to rest on Supe Slayer.

"I'll tell you what. I'll cut you a deal. You tell me who helped you murder the district leaders, and after your sentence, we'll set you up with Paranormal Being Protection Unit. The vamps and Topher won't be able to find you."

"That's a solid offer, right there," Seth said from behind me.

Leo kept a blank stare.

My blood warmed. My fingers tightened on my

gun; I was growing impatient. I wanted to off the mother fucker right there in the interrogation room, but my gut told me he had information. And if that information led to Kay, then I had to pry it out of him-one way or another.

Seth came to my side. He dropped a heavy file on the desk in front of Leo. "You recognize any of these people?" He opened the folder and stabbed a finger at the countless Missing Persons flyers. "Are they the same people being held at the farmhouse?"

Leo's eyes drifted to the papers before him. "Don't know. Don't care."

My jaw ticked, my hand shook...but instead of blowing Leo into confetti, I reached into my back pocket and grabbed my cellphone.

Pulling up an image of Kay, I thrust the phone into his face. "Do you know this woman?" My voice broke. "Do you?" My ears rang as I waited.

His eyes barely swept across the trembling screen. "No."

Seth touched my back. "Let it go, Edy." Slowly he lowered my hand. "We're getting nowhere with him tonight. Let's drop him in a silver cell and see how he feels in the morning. Perhaps a few hours behind scorching metal will change his mind."

I looked at my phone screen. Kay—with that carefree smile of hers glinting up at me—stoked my desperation for answers.

"New deal," I said through clenched teeth.

Leo glanced up. Hope lanced through me. Maybe I had a chance after all. I composed myself as best I could. "You only have to answer one question," I hedged carefully, holding the phone out to him again.

"Is she alive?"

"Edy," Seth interjected.

I waved him off. "Answer that, and I'll let you walk on the vamp murders."

"Edy!" Seth put himself between me and Leo. "Are you insane? Captain will have your badge if you let him walk. Not to mention the vamps—they want justice. And if they don't get it…"

"What? What will they do?" I challenged.

"Seek revenge. It's what they do."

That snapped me into clarity. Vampires are cruel and incapable of feeling true remorse. If justice isn't served for their district leaders, they *will* riot. There was no doubt about that.

I shifted my eyes to Leo. "Throw him in a cell. I'm done with him for the night."

I stormed off, my boot heels tapping furiously down the precinct hallway. I needed space from everyone. If I didn't get it, then I was liable to punch a hole in the wall or through someone's skull.

Vick came out of nowhere. "Did you get him to talk?"

I brushed right past him and entered the main headquarters. I glanced up at the clock on the wall. Quarter to six. Another sleepless night. I could feel the siren call of sleep stirring behind my eyelids, but I refused to give in to it. *Coffee will help,* I thought, stifling a yawn. Captain's allies had been trickling into town, and all due to the precinct at seven o'clock sharp.

Someone had already arranged chairs around the corkboard stationed in the center of the room. Seth came up beside me.

"Leo's in a holding cell. We'll get him to talk after

everything's said and done."

"I'm hoping we won't need him to," I said before taking a seat toward the back of the room. Seth walked away, leaving me to fume alone. I should be relieved to have Leo behind bars, but his refusal to answer any questions had my mind reeling. *Where was Kay? Was she still alive?* My heart squeezed painfully in my chest.

The allied agents started filtering in. Vick seemed to be the voice box for our unit, introducing himself to everyone, and inviting them to settle themselves comfortably in front of the board. I didn't bother to get up. I wasn't in the mood for fake smiles and putting on airs for strangers. Sure, they were going to help us take down the vamps, but that didn't mean I had to pretend I was professional or remotely friendly for that matter.

Captain suddenly thundered out of his office. His tie undone and hanging around his neck, and his hair disheveled around his flushed face. If it was anybody else but the Captain, I would have thought something sordid happened behind the closed doors of the office. But because it was him, I figured he had locked himself inside to privately stress over the horrible situation at hand.

He caught hands with each detective as they momentarily exchanged pleasantries. His history with each member was evident as he spoke to them, recalling names, and lightning flashes of shared memories before he moved on to the next.

I hung back, hesitant to inject myself into the flurry of introductions and briefing for fear I'd let some snide comment slip, and that would be the end of our allied efforts.

The detectives were from different PCI units that spanned from New Mexico to Canada. Some had used special PCI jets and choppers to get here so quickly. Captain knew them all, but the only person I recognized was Rashaun Blakely, a detective from the Canadian border precinct.

I met her about a year ago, while assisting with Carl's rehoming case. That's when the PBP chose the remote Canadian border after humans spotted the Sasquatch near a popular RV site in Illinois.

Rashaun was lovely in a very *non-obvious* way. She wasn't overstated or slinky when she moved, but with her headful of long, copper-tipped dreadlocks, and sharp as blade cheekbones, you couldn't help but do a double-take whenever she walked into the room.

I remember my initial reaction to her. I thought she was a bad bitch. Now mind you, she wasn't rude or demanding. She didn't come off entitled or even self-absorbed. In fact, she was quite the opposite. She seemed…humble and compassionate. But the intrusive way she regarded everyone, like a hawk investigating a weakened rodent, made her seem almost predatory.

Rashaun had her shit together and expected everyone around her to do the same. She was hardened and seasoned in our field, and she wasn't one to fuck with. She wasn't merely a bitch. She was *the* bitch.

Rashaun barely acknowledged Vick as he introduced himself. This made me like her even more. He frowned, but she didn't even notice; her gaze was already fastened onto the information board. She folded her slim arms neatly and stepped closer to the board. She studied it with a shrewd eye, the mechanics of her thoughts apparent in her harsh expression.

I held in a smirk as I watched Vick slink away. His so-called charm was totally eclipsed by her interest in the case. Rashaun was a pit-bull in the PCI. Relentless with cold cases, she earned herself a reputation as the "corpse whisperer" because she had solved a record number of long buried crimes.

She inclined her face up at the board, her features pinched in careful concentration as she scanned every bit of information. The board was nearly swallowed whole by dozens of pinned reports, maps, and an enlarged mug shot of Leo.

She peered closer and pointing at a report, she glanced over her shoulder, clearly looking for someone to ask a question to. Vick was more than happy to oblige, sweeping in gallantly and answering whatever it was she asked.

I switched my gaze around at the other detectives, but then my gaze snagged on Seth. He was standing near the water cooler, chatting to a cluster of detectives, probably formulating a plan, or exchanging theories. He must have sensed my stare, because he turned his face to find me, and shuttered one eye in a quick wink.

I tried to smile back, but my nerves were so completely wrung out, it came out tight and painful across my face.

Seth's brows cinched a little, and he excused himself from the discussion. With clipped strides, he crossed the space between us, politely nodding to anyone he passed in the process. Taking my shoulder into his grip, he leaned in close.

"What's wrong?" he asked, in a hushed tone.

I shook my head, staring but unseeing at the mingling bodies in the room. The vision of the blood-thirsty vamps clung to my mind like an anchor, sinking me deeper and deeper into a depression I knew I wasn't strong enough to pull out of. *Was Kay on that farm?*

The screams of the victims drowned out my thoughts, and I couldn't help but worry that Kay was one of those people imprisoned in the barn during the day. Tears burned and clawed like nails against my eyeballs. I gulped, clenching my trembling hands into fists.

He squeezed me tighter. "You breaking down on me?"

His words snapped me into focus. Although the answer was clearly *yes,* I casted my eyes up, scowling at him as I hissed, "No."

His eyes hardened, searching my face for the truth. By the way his mouth thinned into a curt little line, I knew I'd been caught. I cursed my emotions for betraying me.

"Edy," Seth started, his voice disgustingly gentle, as though he were coaxing me off a ledge.

I held up my hand in protest. "Don't." I stood abruptly, knocking my chair to the floor with a crash. "I'm fine as fuck all right? I don't need you looking at me all sad-eyed, like I'm some pathetic female who needs a god-damn hug or something."

The room quieted as dozens of pairs of eyes turned to measure me. I knew they were silently judging me. I was a walking mess—and I knew it. Heat crept up my neck and warmed my ears to an uncomfortable degree. I swallowed, barely able to meet the stares in the room, but I knew Captain was watching me.

I could feel the scorn radiating from his general direction. I flicked my eyes to him, and sure enough, he was glowering at me, his stare simmering and marked with a warning to get my shit together or there would be hell to pay.

I needed a minute alone to do that. I couldn't gather a semblance of composure with all those damn eyes on me, so I dashed from the room and out into the hall. A few people lingered around, so I ducked into the restroom.

The small bathroom was empty, so I flung myself into the closest stall and pressed my back against the door, trying to right my hammering pulse and quickened breath.

The stress of the past few weeks was suffocating me. Every day that passed without Kay was slowly sealing off my airway and driving me fucking insane. I was surprised I held it together for as long as I had, but I couldn't allow myself to break down today.

Not today, I told myself. *Not today, God-dammit.* We were so close to cracking the case wide open, and possibly finding Kay. I had to hold it together until I found her. Until I could wrap her in my arms and deliver her safely back to her mom.

Again, I welled up, but to keep the tears in, I pounded my fists on the stall door, rattling it, not caring who heard me. There was an edge burning inside of me that demanded to be dulled. A need that begged to be released.

I choked back a scream and tore out of the stall. I needed air, and the stuffy confines of the bathroom walls were stifling me. Before I yanked the restroom door open, I glimpsed myself in the mirror, and it stopped me in my tracks. My eyes were wild and jumpy. Primal even. I knew this look well. Desperation had fueled my demons, and it was a matter of time before they needed to be dealt with.

I released the handle of the door, allowing it to swing softly back into place. I stepped up to the sink and gazed at my reflection. My hair was coming loose from the long braid that flowed over my shoulder. My once slick black eyeliner was now smudged gray, like bruises around my lids. My eyes were bloodshot from exhaustion and my face gritty and dirty from hiking in the woods.

I looked like a damn junkie. A shiver slid through me. That was exactly how I looked after drinking myself into oblivion and waking up in a strange bed, next to a man I barely recognized.

I washed my face, hoping it would help regain my thinning grasp on my composure. If I looked less like a wild animal, maybe I'd feel less like one cooped up in a small cage.

My reflection may have looked better, but adrenaline still coursed thickly through my veins, making me feel jittery and tight. *Speed, booze, or sex...which will it be today?* Sighing, I realized with harbored revulsion...I was still a damn junkie...

Chapter 35

When I stepped back inside the command center, I sensed a change in atmosphere. A flood of energy rippled through everyone, and they seemed to have forgotten about my little episode. With his booming voice and commanding aura, Captain held the attention of everyone, briefing them on the crimes and the severity of the mission.

I lingered toward the back of the crowd, my skin crawling with so much pent-up energy, I felt as though I was going to crack.

Guilt threatened to swallow me whole as I pictured Kay being ripped from the sidewalk, screaming, and begging for help. I imagined her terrified—imprisoned in the relic of a barn, with fleeting hope whenever the doors swing open, and she's allowed to run as free as the electric fence will allow.

I glanced down at the nearest desk. Leo's mug shot stared back at me The Were's smug face mocked me from the page. I muttered a *fuck you asshole,* just before crumpling the paper into a ball. Out of the corner of my eye, I caught a glimpse of Seth in the midst of the crowd. He was watching me, concern wrinkling his forehead and tugging the corners of his mouth down. I turned away, fisting the ball of paper tighter.

The voices in the room buzzed like annoying bees in my head. Nothing made sense. It was happening again. My need for instant gratification grating my nerve ends like sandpaper. I felt compelled to flatten my palms over my ears. *Calm down,* I instructed myself. I closed my eyes for a beat, tamping down the mounting panic that clawed away at my gut.

Someone cupped my elbow, and my eyes flew open to see who dared to touch me. It was Seth.

"You okay?" he whispered.

I didn't have the strength to lie, so I gave a weak shake of my head.

Still gripping my elbow, he hauled me away from everyone. I was distantly aware of Captain's voice trailing behind us, answering questions, and addressing any potential dangers of storming the barn. I thought it was crucial we listen to that portion of the meeting, but he led me away anyway.

Alone in the hallway, he held onto me firmly. "Edy, you're exhausted. You're not fit to handle this takedown."

I glared at him and shook out of his grip. "Who the hell are you to tell me what I'm fit for, and what I'm not?"

His eyes were wide, but hard. Determined and not afraid to be frank. "Damn it, Edy, now is not the time to be stubborn. We're about to head straight into a goddamn vampire lair, and the last thing I need is for you to hesitate one second too long, and..." He fixed his jaw tight, breathing harshly through his nostrils. His chest heaved uncontrollably, and he practically whispered his next words. "And something happen to you."

My anger vanished. Looking at him, scrubbing the back of his neck, bearing himself to me, vulnerable and honest, I pinched my lips shut. For once, I was speechless.

"I don't know what I'd do if something happened to you." He paced the hallway and raked his fingers through his hair. "Actually, I do," he added, hooking a hand behind his neck. "I'd slaughter every last vamp in that God-forsaken place before burning it to fucking ground." He stopped and turned to look at me. "I'd burn every last vampire to ash just to prove a point."

He slowly stalked forward, his hazel eyes glimmering a shade darker than normal. The fluorescent lighting overhead bared down on him, casting him a sickly, yellow glow, but somehow he made it look enticing. Sexy even.

The swell of need unfurled within my gut, begging me to act upon the ferocious urge with hurried and completely hot sex. Needing space before I acted on that impulse, I backed up until I felt the wall come flush behind me. "And what point is that?" I licked my lips, trying to relieve the dryness that caked the roof of my mouth.

Seth stood before me, and placed on palm flat against the wall beside my head, partially caging me in.

"That you're mine," he murmured, tracing a finger along my jawbone. "And that *no one*, mortal or immortal, touches what's mine."

I swallowed, and his eyes shifted to my neck. His fingers trailed achingly slow down the column of my throat, and every nerve in my body tingled with awareness. His face inched closer, and for a brief moment, we shared the same sliver of air. I shuddered as his lips brushed against mine, hesitating to take it further.

"You are mine, aren't you Edy?" he asked against my mouth. His hand moved to stroke my hair. I was mindless with desire, yearning to wrap my legs around his waist and offer myself to him right there in the hallway. I slid my hands up to Seth's shoulders and around his neck, drawing him down to my face.

"Yes," I breathed, before pressing my mouth roughly against his. He retaliated wonderfully, his lips rising and falling against mine as if following a familiar dance.

He splayed a hand across my lower back and pulled me against him. My blood rushed beneath my skin, heightening every sensation to a blinding crescendo. *God, I want him so bad right now.*

"Jesus," said a voice down the hall. "Really?"

He released my mouth, kissing me once more before completely breaking away. We turned to find Vick standing near the double doors of the command center, one hand holding the doors ajar.

Vick barked a laugh. "Grooms? Of all the fucking men, you pick *Grooms*?"

Seth straightened, pushing his shoulders back and tossing his head back just enough to look down his nose at Vick.

I slipped my fingers into Seth's belt loop, and hung on, unable to come up with anything worth saying. My mind was turning silly loops, drunk from his kiss.

Vick divided a look between us both. "Captain wants you two in here." With a shake of his head, he added, "*Now*."

When the command room door swung closed, Seth turned back to me, an amused, crooked smile breaking across his face.

"What?" I demanded half-heartedly, still riding my high like an addict.

"Of *all* the fucking men?" he replied, his brow arched in interest. "Should I be worried?"

I yanked his belt loop, snapping his body against me. "No," I answered, nuzzling the tip of his nose with mine. "If there are other men, I don't see them. I don't see *anyone* but you."

He captured my lips. His kisses were so incredibly tender and full of unspoken emotions, I wished we could communicate that way forever—with just kisses and embraces that said everything words could not convey.

We parted all too quickly for my liking, but we both knew not to keep Captain waiting. I untangled my fingers from his belt loops and unhitched myself from the wall. I smoothed my hair for good measure before heading back into the command center on trembling legs.

Seth was the only man to shake me to my core like that. To leave me burning from the inside out with lust so rampant I thought I'd disintegrate under his touch.

He followed two steps behind, but by my flushed cheeks and his cocky little grin, I figured the entire room knew what we were doing. Captain glared with crossed arms, his eyes tracking us like laser beams. I found an empty space and clasped my hands in front of me. Seth stepped up beside me, his hands shoved into pockets innocently.

"Glad you two could join us," Captain grumbled, ambling back around to face the information board. Once his back was to us, Seth caught my eye, and smiled.

I smiled back, acutely aware the vibration of adrenaline that ran through me earlier had reduced to a tolerable, gentle humming in my veins.

I looked away from Seth, trying to make sense of it all. His kiss knocked the edge away. Just a simple kiss. *What does this mean exactly? That I no longer need liquor, adrenaline highs, or orgasms to see clearly? That just having Seth is enough?*

I chewed my lip, pondering, as Captain's voice droned on and on. Seth nudged me with an elbow, shaking me from my thoughts.

I blinked and darted my eyes to Captain. His brows nearly touched one another, and his mouth was set firm in his perpetual frown. He was rambling about Leo, his rap sheet, and the possibility of more werewolves being on the farm. This, of course, posed a problem for a sneak attack. There was only one way a take-down was going to work. PCI had to strike quick, and we had to strike hard.

Captain explained our plan of attack thoroughly to an enrapt squad room. I, on the other hand, paced the floor, unable to stay still. *I'm coming for you Kay,* I'd think over and over, ready to get on with the mission. When the room suddenly fell silent, I turned to find Captain staring out at the sea of grim faces,

"Be safe out there," Captain said in closing. "Use your heads, and don't take any unnecessary risks."

I scoffed silently in my head. *Unnecessary risks? Everything we DO is an unnecessary risk.*

"I want this mission to end with the same amount of PCI bodies that it started with." Captain's eyes drifted across the faces before him, allowing them to touch on everyone individually.

It was the first time I had ever seen a fraction of emotion from him. He actually looked like he *cared* about us. "Don't be a hero," he added, his gaze settling on me without subtlety. "And don't fuck up." He raised his arm and motioned toward the center's exit with an extended finger. "Fall out!"

Chapter 36

Everyone broke apart. Most filed out of the command center, while others headed straight for the weapons room.

I started toward the weapons room myself when Seth touched my shoulder, stopping me. "I've already collected your gear," he said, jerking his head toward our desk, where his duffel bag sat. "You stood me up by the way."

"Sorry," I replied meekly.

He went to the desk, snatched the bag off the floor, and then jogged back to me. He didn't waste any time unzipping the bag and handing me equipment hurriedly. I shoved them into my pockets, noticing my heartrate was speeding up. My body was again reacting to the adrenaline spike, and I needed to move. *Now.*

We moved in unison, both striding with determined steps through the hallways and out the precinct's doors. My boot heels clomped across the asphalt as I rounded the front of my car and swung into the driver's seat. Seth slid in beside me, pulling the seat belt across his chest in one smooth motion.

"You ready for this?" he asked.

I gave him a hard sideways glance and steeled my voice. "Hell yes." I threw the car into drive and stomped on the gas, tossing Seth back into the headrest. He gritted his teeth, and with a white-knuckle grip, he held the edge of his seat as if he was withstanding some sort of torture device.

Usually I found humor in his prissy behavior, but under the current dire circumstances, I just couldn't. I was too far gone. Too amped up on adrenaline, and too busy running through the list of possibilities the day would bring. I could find Kay alive. I could find her dead. Or I wouldn't find her at all…

We flew down the road, trees blurring as we whirled past them, ignoring every speed limit sign along the way. Thanks to the mind scrambler, I didn't have to worry about mortal cops getting in the way. I was free to press the pedal flush to the floor. And against Seth's pleas, I did just that.

The captain didn't mark the mission as urgent in the sense that all units were to rush to the scene as if a crime was in progress, but I wasn't about to dawdle my way through town. The rest of the squad can hang back and follow the rules if they wanted to, but Edy James doesn't wait for anyone. Nor does she follow rules very well.

"You trying to be the first on the scene?" Seth questioned through tight lips.

I shifted gears and glanced at my side mirror. Not a PCI unit vehicle in sight. "Is there a problem if I am?"

"No," he answered stiffly. "As long as you plan on waiting for backup before storming the place."

I adjusted my jaw, considering his words before I spoke again. "Listen," I started.

"Oh no," he groaned, lifting his face to the ceiling.

I pushed on. "I was thinking we could possibly release the hostages before we storm the farmhouse."

He looked at me again, clearly struggling with my

logic. "Why can't we do that *with* the unit there?"

"Too conspicuous," I insisted. "Once the unit shows up, the mission is going to go into overdrive—fast. We release the hostages, and then the squad raids the house."

"It sounds risky, Edy. We already know the place is patrolled by Supes."

I didn't say anything, instead, I just slowed the car, and turned onto the desolate road the led parallel to the property. Streetlamps that could have been labeled as antiques, dotted the side of the gravel road ahead. The tree-line looked like sprawling ominous shadows even in the daylight.

I put the car in park long enough to punch in the coordinates. I needed to remember to thank the PCI technology geeks who had pin-pointed the farm's location by satellite.

I probably could have found it again on my own, but I wasn't wasting any time, besides, I planned on driving straight up to the property, no more of this slinking around in the shadows. I'm more of direct, straight-to-the-point kind of girl. It suited me better.

"Edy," Seth said urgently. "Did you hear what I said?"

I stared at the small electronic screen as it pulled up a digital map and aligned our location to it. The robotic voice indicated we were approximately four miles from the destination. I eased the car back onto the deserted road and followed the automated instructions.

"Travel one point four miles, then turn right," the monotone voice directed.

Seth grumbled irritably beneath his breath and turned to look out his window. My stomach twisted. I *wanted* to reach out and take his hand. I *wanted* to tell him I'd be sensible and wait for backup, but the truth was...I'd be lying. The moment I stepped onto the farm, I was going to look for Kay, and I was going to take down any Supe or any human who got in the way.

"Turn right," the voice instructed, cutting into the tense air of the cab.

The car swung onto a road more isolated than the last. The gravel ended, and other than the worn grooves along the dirt path, there was no other indication that the road was ever traveled. Again, the voice instructed me down another road. With every turn, the GPS device was leading us deeper into the belly of the forest. The road seemed to carve through the center of it, thrusting towering pine trees on either side of us.

I glanced up at the GPS. We were getting closer. The small blip on the screen that represented my car, hovered near the flagged final destination marker.

Up ahead, the silo of the farm took form. My chest cinched as if I'd been fitted for a corset. I slowly eased the car off the side of the road, shut off the engine, and palmed the keys after I pulled them out of the ignition.

Seth didn't move. He remained sitting quietly, his seatbelt still locked into place across him. I unclicked my own seatbelt, the strap slipping back into place as I lifted my hand to the car door handle.

"Edy," he said in a low voice. The way he said, it caused me to pause. Raw emotion steeped into that strained voice. *Edy*. As if my name alone held the strength of a prayer. I turned to face him. He grabbed my arm, anchoring me into place. "Captain said not to play hero."

I looked down at his fingers on my sleeve, closing

my eyes for a beat. "Seth," I breathed, before fixing my gaze on him firmly. "I'm not trying to play hero. My best friend could be in there."

"So let the PCI do its job," he argued.

"I will." I opened the car door. "I'm just going to make sure they don't fuck anything up while doing it." With that, I stepped out of the car. I zipped my coat up higher to ward off the icy chill the clung to the air. I performed a quick check of all my equipment, first tapping Supe Slayer at my hip.

Then, I lightly touched each pocket, ensuring everything was in place. Were mace in my inner coat pocket. Ground garlic, to temporarily blind a vamp, in my back pocket. And a vial of holy water, along with a dozen silver bullets in my right coat pocket.

The sound of muffled static came from Seth's duffel bag. He glanced down. "Squad's here." He reached down into the bag and removed a walkie-talkie, mashing the side button before lifting the receiver to his mouth.

"Grooms and James," he said. "Go ahead."

More static, then Captain cut through the feedback. "What's your position?"

"Near the barn where the hostages are held."

"Hold your positions."

"Captain," Seth pleaded. "We're going to release the hostages and ensure they get to safety. We will be in touch should you need more feet on the floor at the house."

Radio silence. I chewed my lip as Captain considered.

"Ten-four," he said. "I'll send some agents to patrol your area. And Grooms?"

"Yeah, Captain?"

"Don't let James get you killed."

Scowling, I flipped the walkie-talkie the bird before reaching into the duffel bag and taking out a pair of hand-held bolt cutters. I slipped it into my back pocket for safe keeping.

Seth clipped the walkie-talkie to his belt and readied his gun. "Ready?"

I gave a curt nod, raising Supe Slayer over my shoulder. "Ready." We ran toward the barn. My gaze swung back and forth, scouring the area for guards. Luckily, there was none. The door was heavily barricaded with thick chains and locks.

I was snapping the metal in two with the bolt cutters, moving on to the next lock when I heard radio static.

"We're closing in on the farmhouse," a voice said.

"Roger that," came another voice.

"The squad is about to rush the house," Seth whispered. "Hurry."

The last lock broke and fell to the dirt.

As the barn doors swung open, I expected the hostages to pour out like before, but this time, nothing happened. I poked my head inside. The barn was a vast structure and had very little ventilation. I gagged. It reeked of human waste, and ancient sawdust.

"Hello? Is anyone in here?"

Nothing.

I looked back at Seth.

"Cover me?" I asked.

Seth shot me a grim look, but he knew I was going with or without him. If there was even the flimsiest possibility that she was somewhere in there, nothing, not even Seth, was going to stop me from going in after her.

"Don't I always?" he said, his eyes moving to the barn behind me.

The walkie-talkie crackled. "We're moving in on five."

I swallowed and then turned back to the barn. *Five minutes before the squad storms the place, possibly causing all-out war.* On a deep breath, I slid the safety off Supe Slayer and stepped inside. My boots crunched on the dirt, and dust that covered the floor.

I cast my gaze around the dimly lit barn. Several holes in the roof allowed pin pricks of light to shine through, but it wasn't enough to illuminate the rafters or dark corners. I took a few more steps. Dozens of humans cowered in the corners, some whimpered like injured animals, while other openly wept in fear.

There was a second level to the barn, and even from below, I could tell it held at least a dozen more hostages. I scanned the filthy faces of the prisoners, searching for Kay. Though all were different, each face resembled one another. Pale, sunken, and smudged with grime. They all told a tale of horror and lost hope.

I crept forward, adjusting my gun in my clammy palm. The hairs on my neck stood erect as I sensed movement above me. An old ladder leaned against the second story floor, and I tested the first step. It creaked beneath my boot, and I thought better of climbing it for fear it would make me an easy target for any Supe lurking around.

I caught a glimpse of a shadow swinging from the rafters, and instinctively, I raised Supe Slayer. It moved fluidly, like fog rolling across stilled water. A vampire.

I fired once, missing the vamp but blowing a massive hole through the aged roof. People screamed as splinters of wood rained down on them.

"You missed me, you missed me...now you gotta kiss me!" called a young voice. Angelica, the teenage vamp from Garon's district stood up on the rafters, her shock of blonde hair bright against the shadows of the barn.

I fired again, but she swooped from the rafter, her supernatural speed making it easy to dodge Supe Slayer's bullet. She clasped another wood beam and swung off, her body sailing smoothly through the air.

She landed in a crouch on the second level of the old barn. Her landing was so soft, it barely stirred a single dust mote in the air. She snarled, glaring down at me before disappearing toward the recesses of the barn.

"Angelica!" I shouted. Before I could make a move toward the ladder, I heard a woman's voice pleading, "Please, no" then a sickening crunch, like bone beneath a boot heel. Angelica's ghastly pale face emerged out of the dark shadows of the rafters, then, with the grace of a dancer, she took a running leap, silently dropping to the floor in front of me.

She watched me for a long moment, her eyes sparkling with a dangerous edge. It felt as if she could read my vitals by just looking at me. Counting each quick pulse pounding away at my neck and wrists. I tightened my grip on Supe Slayer and held my breath as I waited for her next move.

My gaze traveled to her arms where she held a woman's body. She dropped the woman to the ground with a heavy thud. I inhaled sharply. A sick smile was plastered on Angelica's red-stained lips, and her eyes were transfixed on mine, as if relishing my reaction.

I slid my gaze to the woman on the floor. The build didn't resemble Kay's, but my stomach churned anyway. The woman was unconscious. Mousey brown hair fell across her face, obscuring any features. Blood soaked through the strands of matted hair that lay across her cheek. Her jean skirt was torn and streaked with dried mud. Her knees were scrapped up and covered with bruises.

"Soon, there will be farms like this one all across the world," Angelica said. "Vampires will take their rightful place at the top of the food chain, and your people will scatter like the parasites they are."

I was getting really sick of hearing humans being degraded. I arched a cynical eyebrow. "Parasites?" I replied. "Bold words from someone who relies on us to live."

She cocked her head, as if considering my words. "Merely shows how insignificant your kind is. You only provide nourishment for a stronger species."

My trigger finger itched to be used, and I felt like snarling myself. *I'll show you who the stronger species is, bitch.*

"In time, your precious little PCI won't be able to hold back the inevitable. The de-ranking of mankind to nothing more than blood warmers." She barked a sinister laugh.

I leveled my gun to the center of her forehead. It may not kill her, but it would slow her down. Before I could squeeze the trigger, Angelica kicked the body at her feet viciously, stopping me in my tracks. The tangled, brown hair slipped away, revealing the bloodied face of a middle-aged woman. My eyes widened with recognition. *Rita.* My stomach twisted violently, bile collecting at the back of my throat.

"Who runs this?" I demanded.

Angelica chewed her gum, glaring at me in total silence.

Somewhere behind me, I heard the sound of dozens of feet trampling toward the barn. Time was up. The PCI were coming. They were storming the farmhouse, and I was about to lose any chance of learning who was at the helm of this gruesome place.

Angelica's eyes flickered to the barn doors, then she bent and yanked Rita's wilted body up by the crown of her hair. She settled her gaze dead upon me, then took the gum out of her mouth just before sinking her fangs into Rita's neck.

"No," I shrieked, lunging forward. She dragged Rita back a few steps. Taking a deep pull, Rita's body convulsed as if startling awake. Rita's eyes flew open, locking onto mine, portraying a look of sheer pain and confusion.

Angelica sank her teeth deeper, and like a hungry shark, she tore off a chunk of Rita's neck. Rita's scream died on her lips, and blood ran in rivulets down her shoulder and chest. Angelica lifted her blood-smeared face from Rita's neck and tartly popped her gum back in her mouth just before dropping Rita to the floor.

Chapter 37

I stood frozen, staring at Rita's vacant eyes. Guilt swallowed me whole as I recalled all the rotten things I ever thought about Rita, and all the mean names she'd been called. She didn't deserve to be called a lush or a hot mess. Rita was a person battling demons, and the only way for her to stay afloat in her misery was to drink them away, just like me.

"Edy!" Seth hollered, cutting into my dark thoughts. He was running through the barn with his gun drawn, his eyes darting wildly around him. Angelica disappeared into the dark recesses of the barn.

"Open those doors as wide as they will go," I shouted to him.

He seemed to understand, doubling back to prop the barn doors wide. Sunlight spilled across the barn floor like a golden tidal wave.

I chased after Angelica, plunging deeper into the barn. Old, rusty equipment hung from the walls, and long forgotten bales of hay laid scattered in one corner. Behind me, I could hear the PCI moving quickly to remove the hostages. I was relieved they were there and prayed they'd get all the people out in time. Kay's sweet face flashed in my mind, and I hoped she was among the survivors being pulled from the barn.

I figured the best way to flush Angelica out was by bluffing that I already knew who was in charge, playing into her ego, or flat out pissing her off. Just so happens, I excelled at option three.

"So, what role do you play in this operation?" I asked into the darkness. I was careful to hover around the small pockets of sunlight that trickled in from the holes in the roof. "Decoy, maybe? Seems like a shitty role if you ask me."

The smell of the place was like acid, burning my nostrils and throat. I wondered how toxic the air was, and how damaging it was to the hostages who had been held here. The barn was a collection of filth. From the scattered rat feces on the floor, to the layer of thick dirt on the rafters, you could practically choke on the dust motes floating through the air.

"Is Garon responsible for all this? Is he sleeping the day away, while you're in here fighting his battles?" A few more strategically placed steps. "I hope he at least made you second-in-command after Claudette was ashed."

A grumbling noise came from the shadows.

I kept my feet planted in the small beam of sunlight as I dipped my fingers into my pocket, taking out the bottle of crushed garlic. "You'll be taken into custody too, Angelica. With any luck, you'll both be tied to the same stake. You'll burn together."

A savage growl erupted, just before the vamp pounced. She knocked me backwards, sliding me across the worn wood floor. I was back in the shadows, but a faint trail of sunlight sank into her shoulder. Her skin crackled like a fading campfire, but she kept coming for me, nails raking down my jacket, tearing slices in the fabric, and her lips peeled back over her serrated teeth.

Somehow, I was still clutching the bottle. With

clumsy hands, I threw the ground garlic into her face, sending her shrieking back into the darkness. Reacting on pure adrenaline, I didn't let her get far, blasting a hole through her back with Supe Slayer. The holy water infused bullet sizzled as it pierced her skin, and she howled in pain.

Sinking to her knees, she writhed and screamed. Taking advantage of her sudden weakness, I seized a fistful of her blonde hair. I yanked her head back and shoved the barrel of my gun into her mouth.

PCI agents kept pouring through the barn doors. Their guns raised, ready to take down anything Supernatural in their path.

"Make another move, and I will blow your goddamn head off," I said, my words coming out in shallow pants. My veins felt hot, like my adrenaline had manifested into lava. It was almost unbearable.

Seth came running up, a string of garlic clasped in his hands. He worked quickly wrapping them around Angelica's wrists, and around her neck. Any skin exposed to the string of garlic turned a nasty red and blistered with giant welts before my eyes in a matter of seconds.

She struggled under the garlic restraints, hissing, and throwing spittle all over the place. Her chin seethed red with anger. The other agents worked efficiently, quickly clearing the first floor. Hostages rose to their feet, eager now to get out of the shadowed confines of the barn.

Seth took Angelica by the wrists. His gaze swept over me, examining me with methodical eyes, as if ensuring every part of me was in place. "You okay?"

"Yeah," I replied, wiping my brow with the back of

my hand. The high of the fight was wearing off, leaving my body spent, and hollow.

He unclipped the walkie-talkie and lifted it to his mouth. "I need a sun blanket in the barn." With his eyes softening, he asked, "Did you find Kay?"

"Not yet. I'm going to look for her upstairs." I cut a glare to Angelica. She squirmed, spitting like a wild cat. "You go get Miss Hiss here loaded up." She lunged at me, but he yanked her back. I could tell he didn't like the idea of me staying behind, but he knew me well enough to argue.

"I'll be fine," I assured him.

"Five minutes," he said, his lips threatening a grin, but it died before it could form. He shoved Angelica forward, leading her toward the barn doors. "No," she snapped. "I will not leave him. He needs me! He has visions that I must help him fulfill."

She whipped her head back and forth, fighting against Seth, but the garlic was doing its job; weakening her to a manageable state. In normal circumstances, pound for pound, the brute force of a vampire was no match for a mortal.

"Who?" I asked sharply, suddenly losing my cool. Enough of this grand-standing and unnecessary drama. We weren't in a movie, god-damnit. This was real life. I glowered at her, feeling the heat rise from chest to the top of my head. "*Who* are you talking about? Is it Garon?"

Her mouth worked into a snarl, glaring at me with the look of pure hate.

"We will find him," I said to her. "I guarantee that. We *will* find him, and he *will* pay for this."

A PCI detective I didn't recognize walked up to

Angelica toting a special sun-blocking blanket. He threw it over the vamp and helped Seth wrestle her out into the daylight. I watched as they shoved her into an awaiting PCI squad van. They slammed the doors shut, and the entire van rocked back and forth with the force of her thrashing.

I finally returned my gun to its holster and turned back around. The first level of the barn had been cleared out. All that was left was the sawdust that covered floor, and threads of spider webs clinging here and there. The PCI were already assisting hostages from the second floor. A string of bedraggled people slowly descended down the ladder. With trembling legs and ashen faces, they were clearly shell-shocked from the turn of events.

Detective Rashaun was waiting at the bottom rung, handing the hostages off to other agents. If they seemed healthy, other than being dehydrated and malnourished, they went with a PCI detective. If they were injured or appeared extremely ill, they went directly to an PCI emergency care worker.

My body felt restless, waiting for each body to amble down the ladder. Waiting for them to swing around and show me their face. *Come on*, I thought. *Please be here.*

A woman's voice above me croaked out a strained, "Edy." It was weak, but I recognized it immediately. I glanced up, and my heart nearly burst in my chest. *Kay!*

She had on the same powder blue sweater she wore that night at the pub, but now it was covered in grass stains and dried mud. Her auburn curls hung in greasy clumps, and my stomach soured at seeing her that way. I ran to the ladder, knocking Rashaun out of the way.

"Hey," she cried, startled.

"I'm sorry," I murmured to her as an afterthought, hurdling myself up the ladder as fast as my legs would take me. As soon as my boots touched the floor, I flung myself at Kay. We collided, folding each other in a joint embrace that almost squeezed the breath right out of us.

She was crying uncontrollably, hiccupping and gasping painfully. I shushed her, smoothing her disheveled hair from her face. I breathed her in, and although she no longer held the scent of her familiar coconut shampoo, she still smelled distinctly of Kay.

"You're okay," I reassured her, feeling the tears jump to my eyes as well. They felt hot, feverish, and untamable. "I found you." The words came out sloshy as the tears finally won out, falling down my cheeks and slipping over the crease of my lips. "I found you," I said again, as if saying it twice held more validity.

Kay felt tiny in my arms, her frame now gaunt and frail.

"So many died," she murmured into my shoulder. "Horribly." The air sucked out of her sharply, as if remembering something vital. She snapped back, taking my hands, and pulling at me anxiously. "What time is it? We have to go." Her blue eyes were round and full of terror. Tears streaked clean tracks down her dirty face, and her lips quivered as if she were shivering.

"It's better to be in the middle. The first ones out are the first to die, and the last ones out are easily captured." Her fingers were cold in my grip, and they felt brittle, like fragile heirlooms. "The middle," she repeated. "The middle is best."

She tried to drag me toward the ladder, but I

stopped her, grabbing her hard by the shoulders. My chest was tamped with guilt and sympathy. For the moment, she was broken. If allowed to stay this way, her memories would forever haunt her, and she'd never be the same again. Nightmares would consume her, and soon she'd be crazed with the vivid details of the horrors she'd witnessed here.

Vampire victims almost always had to be mind-scrubbed. Their acts were so violent, so vicious, the PCI was forced to erase any memory the vics had of the incident. Suicide rates amongst the victims whose memories weren't erased, were a staggering, ninety-eight percent. *Ninety-eight percent.*

"It's over," I said, looking at her levelly. "You are going to be all right." I cast my gaze down to the first floor. "See all those people? They are detectives from my unit. We are *saving* you. It is *over.*"

Her eyes skipped around the room frantically. Worriedly. She didn't seem to fully grasp my words. I felt as though I'd ingested an anchor. *What have you gone through?* I wanted to ask, but I knew it would be disastrous. She was already treading a thin line between sanity and full-blown psychosis, so she had to be handled delicately.

"Kay," I said gently. "You are safe now. I promise."

Her gaze snapped to my face, searching with a desperation that wrenched my gut. Her fear, and survival instinct was overriding everything in that moment. I slipped a hand off her shoulder and held it up a pinky finger between us. "Pinky swear."

A very pre-teen thing to do, but it was something we always did, and I felt in that moment, she needed something to remind her she was indeed alive. Something that reminded her, she was human. That she was Kay.

I could see the workings of her throat as she swallowed, and ever so slowly she brought up a shaky hand.

"Pinky swear?" she asked, her voice wobbly and unsure.

"On my life." I hooked my finger tightly around hers.

"Edy." Seth's voice came from below. I looked down to find him looking up at us. "The sun will be setting soon," he called up. "We need to get everyone out. Now."

I noticed the flow of people had thinned. All that remained was a few officers doing a final search of the barn and us. I glanced outside the barn's open door. The sun was sinking low to the west. There wasn't much time. My heartrate kicked up a notch. I turned back to Kay. "You have to go. These people will take care of you. Make sure you stay safe."

"You're not going with me?" Her eyes went big and fearful.

"I have to stay," I countered, tightening my pinky around hers. I stared straight into her eyes. "I am finding who did this, and I'm going to make them pay."

She was on the verge of tears again; I could tell by the glimmer in her eyes.

"Edy," Seth urged.

"Go," I said urgently. "Get out of here." I shoved her toward the ladder. "Now!" Seth helped her down. He held fast to her, bearing much of her weight as she collapsed against him. "Get her to the med team," I directed, quickly climbing down the ladder. Clouds of dust circled my feet as my boots landed on the floor.

"The farmhouse has already been cleared," Seth told me.

"Was Garon in there?"

He shook his head.

Frustration bloomed in my gut. "Did they check for a basement?"

Seth nodded again.

"He's behind this," I said. "I know it. First Claudette, then Angelica. The only reason he brought Leo to us was to shake us off his trail…" Dawning hit me. "Of course, he's not here." I started striding away from the barn, back to the direction of my car. "He's an Epoch. He hasn't risen yet. Come on!"

Chapter 38

Seth and I ran through the farmland. PCI Agents swiveled their heads, watching after us as we blew past them. My car was in sight when Captain stepped out of the forest.

"Where the hell are you two going?" he asked, crossing his arms over his chest.

Halting to a sudden stop, Seth answered, "Going to get Garon. We think he's still in his sleeping chambers."

I went to move past Captain, but he lifted an arm, blocking my way. I whipped my head to the right, looking him in straight in the eyes. "What are you doing?"

"You don't have a warrant."

"To hell with a warrant," I countered. "We need to take that asshole down. Now!" The Paranormal Crime Investigation squad often had to rely on hunches and swift action, so technicalities, like warrants and other legalities, often had to be overlooked until after the fire was put out. Today, that fire was a powerful, ancient vampire named Garon Walker.

"Time is against us here, Captain," Seth said urgently. "It won't be long until he finds out we stormed the farmhouse. He's a flight risk. We need to strike now."

Captain and I glared at one another. I wasn't

309

willing to back down, and neither was he. He stood there, combative, perspiration dotting his forehead. This was a waste of valuable time. My heart wrung tight within my chest. Shoving his arm away, I attempted to brush past him.

Again, he blocked me.

I blinked back at him, confused.

Captain then reached into his coat pocket, withdrawing a shiny handgun. "Drop your weapon."

I felt a gasp escape me.

"I said, drop your weapon."

"Fuck you," I spat, backing away from him.

He aimed the gun lazily at me. "Hardheaded women," he said, "are a pain in my ass."

"Captain," Seth questioned. "What are you doing?"

Captain shifted his gaze to Seth. "Protecting the Master," he answered simply.

"What?" My stomach soured. "You're in on this?"

"Garon promised me a position in the New World."

"What position?" I asked.

"Overseer." Captain's face hardened into stone. "Won't be much different than what I do now. I'll keep law and order in place at the blood farms."

I felt sick. "How could you?" My head swam with this information. "How could you turn on your own people like that?"

Captain shrugged. "Somebody has to do it. Why not be me? Now, drop your goddamn weapon!" Captain swung the gun in Seth's direction, the barrel pointing at his torso. "Do it or he's dead."

Fear gripped me. Seth froze, raising both hands in the air.

With a shaky hand, I removed Supe Slayer from

the holster and dropped it to the grass.

"Good girl," Captain said.

"And now you," he told Seth.

Seth tossed his gun to the ground and asked, "Did you help Garon with the vamp murders?"

Captain grunted, amused. "You think I'm going to spill all my secrets to a damn newbie?"

I wanted to punch him in his throat. I squeezed my hands into fists, adrenaline spiking through me like ice water. I rushed to put the pieces of the case together. Surging to the forefront of my thoughts was the cherub's ominous warning: *stay vigilant of those who surround you. Not everyone is what they say.* The warning wasn't about Seth. It was about Captain. My heart was crushed. Sure, the man was maddening, and perpetually prickly, but he was the Captain. The man who'd mentored me since my start with the PCI.

His so-called "good-will visits" to Saint Ambrose were just a farce. He was there, likely forcing the monks to bless more steel for the vampire leaders mass murders. Fury built up within me. At any moment, I was going to totally lose my shit.

I glanced at Seth. He wasn't ruffled at all. He stood tall, talking calmly to Captain, buying us more time. "You provided the Smite, didn't you? The Smite that killed the vamps?"

As Seth distracted Captain, I ever so slowly, reached into my back pocket, removing the switchblade I kept there for emergencies. The same switchblade I used on ole Pubes back at the beginning of this whole mess. My heartbeat roared against my eardrums, drowning everything except my own breathing. With a quick flick of my wrist, the blade swung out, ready to tear into someone's flesh like a rabid animal.

I hurled the knife at Captain, thankful when the blade hit its mark, sinking deep into his shoulder. He bellowed and staggered back a few steps.

Seizing the moment, Seth surged forward, tussling with Captain. The crack of gunfire went off, echoing around us in the quiet forest clearing. I lurched forward, grabbing clumsily for Supe Slayer. I clutched it tight, though my palms were damp. Feeling the familiar weight of it, I was relieved to have it back in my hands.

Captain stood over Seth, his face twisted in anger. "I warned you not to let James get you killed." He lifted the gun, aiming it Seth's head.

Wrapping both hands securely around Supe Slayer, I squeezed the trigger without hesitation. The bullet punctured Captain squarely in the heart. With eyes bulged wide, he collapsed, bleeding out from the chest and shoulder. It was then that Supe Slayer felt heavy. Too heavy.

I slipped it into the holster, ignoring the heat from the barrel as I ran to Seth, falling on my knees beside him. "Seth!" Everything around me fell back into obscurity. Seth was the only thing that mattered. Seeing him lying there, injured, tore at my heart. "Oh my God. Please tell me you're okay."

He groaned, pulling himself upright. "It's just a graze," he said, wincing as he shifted his leg.

I covered his face with kisses. "When the gun went off, I..I.." My throat constricted at the thought of losing Seth. I had loved him for such a short while, but the thought of losing him was agonizing. Tears threatened to well, but I sniffed and blinked them back. "I thought he had taken you from me."

His mouth twitched, and he gently touched my cheek, his fingertips playing softly against my skin. You can't shake me that easily." He shifted, and his smile melted into a tight grimace.

I looked down at his leg, fresh blood seeped through the fabric of his jeans. "We got to stop the bleeding." I dashed to my car and flung open the trunk, shoving everything aside as I searched for something to use as a tourniquet.

I found an old t-shirt and ran back to Seth, but not before pausing at Captain long enough to extract my switchblade from his shoulder. After cleaning his blood off with his own coat, I quickly shredded the t-shirt into strips and sank down at Seth's side. I wrapped a piece around the wound and tied it off, hoping it would soon stop the bleeding.

"We need to go," Seth said. "Garon is going to rise soon. We need to be there when he does."

"But your leg," I disputed. "We need to get you to a medic."

"No," he said. "We need to finish this, Edy. We need to get Garon. For Kay."

Struck for a moment, I stayed kneeling, the weight of the world felt like it rested on my shoulders. *For Kay.* I thought about her frantic eyes and the way her clothes now hung on her frame.

"Come on, we don't have much time."

I helped him to his feet, bearing much of his weight as we made our way to the car. After settling him in the passenger seat, I wasted no time strapping myself in and revving the engine. Throwing the car into gear, the tires chewed up the dirt paths leading us away from the farmhouse and closer to Garon Walker.

****

On our drive, I radioed the squad to tell them about Captain. My account was brisk but to the point. I gave them the location of his body, knowing the Sweepers would handle it from there. I also asked for backup and a medic. With Seth lame, I wasn't certain I'd be able to tackle Garon on my own. Who knew how many vamps were in the house.

When Garon's mansion came into sight, my heart ramped up with anticipation, and not to mention fear. Garon was an Epoch, so he was going to be hard to take down. The car skidded to a stop on the gravel driveway. I threw it in park and reached for ammo. "You up for this?" I asked Seth as I reloaded Supe Slayer. He grimaced but gave me a solid nod.

I slipped out of the car as soundlessly as I could. If I was going to smoke a few vampires, it would be best to catch them by surprise.

Seth ambled out of the car, trying his best to keep up. "Cover the door," I called back to him. He was still several paces behind when I kicked the front door in. A few vamps scattered from the living room; others hissed and advanced on me. I blew through them, the holy salt igniting them into smoke on the spot.

"Where's Garon?" I called out, lurking around a corner with Supe Slayer poised and ready to fire off another round. "All I want is him."

The house was quiet, save for my own breathing.

Peering around the corner, I saw several vampires closing in on me. Their chins flared an angry splash of red, so I knew they were smelling Seth's blood from the front door. I reached into my pocket and pulled out a bottle of ground garlic. Uncorking it with my teeth; I clutched the bottle close to my chest and waited.

When I heard the wisp of their movement, I stepped out and threw the garlic into their faces, sending them shrieking back. Firing again and again, I evaporated each and every one of them.

Garon surprised me by speaking. "Impressive, Agent."

I whirled around, leveling the barrel between his eyes.

"You're under arrest for violating Otherworldly Laws."

Garon just laughed, the sound sharp, like the fangs that hung from his lips.

"All of PCI is gunning for you, Garon. You can make this easy, or you can make this hard. Which is it going to be?"

He glared daggers at me, then, without warning, took off upstairs. I knew he was leading me into an ambush, but I followed anyway. There was no way in hell I was letting him get away.

I took the steps two at a time before coming to the landing. The second floor was still, unsettling me. I crossed the floor slowly, taking measured steps as I searched the shadows for Garon. Through a far window, I noticed the sliver of golden sun peeking over the horizon.

A savage growl erupted from the shadows, just before Garon pounced, knocking me backwards, sliding me across the worn wood floor. My vision went fuzzy. I shook my head, trying to sharpen my focus. Garon stood over me, his chin drenched scarlet.

"I will feast on your blood, just as I have feasted on so many others before you."

Somewhere close the crack of gunfire broke loose. Garon opened his mouth wide, his fangs stretched out into twin blades. He descended swiftly. I recoiled, bracing myself for the sting of his bite, but instead I heard several blasts of a gun go off, then a deathly silence.

The shooter dropped Garon all right, but unfortunately it was on top of me. His weight snatched the breath from my lungs. Since he didn't turn to ash instantly, I realized with horror that the bullets that hit him weren't designed for vampires.

Seth stepped into my field of vision, his leg slowing him to a hobble. "Ran out of vamp bullets," he explained with a shrug.

"Where's your goddamn duffel bag when you need it!" I ground out a curse and my survival instincts went into overdrive, thrashing and struggling beneath him. He would soon regenerate and be mad as hell once he did.

Garon's neck bore a gaping hole, his blood dripped onto my chest, soaking my shirt. With difficulty, he raised his lolling head, his chin an angry shade of red. His fangs glistened as he curled his lips over them in a snarl.

I fought against him, but it was like beating against a stone wall. His weight kept me pinned, and there was simply no way to move him.

"Get off of her!" Seth shouted, pressing the gun barrel to the back of Garon's head. The vampire growled, and with a swiftness I could barely register, whirled and back-handed Seth, sending him sailing through the air and crashing into the far wall.

Seth slid to the floor, but somehow the blow had

not killed him. He touched the back of his head and drew back fingers wet with fresh blood. Garon's chin darkened, marking his hunger.

Fear nearly swallowed me whole. Now that Garon thirsted for blood, his need for it overruled everything. No longer was he just fighting for his cause or to keep from being imprisoned by the PCI. Now he needed to feed. And he'd kill Seth after he had his fill. I reeled back and with all of my remaining strength jabbed my thumb into the regenerating hole in Garon's neck. He winced and hissed through clenched fangs.

"Fucking bitch," he seethed, easily prying my fingers away from his wound. My hands were slick with his blood, but his grip on me was as tight as steel. He adjusted his neck, the skin regenerating quickly, filling the bullet wound right before my eyes.

Seth had crawled closer. His eyes were hooded with an impending concussion, but he stubbornly blinked it away. With fingers outstretched, he taunted Garon with his own blood. "Hungry motherfucker?"

Garon grinned at that, his teeth glimmering dangerously. Glaring down at me, he ran a finger from my earlobe to my collarbone. "First, I'm going to drain your boyfriend. Then, you'll be dessert." Lifting off of me, Garon turned his attention on Seth. His eyes were black with bloodlust. Seth scrambled back, trying to put distance between him and the advancing vamp.

Finally able to free Supe Slayer from the holster, I lifted it, taking aim at the vampire's broad back. The gun clicked. I tried again, and again it clicked, the hollow sound causing me to panic. *Shit!*

Garon lifted Seth from the floor like he was nothing more than a rag doll. Seth squirmed and kicked, but the struggle only seemed to enflame Garon's hunger. *It really is all about the hunt,* I thought with sickening realization.

I glanced around, frantic. My eyes lighted on Seth's forgotten gun. I snatched it up. I could shoot the vamp again, but it would only slow him down. With my heart in my throat, I lifted my eyes to the ceiling to pray for the first time since my parents died. As Seth screamed, I suddenly knew what to do.

Raising the gun over my head, I unloaded the magazine until it was spent. Roofing blew apart, splintering and crashing all around us. The rays from the lingering sunset poured in, flooding the room in golden light. Garon didn't even have time to scream. He vaporized instantly, leaving just motes of ash swirling in the air. Seth dropped to floor like a bundle of wet blankets.

I scrambled to my feet, rushing to check on Seth. I touched his shoulder. "Seth?"

He groaned, stirring slightly.

I brushed some plaster from his hair. "You okay?"

"Yeah, I'm good." he answered, lifting his gaze to meet mine. There was a trickle of blood coming from his nose. "You?"

I gave a little laugh, remembering our encounter with the Jersey Devil. "This conversation sounds so familiar."

He chuckled. The scream of sirens came in the distance, growing nearer and nearer. "Backup," he said. "Finally."

"My backup is already here." I leaned in and gave him a kiss. He returned the kiss, reaching up and cupping my face gently. We pulled apart, and I looked deep into those hypnotizing eyes of his. "Seth," I started.

He clasped my hand. "I know, Edy. It's okay. You don't have to say it."

I bit my lip, pondering. He knew how I felt about him. Did I have to say it out loud? Though we were knee deep in vamp territory, covered in dust, vampire ash, and blood…it was time. The perfect time to say those three little words.

"Love you, Newbie."

Seth's eyes glimmered, and a smile broke across his handsome face. "Love you too, Badass.

****

The radio scratched before the dispatcher's voice came across the airwaves. "There's a five-oh-eight in progress on the south end of Cloverfield. Mortal law enforcements are enroute." Agent Marshal and Agent Jackson responded, confirming they'd handle the crime involving a poltergeist, a pedophile, and the not-so-unfortunate use of a Christmas nutcracker.

"Never a dull moment with Supes," I said to Seth, who was riding shotgun as my permanent partner. We were parked at the post office. I had a quick errand to do before our shift officially began.

He laughed that great laugh of his and flicked his gaze out the windshield, taking in the busy streets of Cloverfield. I was about to unbuckle my seatbelt when my cellphone rang. I lifted it to my ear. "James."

"Edy. It's Franco."

"What's up?" I asked, sensing the tightness in his voice. "Did something happen to Carl?"

"Oh no. Carl is fine. Loves Montana."

"Great," I said with a relieved smile.

"But that's not why I called."

"Oh?" The radio in the cab crackled again. This time it was dispatch requesting Sweepers at a nearby hookah bar. A group of Supe youths were given drug-laced sugar cookies and started hallucinating caterpillars wearing wooden shoes were crawling all over them. They totally trashed the place swatting at the imaginary bugs.

Franco spoke again. "Got the perfect place for your Were-should you ever let him out of his silver cell.

I cut a glance at Seth. Leo wasn't responsible for the human slaughterhouse, nor did he actually kill any of the mortals held captive there, but he was an accessory to the horrific crimes that occurred on Garon's farmland. Plus, it was determined that he was in fact, the murderer of district leader, Tek Ronboi. Leo wasn't going anywhere for a long, long time.

"Thanks, but Leo's not going anywhere anytime soon," I told him. "Besides, if PCI ever decides to release him, Topher and his entire pack will be waiting for him."

"Roger that. Hey, how's your friend?"

I pinched the bridge of my nose. "She's good." I closed my eyes for a beat, reminded of the day I found Kay, dirty and almost feral. "We had to use the *EVAP* on her, so that makes it easier. For her anyway."

Franco whistled. "Shit. Well, at least it's all over. You did a good job, Edy. You're a damn good agent. You be careful out there." He bid me goodbye and hung up.

I slipped my phone into my jacket pocket. "Franco says Carl likes Montana," I told Seth with a smile. I unbuckled and grabbed a grocery bag from the backseat before stepping out of the car. Striding to the passenger window, I bent to press a kiss to Seth's lips. "Be back in five, Newbie."

He winked and said with a laugh, "I'll be waiting for you."

I walked into the post office with two bags of jumbo marshmallows in hand. I jotted a quick note to the big furry guy: "Stay out of trouble." With a fond smile upon my face, I sealed the box and scrawled the vague Montana address across the top. I was keeping my promise to Carl. Now it was up to Carl to keep his.

If only it were that easy to keep all Supes out of trouble," I thought as I dropped the package in the mailbox. As I walked out of the post office, the two-way radio crackled on my left hip. With that familiar rush of adrenaline, I rested my hand on Supe Slayer, readying myself for the night, and yet another call for the PCI.

A word from the author...

I work full-time as a zoo curator, so when I'm not running a zoo, I'm trying to tame the one I live in! I have two kids, and a husband who sometimes acts their age.

I can usually be found jamming to Elvis Presley tunes or diligently chipping away at my never-ending "to be read" pile.

I tend to gravitate toward anything paranormal. I love creatures who fly and characters who sprout fur or fangs. Sprinkle some romance and magic into the mix, and I'm a happy girl!